SINS OUT OF SCHOOL

SINS OUT OF SCHOOL

A DOROTHY MARTIN MYSTERY

Jeanne M. Dams

Walker & Company
New York

First published in the United States of America in 2003 by Walker Publishing Company, Inc.

Published simultaneously in Canada by Fitzhenry and Whiteside, Markham, Ontario L3R 4T8

For information about permission to reproduce selections from this book, write to Permissions, Walker & Company, 435 Hudson Street, New York, New York 10014

Library of Congress Cataloging-in-Publication Data

Dams, Jeanne M.
Sins out of school / Jeanne M. Dams.
p.   cm.
ISBN 0-8027-3379-4 (alk. paper)
1. Martin, Dorothy (Fictitious character)—Fiction.   2. Women detectives—Indiana—Fiction.   3. Retired teachers—Fiction.
4. Indiana—Fiction.   I. Title.

PS3554.A498 S56   2003
813'.54—dc21
2002034698

Series design by Mary Jane DiMassi

Visit Walker & Company's Web site at www.walkerbooks.com

Printed in the United States of America

2 4 6 8 10 9 7 5 3 1

SINS OUT OF SCHOOL

1

ow, let's see." I sat at the kitchen table with my shopping list in front of me, talking half to myself, half to my husband, who was finishing his second cup of coffee. "I've ordered the turkey, but I'll have to pick it up at the last minute. It's too big to fit in the fridge. Thank goodness the care package came from Hillsburg last week. I don't know where I would have found the fresh cranberries, or the cans of fried onions. So. Celery, yams, green beans, pumpkin . . . and I'd better get some more onions for the stuffing . . ."

The phone rang. Alan put down his coffee cup and reached for it. "Alan Nesbitt here."

I continued thinking out loud. "Oh, and little boiling onions to cream . . ."

Alan handed the phone across the table. "Sorry, love, but it sounds urgent."

I made a face and put down my pen. "Yes?" I said curtly into the receiver.

"Dorothy, thank God you're there! Are you all right?"

"I'm fine," I said. What else would I be, for heaven's sake? "Who's speaking, please?"

"Oh, sorry, sorry! It's Catherine, Catherine Woodley, and I'm in a bit of a stew. Are you sure you're feeling well?"

"Catherine, what *is* the matter? Of course I'm well."

"There's no 'of course' about it, my dear. Half the town is down with the flu, and that's why I rang. One of my teachers simply failed to turn up this morning, and I've gone through the entire list of supply teachers. Do you suppose you could possibly fill in for an hour or two while I try to find someone?"

"What, *now?* My dear woman, it's three days before Thanksgiving!"

"Thanksgiving?" There was a silence at the other end of the phone for a moment before Catherine said doubtfully, "Oh, yes, the American holiday."

"Yes, indeed, and I'm having ten people for dinner, and I'm up to my ears in grocery shopping and cleaning and—"

"Dorothy, I'm up to my ears in nine-year-olds! I'm desperate, truly, or I wouldn't have bothered you. It's not even legal for you to teach, you're not officially qualified, but we can pretend you're an aide, and I don't know what else to do!"

She ended on something very close to a wail. I rolled my eyes at Alan and sighed. "Very well. I have slacks on, though. Don't your teachers usually wear skirts?"

"At this moment I'd welcome you in a bathrobe. Yes, Jeremy, just a moment—oh, well, then—look, Dorothy, I must go. Ten minutes?"

"Twenty," I said into nothingness. She had hung up.

"Catherine Woodley," I said to my husband. "There's a crisis at St. Stephen's. She wants me to fill in for an hour or two."

"I gathered you had once again been roped into something. What about the supply teachers?"

"The flu epidemic's used them all up. Look, could you drive me over? I don't think it's at all easy to find a place to park there."

It's never easy to find a place to park anywhere in Shere-bury. A beautiful little town, called a city only by virtue of its cathedral, Sherebury was laid out in the eleventh and twelfth centuries, and somehow the town planners (if there were any) failed to take the automobile into consideration. World War II bombs created instant parking lots in many English cities and towns, but Sherebury was largely spared, so parking is always an adventure. Usually I walk or take one of the effi-cient little minibuses, but this was an emergency. I made a quick trip to the bathroom, not sure when I'd get another chance, and put on the first hat that fell to hand as Alan got the car out of our diminutive garage.

I'd known Catherine Woodley for three years or so. She was head teacher at St. Stephen's, the local primary school, and we'd met at a cocktail party. When I was introduced as an American and a retired teacher, our common interests had led us into conversation. I'd learned a lot about the English educational system, though I'd gone home somewhat more confused than before.

I had, since, figured out a few things. One was that the system had been undergoing constant change for the past generation or so, and expatriate Americans weren't the only ones who were confused. Simply put, however, it seemed that there were essentially two strata of English schools. Wealthy and/or influential parents sent their children to prep schools and then to "public schools," in their sense of the term. We would think of them as private schools. They were usually boarding schools and were often, though nowadays not al-ways, segregated by sex. The rest of the school-age population went to state-run schools, which were inexpensive, though not entirely free. They might or might not also be affiliated with a church (depending on the history of their develop-ment). These most closely resembled public schools in our use of the term, although even in schools with no church affiliation the students were required to participate in a "Col-lective Act of Worship" every day. As an American, accustomed to rigid separation of church and state, I found this startling.

There was also a handful of entirely private schools run by "nonconformist" (neither Church of England nor Roman Catholic) religious groups. These had no state support and were patronized almost entirely by members of the churches in question. Even these small schools, though, however nonconformist in any sense, were required to conform to the standards of the national curriculum.

I had never actually been inside St. Stephen's. I knew it was, despite its name, not associated anymore with any church. I had only the vaguest idea of what Catherine's job actually was, though I knew that "head teacher" was more or less equivalent to our "principal."

I was about to learn a great deal more about the system and how it worked. Or didn't.

I had no time at first to talk to Catherine, whose tiny office when I walked in was a scene of chaos just barely under control. The phone was ringing, two children stood in front of the desk looking scared, and a woman waited impatiently in one corner while a man stood arguing with Catherine.

She detached herself, greeted me with a harried smile, and said, "My dear, you *are* a lifesaver. I'll come along in a bit and see how you're getting on, but just now—well, you can see, can't you? Ravati," she said, snaring a little passing girl, "can you show Mrs. Martin to Mrs. Doyle's room, please? And take her coat and hat and hang them up? Thank you, dear." She had turned to deal with the next crisis before I had time to decide whether the thanks were directed to me or the child.

Ravati escorted me to the classroom, flashed a shy, bright smile, and disappeared around a corner, leaving me to my fate.

The room was about half the size of my last classroom in America. True, there were fewer children, only about twenty, but the room was still crowded. There were no desks, only a few scarred worktables and chairs scattered about. The dim light fixtures suspended from the ceiling did little to disperse the gloom of a late-November day, and the skimpy windows didn't help, either. There was only one small chalkboard, chipped at the corners, and no bulletin boards at all. Children's work was taped to the walls. A bookcase built of bricks and planks held a collection of well-worn books and one world globe.

At my entrance the children, who had been behaving about as one would expect with no teacher present, became quiet and sat down on the floor. They left little space, but I took a deep breath and threaded between them to the front of the room.

"Good morning." There were a few giggles at my accent, but the response of "Good morning" was polite enough.

"My name is Mrs. Martin, and I am, as you can tell, American. Mrs. Doyle is ill today, and since there are no proper teachers to take her place, you'll have to make do with me. I'm a retired teacher, though, so we should get along all right." More discreet giggles, which I ignored. "Now, who can tell me what you do first thing in the morning?"

A sea of hands. I pointed to a little blond boy in front. "Please, miss, Mrs. Doyle calls the roll."

"Good. What's your name?"

"Peter 'Arris, miss."

"Fine, Peter, come up here and see if you can find Mrs. Doyle's list of pupils." I didn't know if it was called a class roster or a roll book or what, and I had no intention of calling down further amusement by my ignorance. "And while he's doing that, will you"—I pointed to a girl who looked reasonably bright and responsible—"find some paper and pencils— or markers would be better if you have them—for everyone to make a tag with your first name on it. That will make things much easier for me. Print, please, and nice big letters so I can read them."

The classroom might be small and shabby and the supplies pitiful, but children everywhere are much the same. Though it had been a number of years since I'd taught, we settled easily into a routine. The small class made it quite pleasant, actually. Fourth-graders—"nines," they called them here, since most of them were nine years old—have always been my favorites. They're old enough to be really interesting people, with individuality and creativity, and young enough not to be smart alecks yet—well, most of them. There's at least one in every class, and you can spot them at a glance, but the two I was saddled with today were, fortunately, still bemused by my foreign accent and manner and gave me little trouble.

The first subject on the agenda was arithmetic ("maths"). Well, that was no problem. We struggled with long division, which they were just beginning, and I flattered myself that I taught them a trick or two. Geography, after that, was interesting. The children were, of course, far more familiar with the map of England than I was, but I had often visited Salisbury and its famous Plain, and most of them had not. We enjoyed swapping information.

The next item, however, was history. They were studying the Napoleonic wars and there I met, so to speak, my Waterloo. I know virtually nothing about Napoleon except that he crowned himself emperor, and I know that only on the basis of a painting in the Louvre, which may be inaccurate.

My teaching methods have always involved acknowledging my shortcomings and playing to my strengths. "Right," I said when Terence had told me where they were in history. "I'm afraid I'm a little fuzzy on the details of some of those battles, so suppose I teach you some American history? There's a very important American holiday coming up soon, and I'll bet none of you knows anything about it."

They relaxed. A lesson about something one doesn't have to know is always more fun. So I told them about the Pilgrims and the Puritans and the Indians. "Indians?" queried Chakra, a puzzled frown on his face.

"Sorry, Native Americans. Red Indians, I think they're sometimes called in England, to distinguish them from real Indians like your people, Chakra. You remember, Columbus thought he'd sailed to India, so he called the people he found Indians, even though they weren't at all. They were very helpful to the first English settlers, though."

And we went on to turkey ("No, I don't think they come from Turkey. I don't know why they're called that") and corn ("You call it maize, or sweet corn") and lima beans and squash, and the first feast of thanksgiving for the harvest, meager though it had been.

"There, now," I said when we had finished. It was nearing lunchtime, and no one had shown up to relieve me. "You know something the other kids don't. You can tell them all about it at lunch."

"Please, miss?" Fiona, she of the bright red braids and freckles, one of the potential troublemakers. "Why isn't Mrs. Doyle here? She wasn't ill yesterday."

"I don't know, dear. Mrs. Woodley didn't tell me."

"Will she be back tomorrow?"

"I expect. Oops, there's the bell." I didn't have to ask the procedure for getting them to the lunchroom. They lined up without being told and filed out in an orderly fashion. I heaved a huge sigh of relief and joined the teacher from the next room. "Are we supposed to eat with the children?"

"No, thank God," she said crisply. "The lunch ladies look after them. Come with me to the staff room and I'll show you the drill."

The staff room was as shabby as the rest of the school, but it was large and clean. Most of the teachers had brought sandwiches. I saw why after one look at my school meal, brought to me by a "lunch lady." Consisting of a large piece of breaded mystery meat, SpaghettiOs, Tater Tots, and for dessert a thick, pallid slab of something baked, the meal could most charitably be described as edible. Maybe.

I was both starved and exhausted. I ate what was put before me. When I had absorbed a week's ration of fat and car-bohydrates, I gratefully accepted a cup of coffee in someone's mug and looked around for Catherine.

She was chatting with the teachers at the other table, but she met my eye and came to sit in the vacant chair next to me. "I thought you looked as though you should have your meal first. How was the lunch?"

"Awful, but sustaining, I suppose."

"We do try to make the food more or less decent, you know, but with the budget we're given—"

I waved it aside. "It doesn't matter. I ate it, and I do feel a little better. I can't believe how tired I am after only a morning. *And* my voice is giving out. I'm out of condition."

Catherine sighed. "Oh, dear. I really hate to tell you, then, but I'm afraid I haven't been able to find anyone at all to take your place this afternoon. I'd step in myself, but I've a meeting with the national curriculum people. Can you stick it out, do you think?"

I sighed myself. "I'll have to, I guess. Actually it's not too bad. The kids are sweet. Well behaved, responsive. Mrs. Doyle must be a good teacher."

"She is," said Catherine, chiming in with the woman across from me, the one who had shown me to the staff room. Catherine smiled. "Dorothy, I must go and deal with an irate parent, but let me introduce Ruth Beecham, who teaches the other class of nines. Dorothy Martin, Ruth."

Catherine hurried from the room; I exchanged nods with Ruth Beecham, who was an attractive brunette with an intense, mobile face. "More coffee?" she asked.

"When do we have to go back to the salt mines?"

She grinned. "Fifteen minutes or so."

"Then I won't, thanks. I wouldn't have time to drink it *and* go to the bathroom, which I would certainly need to do with that much coffee in me."

"You can leave your little monsters for that long, you know. You're right, they're a well-behaved lot."

"You can tell a lot about a teacher, I always think, by the way her students behave with a substitute. From the way these kids act, I wouldn't have guessed Mrs. Doyle would be the sort to go AWOL."

"She's not!" Mrs. Beecham banged her mug on the table so hard coffee slopped out. "I'm worried sick about her!"

2

THE room got quiet for a moment, and Mrs. Beecham's face turned red. "Sorry," she said, mopping at the spilled coffee. "I didn't mean to make a scene, but honestly, I don't think anyone's taking this thing seriously enough."

"Mrs. Doyle's unexplained absence, you mean? Catherine sounded quite annoyed about it when she called me this morning."

"That's it, you see. Annoyed, not worried. Oh, I do see her point. One can't have one's staff vanishing, and Catherine's first priority has to be the school and the children. But she seems to think Amanda—Mrs. Doyle—has simply done a bunk, and she wouldn't do that!"

"Conscientious, then?"

"To a fault. She's taught here for five years, and the only time she's ever not turned up was when she had appendicitis. And then she rang up Catherine at home the night before to say she wasn't feeling well and might not be in for a few days. She reminded Catherine that the next day would be the children's turn for the library and computer studies, and never once mentioned the fact that she was in hospital awaiting an emergency appendectomy! So you see . . ."

"Yes, I do see," I said slowly. "I suppose Catherine called her when she didn't show up today?"

"No answer. That was when I called the bank where her husband works. They said he'd taken a holiday."

"Oh, well. They've probably gone someplace together—"

"If you knew him, you wouldn't say that." Her voice was neutral, but her face was not designed to conceal her feelings.

"You don't like him."

"I can't imagine that anyone who knows him likes him. Look, Mrs. Martin, Amanda Doyle is my friend. She's a wonderful person. And if I could get my hands on that husband of hers, I'd strangle him!" She sounded as though she meant every word.

Intrigued, I was opening my mouth to pursue the matter when the bell rang. It must have been just outside the staffroom door, because the clamor drowned out everything. I jumped, but the rest of the teachers were used to it; they scraped chairs and rose and headed out to their afternoon's work.

"Why?" I asked, trailing after Mrs. Beecham. "What's he done that's so terrible?"

"Later," she said in an undertone, nodding in the direction of the children, who were crowding close to us, intent on confiding the important events of lunchtime.

"Later" came in the second class period of the afternoon, right after an English lesson in which I failed to distinguish myself. Even after living for several years in England, I still tend to speak and write American. The two languages differ in subtle but important ways. I began in disgrace by leaving the *u* out of "honor" when I wrote a sentence on the board, and the whole thing deteriorated from there. I was glad when the bell rang and Peter, who had appointed himself my mentor, informed me, with a grimace, that it was time for religious studies and we all had to go to the lunchroom.

The whole school gathered in there, about four hundred children ranging in age from four to eleven, and all the teachers, and Catherine. The children seated themselves on the floor in age groups. Chairs were apparently considered an unnecessary expense; I wondered what they had done at lunchtime and decided I didn't want to know. There weren't any chairs for the teachers, either. We stood near our classes to keep an admonitory eye on them. Supervision was necessary; the children were bored and therefore restless.

"They don't like this part, do they?" I murmured to Mrs. Beecham as they were settling.

"Not much. It's pretty bland, I have to say. One-size-fits-all religion, you know."

"Oh. I thought it would be Church of England."

"No, nondenominational. Not even necessarily Christian. A lot of the children are Indian or Pakistani, therefore probably Hindu or Muslim. There's a fair sprinkling of Buddhists, too, amongst the Chinese. And the Japanese—Masako, turn around and pay attention! Mrs. Woodley is about to begin!"

The session seemed harmless enough, even fun. With the Christmas holidays drawing near, the children were learning several carols and sang them lustily, if not particularly tunefully. King's College they weren't, but at least they worked off some of their excess energy.

"I don't see why they don't enjoy this," I said to Mrs. Beecham. We had drawn a little away from the children, into a niche where we could talk without disturbing the practice.

"Only because it's required, I suspect. And of course most of the time it isn't music, but watered-down platitudes. Pretty useless, really, and the children know it. You can't fool them."

"I would have thought some genuine comparative religion would be better than vanilla-flavored piety. Or else nothing at all. Of course, as an American, I don't think a public school—

sorry, a state school—is the place to teach religion. The home, the church, yes, or else a denominational school."

"And those can be ghastly, believe me." Mrs. Beecham spoke with passion. I looked at her with surprise.

She drew a deep breath. "You asked me what was so dreadful about Amanda's husband? Well, aside from being a bully and all-round nasty piece of work, he's a religious fanatic, some frightful nonconformist sect. He makes their daughter go to the school run by these raving loonies, and Amanda has to go to the church. Twice on Sundays, and then there's Wednesday nights, weekend prayer meetings, mission meetings, Bible study meetings—the woman can't call her soul her own!"

"It does sound a bit much," I said mildly. The singing paused. I glanced at my charges and hurried over to have a word with Fiona, who was about to drop a marble down the neck of the rather dim-looking little boy in front of her.

"Why doesn't she rebel?" I asked when I rejoined Mrs. Beecham. "Surely she could simply refuse to do some of these things. Maybe she enjoys it."

"She hates it. She tells me that, but she can't tell him. She's a submissive sort of woman, always has been, I'd say, and he's worked on that, beaten her down until she doesn't dare defy him."

"You don't mean he abuses her?"

"Not physically, but words can hurt. And attitudes. He's a harsh, cruel man, and why she ever married him, I can't imagine. He wouldn't even let her work if they didn't need the money so badly."

"Doesn't he have a job?"

"Bank clerk. Terribly respectable and all that, but there's not much money in it."

"I'd think she'd leave him. She'd have only a little money, but it would surely be better than living under such oppression."

"There's some reason why she doesn't. I've never been

able to get her to tell me what, she just sidesteps the issue, but it's almost as if he has some sort of hold over her."

"Well, maybe. But abused women often refuse to leave their abusers, and what she's suffering is certainly abuse, even if it's not physical."

"But Amanda's not that type. Besides, from what I've read about abused women, they also defend their men, say he really loves them, all that rot. Amanda never defends John. Quite the opposite, she—whoops!"

Mrs. Beecham rushed over to intervene in a pushing match, and by the time she'd separated the combatants and persuaded them to repent of their deeds, the carol singing was over and we shepherded the children back to the classrooms for the final lessons of the day. In my case that was supposed to be art, but as my art capabilities are limited to rudimentary stick figures, I gave up the battle and read to them from a Harry Potter book that had somehow found its way into the rather elderly classroom collection. I'd been dying to read it anyway, so we all enjoyed ourselves.

"Please, miss, will Mrs. Doyle be back tomorrow?" asked Peter as the children tidied up the room for the end of the day.

"I don't know. Probably."

"If she isn't, I hope you come back, miss. I like you, and we had fun today!"

Oh, dear. It was delightful that Peter liked me, but fun was not exactly what school was supposed to accomplish. I probably hadn't done my job, and Mrs. Doyle, when she eventually returned, would have extra work to do. Well, blast it all, the woman should know better than to absent herself with no warning.

That was funny, actually. As I said something noncommittal to Peter, I wondered idly if Ruth Beecham's worries might not have some foundation. A conscientious teacher wouldn't just go away, let alone one with a stern, self-righteous husband. Surely he couldn't have harmed her here. Or spirited her away? My imagination, nourished by hundreds of mystery novels, could come up with all sorts of possibilities.

Oh, well. Mrs. Beecham was probably wrong. Maybe Mr. Doyle was just a little too rigid in his views for her taste, and she'd blown the thing up out of all proportion.

Wearily I erased the chalkboard, found my purse, and went in search of my coat and hat.

I found them in the staff room, where Catherine was waiting for me with a cup of tea. "Sit down, Dorothy. You look absolutely frazzled."

"Wiped out," I admitted, dropping onto the sagging couch with a groan. "Oh, that feels good. But I'll never be able to get up again." I took the tea and sipped it gratefully.

"How did you get on?"

"Not too badly, considering. I can't spell, at least not in English, as the children gleefully pointed out to me. And I'm a total loss as an art instructor. But they learned something in arithmetic—sorry, in maths—and in history, though not what was scheduled. And *they* taught *me* quite a bit of English geography. So it was a good enough day, all in all. Mrs. Doyle has prepared them well. Have you heard from her?"

"No, actually, and I've rung several times. There's no one at home, and apparently they haven't an answer phone, or they forgot to turn it on. So I was working myself up to ask if you could possibly consider coming again tomorrow?"

I groaned. "Catherine, you have no idea how tired I am! I'm too old for this, really I am. And I have a house to clean and a festive meal to prepare and a hundred things to do first—"

"I'll send you my cleaning woman," said Catherine. "It's the least I can do. I can't pay you from my budget, since you're not a qualified teacher, but I can pay her out of my own pocket and buy you some time. She's very competent. Do please say yes! You're good with the children, and truly there's no one else, unless everyone in town suddenly recovers from flu. And you'd have my undying gratitude."

I sighed, the memory of Peter's words clouding my judgment. The affection of a child, like that of a cat, cannot be coerced, and winning it always goes to my head. "Oh, very well. But *only* tomorrow, positively."

"Agreed. I'll have Mrs. Finch there for you first thing in the morning."

"Oh, Mrs. Finch! I know her well, as it happens. She's a gem. I can relax about the housework, then. When should I be here?"

We settled the details, Catherine helped me out of the clutches of the couch, and I went to call Alan. I had planned to walk home, but I felt as though I'd been digging ditches all day. He could jolly well pick me up, and in fact stop by a pub and buy me a drink on the way home. I'd earned it.

3

THE next morning I dragged myself out of bed long before the sun and stomped around snarling over every detail of the situation. My knees ached. My head ached. I'd slept badly, with assorted children running through my dreams shouting unreasonable demands. Not only that, it was positively uncivilized to get up before sunrise, and the sun rose ridiculously late in England at this time of year, and I was too old to be teaching, and I wasn't even getting paid, and some people really did take advantage of one's friendship, and for heaven's sake, Emmy, *move!*

Emmy, the senior of our two cats, looked at me, stretched, and sauntered away from her position in the exact center of the top step. She made it very clear that she moved only because she wished to do so, not in response to my burst of temper.

Alan, patient with my grumbles, brewed coffee and plied me with it until I felt almost human. He fixed me a bowl of cereal and even made a couple of sandwiches for my lunch; I had waxed eloquent the night before on the subject of school meals. Then he drove me to St. Stephen's and promised to pick me up right after school.

I stuck my head in the door of Catherine's office to say good morning and found her in conference with a pale, thin woman in a beige sweater and skirt. The skirt drooped at the back and the sweater in front, probably because there was so little to hold them up. They were obviously designed for decency rather than style, as was her severely restrained hairdo. She was the epitome of the drab, washed-out librarian type, and I was surprised to hear Catherine address her as "Amanda." Surely this mousy female couldn't be the competent teacher I had replaced yesterday.

She was, though. I was about to back away when Catherine looked up and beckoned me in.

"Mrs. Martin," she said formally, annoyance inherent in every crisp syllable, "this is Mrs. Doyle. I tried just now to phone to tell you she had come in, but you'd already left. I'm so sorry you were inconvenienced."

She looked pointedly at Mrs. Doyle, whose cheeks took on a faint tinge of color. "I'm sorry, Mrs. Martin," she said almost inaudibly. "I would have phoned you myself, earlier, but I didn't know who took my place yesterday. And I hadn't Mrs. Woodley's home telephone number. I'm really sorry. I hope you have a way home, I don't drive and I must get to the classroom, but I have bus fare . . ." Her voice trailed off as she reached into her purse.

"No, it's all right, I'll walk home." It wasn't all right. I felt very much put upon, but Amanda Doyle looked as tightly strung as piano wire. One harsh word might snap something and create a really ugly discord.

"Very well, Amanda," said Catherine, still crisp. "We'll talk about this later." She dismissed her with a nod, gesturing with her eyes for me to stay.

"Well!" I said when I thought Mrs. Doyle was out of earshot.

"Indeed." Catherine's voice was dry enough to crackle.

"Walks into my office, says she's very sorry she wasn't here yesterday, but it was unavoidable, and starts to walk out again! Not a word of explanation, no worry about what went on with her class in her absence, nothing! Would you believe she refused, actually refused, to tell me why she neither turned up yesterday nor let me know? Just kept repeating that something came up suddenly, and she was sorry. She'd *be* sorry if I weren't so short of qualified teachers, I can tell you that. But I can't spare her."

"But how—extraordinary! If some sort of emergency kept her from getting in touch with you right away, surely she would have called, or had someone call, later in the day, or even last night."

"You'd think so, wouldn't you? She *is* a capable teacher, and so reliable in the past that one might have set the school clocks by her. Now this!"

"Do you suppose there's some family crisis? Something wrong with her daughter, maybe? She looks tired to death, and terribly worried. Mrs.—oh, that other teacher I met yesterday—"

"Beecham?"

"Yes, Mrs. Beecham. I think she said Mrs. Doyle has a little girl."

"Miriam, yes. Nine years old, I believe. She goes to another school, which is odd, because the Doyles haven't too much money, and faculty children can attend St. Stephen's free of tuition. I can't imagine what might be wrong with the child that would cause Amanda to abandon her duties in that cavalier fashion, or that she couldn't talk about. Miriam's had the usual childhood illnesses from time to time, and Amanda has always coped. She also always told us about them, in case we thought she might bring illness into the school."

"Hmm. Well, it's a mystery."

"And will have to remain one, I suppose, unless Amanda decides to confide in me. I intend to have a stern talk with her later, but I doubt I'll get anywhere. She can be terribly stubborn, for all she seems so submissive. Dorothy, I truly am sorry—"

"Now don't start apologizing again. It isn't your fault."

"Well, I'm still sending Mrs. Finch. It'll make up for a little of your trouble." The phone began to ring.

"I'll take you up on that, and I'll get out of your hair. I hope everyone recovers from the flu soon."

I waved a casual farewell and left the office, but I didn't turn toward the front door. Call me a snoop, but I felt I had the right to talk to Amanda Doyle myself, and with the children not yet in school, there was plenty of time.

Once, long ago, when I lived in Indiana, I adopted a family of stray cats. The mother had plainly once had a home. She adapted herself easily to life with humans. But the three kittens were feral, and before they began to accept the idea that I wasn't a mortal enemy, they would freeze whenever I walked into the room, then run and hide under the nearest piece of furniture.

When I walked into Mrs. Doyle's classroom, she looked up from her desk with the same hunted expression I used to see in those kittens' eyes. Fortunately there was no place for her to hide.

"I thought I ought to tell you what we got done yesterday," I said before she could open her mouth. "I was so tired at the end of the day I forgot to leave you a note."

"Oh, that's quite all right—I mean, I'm only sorry you had to come at all—the children will tell me—"

"I'm afraid I didn't quite stick to the curriculum," I said, interrupting rudely. "I don't know a thing about the Napoleonic wars, so we did American history instead, and I'm hopeless as an art teacher, so—"

"I'm sure you coped very well, Mrs. Martin, and the children were well ahead with their work, anyway. Please excuse me, I must go and see to—I must go and talk to—"

Stammering, she fled, brushing past me with exactly the

panicky courage the kittens used to display when I blocked their escape route.

Well, well.

Thoughtfully, I went in search of Mrs. What's-Her-Name—Basset, was it?

Beecham. The name was written on a small card above the room number. She was at her desk grading some papers. When she looked up, her face was set in a tight mask.

"Oh. Hello. Are you supplying for someone else today?"

"No. I didn't know Mrs. Doyle was back until I got here this morning. What on earth was she up to yesterday, anyway? She won't say a thing to Catherine Woodley, and she's scared stiff of something."

"She won't talk to me, either. I'll try again at lunchtime, but . . ." She shrugged. "She's acting very oddly, I must say. I wonder . . ." Whatever she had been about to say, she changed her mind and looked at her watch and the pile of papers in front of her. "Goodness, I must get these done before the children get here."

"Yes, of course. Mrs. Beecham, I—I hope you can persuade Mrs. Doyle to talk to you. I don't know her at all, of course, but it looks to me as though she needs a friend badly."

Mrs. Beecham smiled rather bleakly and went back to her papers.

It was really none of my business where Amanda Doyle had been, or what she'd been doing. And it would take me a good half hour to walk home, and there were things I urgently needed to be doing. If I had any sense, I'd leave the thing alone and get out of there.

As I walked past the school office, across the hall from Catherine's more private cubicle, I saw Mrs. Doyle again. She was talking to the secretary, her back to the open door. It wasn't really eavesdropping if I just happened to walk a little slower as I passed.

"At the beginning of term, then. Miriam, yes; she was nine in July. It would be better if she were put in Ruth

Beecham's room, don't you think? It would be awkward for her to have her mother for a teacher."

She leaned over the desk to sign something, and I hastened away.

So she was enrolling her daughter in St. Stephen's next term.

Well, well, again.

I thought about Amanda and her mysterious absence all the way home, and then not again for two days. My time was completely occupied with joyful holiday preparations. I love to cook, and I love company, and somehow it was especially pleasant to celebrate a holiday when the rest of the town was carrying on its regular business. Not having to clean the house made it even more delightful. I made pies and salads and casseroles, and rose at dawn on Thursday to start the turkey cooking. Things were well enough under control that I could pop over to the Cathedral, which is virtually in my backyard, for Matins. Of course there was no mention of Thanksgiving with a capital *T*. There were none of the usual hymns of my childhood, "We Gather Together" and "Come, Ye Thankful People, Come," but the ritual satisfied me. I said my own prayers of thanksgiving and hurried away, refreshed, to set the table.

The house smelled wonderful. A wave of sage and onions engulfed me as I came in the door. I took a long, appreciative sniff, hung up my coat and hat, and went to get my best tablecloth out of the drawer.

The phone rang as Alan and I were pulling the table apart to put in the leaves. "Oh, I do hope that isn't somebody saying they can't come."

"More likely someone wanting to sell you life insurance. If you'll get it, love, I can manage now."

"Hello, Dorothy, it's Catherine Woodley."

"No."

"I need—what did you say?"

"I said no. I absolutely, positively will not come to your rescue today. Eight guests are going to arrive in about an hour, and I don't care how many teachers you're missing or how deep you are in nine-year-olds, I'm sorry but I'm *not* available."

"Oh, I forgot. It isn't that, Dorothy. It's far more serious, I'm afraid."

I dropped the bantering manner. "I'm sorry. I didn't mean to be frivolous. You're really in some kind of trouble, aren't you?"

"Well, not I. That is, not exactly. It's—" She took a deep breath. "It's Amanda Doyle. Her husband's dead."

I made a shocked noise.

"Yes, and it's worse than you know. He's—I'm afraid there's no doubt he was murdered."

4

I SAT down and drew a deep breath of my own. "Tell me what you need me to do, and if I possibly can, I will."

"Well, you see, it's the little girl. Miriam. There's no other family, apparently, and Amanda is—is talking to the police, perhaps for quite some time."

"Is being questioned, you mean? Catherine, you're not telling me Amanda killed her husband?"

"No, no, of course not!" She sounded very emphatic. "But the trouble is, the police don't know who did, so of course they must ask Amanda a lot of questions. And the child is here, here at school. Amanda brought her here on the way to the police station. I thought perhaps we could look after her, put her in one of the classes for the day. She's enrolled for next term, in any case, so—I'm sorry, I'm babbling. The point is, Miriam has tried to do as she was told, but she's much too upset to work with the other children, and one can hardly wonder, poor little mite. She needs some individual attention, and we're simply not equipped to deal properly with one extremely unhappy little girl. So I thought I'd ask if you could look after her, just until after school, when one of us can take her home. But I'd forgotten about your holiday. Of course you can't possibly."

"There must be friends—neighbors—"

"I've asked Ruth Beecham. She thinks she is literally Amanda's only friend, and obviously she can't leave school and look after the child. She says the family never got on with their neighbors."

"Their church, then. Mrs. Beecham says they're very religious."

"Dorothy, believe me, I've thought of everything. Ruth suggested to Miriam that she might like to go to her own school, the church school, for today, at least. We both thought it might be better to maintain some semblance of normal routine. But Miriam refuses to go."

Catherine was sounding more frazzled by the second. I bit my lip and did some rapid thinking. "All right, look, Catherine. One of my guests is a little girl. Ten now, if I'm counting right, a year older than Miriam, but young for her age. She's deaf, but she's very good at reading lips and can speak a little. If you think Jemima and Miriam would get along, bring her over and I'll manage somehow. Do you suppose she likes cats?"

"Not a clue, I'm afraid."

"Well, we'll work it out. Jane Langland will be here, too, and I've yet to see the child she can't deal with. Can you get Miriam here? I'm afraid Alan and I are both too busy to leave just now."

"I'll bring her myself. You are an absolute angel. I'll be there in fifteen minutes."

I took two of those to phone Jane, my next-door neighbor. "Can you come over now instead of waiting till later, Jane? I need you; there's a crisis looming."

Jane asked no questions. She was at my back door almost before I'd hung up the phone.

"What's up?"

I explained to her and Alan at the same time. When I had finished, Alan cocked his head to one side and looked very thoughtful. Jane, as usual, was more direct. "Did she do it?"

"Good heavens, I don't have the slightest idea! I met the woman only once. I have to say my impression was of someone who wouldn't say boo to a goose. But she's a good teacher. Everyone says so, and I could tell from the way her class acted. And a person has to have a good deal of backbone to teach effectively. Without it, the children will run all over you. Well, you know that, Jane." Jane had taught for years at Trinity School, the secondary school where children went after St. Stephen's, and what she didn't know about teaching and children probably wasn't true anyway.

She waved off the side issue and stuck to the point. "Police think she did."

"It does sound that way, doesn't it? And of course the spouse is always the first suspect."

Alan nodded and sighed. His many years as a policeman had taught him the sad truth about domestic disputes. In his pre-retirement position as chief constable he had not had to deal directly with the wives and husbands who took the quick way out of a marriage, but he hadn't forgotten.

"Well, whether she did or not, the little girl is our concern at the moment. And I think she's here, right this minute, so look cheerful!"

Miriam Doyle was not overjoyed to be foisted on strangers. That was plain the moment she stepped out of the car. Her face was streaked with tears and her chin wobbled. She was not an attractive child, at least not with her long fair hair scraped back as tightly as her mother's. I went out to greet her with trepidation.

She had, however, been taught obedience. When Mrs. Beecham led her to me and introduced us, she shook my hand politely and said, "It's nice to meet you, Mrs. Martin. Thank you for letting me come." Her voice shook. Tears welled up in her eyes. But she was trying.

"I'm delighted to have you, Miriam. Now come in and meet my cats."

"I'm not allowed to play with animals, Mrs. Martin. They're dirty."

"My cats aren't, and when you're in my house you may play with them as much as you like. Or not, if you don't want to. Come along, now. You're getting cold."

Her drab brown jacket was nothing like warm enough for the dark, windy November morning, and when she got inside and removed the jacket, her other clothing was lightweight, too. It looked like a school uniform. Cheap white cotton blouse, short tan skirt, tan knee socks that sagged and wrinkled on her thin little legs. Everything was clean, but threadbare, and I remembered what Mrs. Beecham had said about the strained budget of the family. Poor child! Things would be much worse with the father gone, even if the mother didn't face prison.

Miriam waited, a forlorn little bundle of misery, while I hung up her coat. I gave her a quick hug and a little push into the parlor. "There are some people I want you to meet. This is my husband, Mr. Nesbitt. We don't use the same name; I hope that isn't too confusing. And these are my cats Esmeralda and Samantha, but they're usually called Emmy and Sam. Sam is the funny-looking brown-and-cream one. She's half Siamese, but she looks like the real thing. And this lady is my next-door neighbor and my best friend, Miss Langland. She used to be a teacher, like your mother."

Jane sized her up with a quick, shrewd glance and took over. "You look as though you need something to do, child. Lots of work in the kitchen. Know how to scrub vegetables?" A shy nod. "Good. We'll tackle the potatoes and then do the celery and lettuce."

I picked up my cue. "Lovely, Miriam. And when you've finished, I could use some help setting the table."

The immediate problem solved, I continued getting out napkins, plates, glasses, and silver, for eleven places, now, instead of ten. It was going to be a tight squeeze around the table, but there was plenty to eat, and to spare.

I could hear Jane keeping up a gentle flow of conversation in the kitchen. If Miriam answered, I didn't hear her, but neither did I hear any sounds of weeping. Jane was coping, as usual.

"I wish I knew what was happening with her mother," I said to Alan, sotto voce.

"It depends on the situation," he replied equally softly. "Ordinarily they'd talk to the spouse at the home. If they've taken her to the station, it's because there's a better chance than usual that she's guilty."

I had already figured that out. Having Alan say it didn't make me feel one bit better.

"Of course," he continued, "Catherine might have been wrong. Mrs. Doyle might have been on her way to the morgue, being driven there by the police. She'd have to identify the body, of course. Or there might be another suspect in custody, someone they wanted Mrs. Doyle to look at. Any number of possibilities."

"Thanks, love. I know you're just trying to make me feel better, but thanks."

"I'll tell you what I'll do. The rest of our guests will be here any moment, but as soon as I can get away from them, I'll make a phone call or two and see what I can find out. How would that do?"

I gave him a hug as the doorbell rang.

Tom and Lynn Anderson were the first. My oldest friends in England, they're an American couple who live in Georgian splendor in London's fashionable Belgravia. Then Nigel and Inga Evans arrived, Inga's slender figure hidden behind a bulging tunic.

"Goodness! Not twins, surely?"

"They say not, but I must say I can't imagine one child taking up this much room. I keep thinking they must be wrong about the date."

"Well, heavens, come in and sit down, and if you feel one single twinge, don't be shy about telling us. I'm excited about your baby, and thrilled to pieces that you've asked me to be the godmother, but I'd rather he, or she, wasn't born at my dining table."

Nigel grinned broadly as he escorted Inga to the most comfortable upright chair. At this stage, extricating her from an overstuffed one would be difficult and probably unwise.

As for me, I blinked back a couple of unexpected tears. Childless myself, I was already dotingly fond of this baby-to-be, who might never have happened if not for my tendency to snoop into other people's affairs. You never know what a little interfering may lead to.

Jane and I, with timid assistance from Miriam, finished setting the table while Alan poured drinks. Miriam was as careful as I would have been with my best china, and positively reverential with the crystal. "It's pretty," she whispered to me. "We don't have anything so nice. Maybe it's a vanity, but I don't care! I like it."

I had no time to think what she might mean, for our last guests arrived just then, Meg and Richard Adam and Meg's deaf ten-year-old daughter, Jemima. They, too, had been involved in an odd matter a while back, in which I had become embroiled. We'd been fast friends ever since. I'd even learned a little sign language from Jemima.

Jemima'd been a shy, miserable child once, too, but she'd gotten over it. She beamed when she saw someone her age. The children moved in entirely different circles and had never met, but Jemima immediately went over to talk. Miriam shrank back, but her manners held. She allowed Jemima to talk in her rather toneless voice, and if Miriam whispered her replies, it didn't make any difference to Jemima.

I escaped to the kitchen to take care of last-minute preparations, leaving Alan to explain Miriam's presence. I knew he would be tactful and say no more than anyone needed to

know. One of the reasons Alan rose to the highest ranks of the
police force was his talent for diplomacy.

The afternoon went better than I had dared hope. Miriam
said little and ate less, but Jemima chattered happily, with
mouth and hands. We all caught up on everyone's doings, and
Inga did not, thank heaven, go into labor. When Alan excused
himself for a few minutes, everyone but me supposed it was
for the usual reason, and I deliberately refused to catch his
eye when he returned.

The children were excused as soon as they had finished
eating and played together happily. Miriam had apparently
adapted to Jemima's deafness. The cats, who dislike noisy
children, had always put up well with Jemima, and Miriam
was also quiet, so after a time Sam approached her with a typical Siamese yowl and asked to be petted. I happened to be
watching. Miriam, startled by the almost-human cry, cringed
back, but Sam persisted, coming up to her ankle and sniffing
delicately. She looked at the cat then with interest and, I
thought, some longing, but in the end put her hands behind
her back. "I can't," she whispered, and then looked around as
if ashamed to be seen even talking to a cat.

The adults were still lingering around the table when the
doorbell rang. I hoped it would be Miriam's mother coming
herself to pick up the little girl, but it was Mrs. Beecham. I
stepped out onto my little front porch and closed the door behind me.

"Any news?" I asked softly.

"Quite a lot, actually, and none of it good. They're keeping Amanda in custody overnight. I'm going to ring up our solicitor as soon as I get home, see if we can't winkle her out
somehow. It's absurd! Amanda no more killed anyone than I
did! How's Miriam?"

"Doing pretty well, considering. But what are you going to
do with her? She can't go home—to her house, I mean, with
no one there."

"No, she's coming home with me. She's stayed with us

once or twice before, so she'll be comfortable, and we'll work out something for tomorrow. It was really good of you to take her in today."

"A pleasure," I said, only somewhat insincerely. "But she'll be happier with someone she knows, I'm sure. Come in."

We got Miriam bundled back into her coat, and I insisted that Mrs. Beecham take a package of turkey and several pieces of pie. "I have way too much, and you have an extra mouth to feed."

"But not for long."

I said nothing. It seemed to me it might be for very long, but I didn't know the facts, and an unpleasant truth can wait.

Miriam was polite to the end. "Thank you very much for my dinner, Mrs. Martin. And I'm sorry I didn't play with the cats, but Daddy wouldn't like it—wouldn't have liked it." I thought that would bring fresh tears, but her voice remained steady. "And please say good-bye to Jemima, and tell her I'm sorry she was so wicked that God punished her by making her deaf. I'll pray for her to repent. Good-bye."

And as I stood there with my mouth open, she walked sedately to the car, her hand in Mrs. Beecham's.

5

AT least neither Meg nor Richard had been close enough to hear. Both of them had tempers, and I hated to think of their reaction to Miriam's twisted little bit of theology. Shaking my head, I went back inside and assumed a cordial attitude toward my remaining guests.

Unfortunately I've never been much good at hiding my feelings, no matter how hard I try. Somehow my friends got the idea that I'd love to be rid of them. They began to make the usual excuses and preparations for leaving. Nigel and Inga promised to let me know the instant anything started happening. Meg and Richard were profuse in their thanks, and hinted that they might also have some news soon in the baby department. Jemima thanked me in sign language and taught me a new sign, apparently the digital equivalent of "s'aright, mate." Tom and Lynn were the last to leave. Tom enveloped me in his usual bear hug, and then held me at arm's length and looked at me critically. "You're up to something, D. I can always tell."

"If I am, I'll tell you when the time's right."

"And not *one* moment before," said Lynn, giving Tom a poke in his well-rounded stomach. "Come on, nosy. The traffic getting back to London is going to be *horrendous.*"

Jane stayed behind.

"Right," she said when everyone had left. "So?"

The question was addressed to Alan. He replied with a sigh. "Not good. Not good at all. Dorothy, my love, why don't you make us a fresh pot of coffee? I think we could use a little stimulant."

I made it extra strong to counteract the amount of food we'd consumed, and the champagne we'd had with it. When we had heavy white mugs of restorative in front of us, he gave us the worst.

"I talked to Morrison; it's his case." Chief Detective Inspector Derek Morrison, who had been Alan's right-hand man when he was chief constable, was still a pillar of the force. "It's about as bad as it can be. Doyle died at home, sometime last night. They can't get closer to the time until they've done the postmortem. Mrs. Doyle is no help with the time. She says she came downstairs this morning and found him on the kitchen floor. He was lying facedown, a kitchen knife in his back."

I made an involuntary noise. Alan looked up. "Nothing," I said. "It's all right. Go on."

"The knife was not in the body when the police came. Mrs. Doyle says she couldn't leave it there, could she, not all messy. John liked the kitchen to be tidy. She told Morrison that as though it were a complete explanation for why she took the knife, washed it well in soapy water, dried it carefully, and put it back in the drawer. She took it out of the drawer and gave it to the SOCOs when they asked—sorry, Scene of Crime Officers."

I nodded.

"Of course, they'll find the blood on the knife. It's almost impossible to wash all of it away. But the only fingerprints, now, will be hers. Not only that, she had, for good measure, moved the body—'Well, it was lying in the middle of the floor, wasn't it?'—covered it with a sheet, and scrubbed the floor."

I closed my eyes and shook my head.

"And to put the absolute lid on it, both doors to the house were locked when the police arrived. Mrs. Doyle insists they were that way when she came downstairs, or at least she hadn't touched them, and there are no keys except hers and her husband's. His was in his pocket; hers in her handbag."

"Spring locks?" I asked in a last-ditch effort.

"The back door is. The front door is a dead bolt that locks only with a key from either side. So yes, a murderer could have left by the back door and it would have locked behind him, or her. But Mrs. Doyle says the house was always kept locked up, and that Mr. Doyle was not in last night by the time she went to bed, around midnight. He was at a church meeting of some sort. She helped Miriam with her homework and then, after the little girl went to bed, stayed up late grading papers. She says she was very tired when she went to bed and didn't hear her husband come home."

"She didn't even know that he didn't come to bed?"

"They have separate rooms, it seems. One of the bedrooms is divided to make tiny rooms for Amanda and Miriam, and Doyle had the other one. She was quite shy, talking about that, Derek said. A married woman in this day and age; it's almost beyond belief. At any rate, if she's telling the truth about that meeting, and it'll be easy enough to check, we can find out when he came home last night, or near enough. But as for the rest of her story, it's so thin as to be nonexistent."

"She hasn't admitted to killing him, has she?"

"No. She keeps on denying everything and sticking to what she said at first. She's asking us to believe that someone came home with her husband, someone he trusted enough to let him—or her—into the house very late at night, and this person then stabbed him in the back—making so little noise, mind you, that neither Mrs. Doyle nor the little girl, who the mother says is a light sleeper, heard a thing."

We drank our coffee and considered the matter. Finally Jane said, "Motive?"

"Oh, she freely admits that she hated her husband and isn't sorry he's dead."

Jane nodded thoughtfully. I gathered she was somewhat familiar with the Doyle ménage.

Alan went on. "She says, and I quote what Derek told me, 'Perhaps now Miriam and I can have a life.'"

I took a deep breath and let it out in a gusty sigh. "It doesn't seem very likely, does it? For either of them."

We washed the dishes rather silently. There didn't seem to be much more to say about the Doyle family tragedy.

I slept badly that night, though I was very tired. I couldn't stop thinking about that repressed, unhappy woman, and that oddly sweet little girl with the warped religious views. What was going to happen to her if her mother went to prison for murdering her father? Surely there must be some family somewhere, grandparents or aunts and uncles or someone. She needed to be looked after, loved, weaned away from the bleak credo in which she had been raised.

No, I had no right to say that. Her beliefs were her own business, repellent as I found them. What on earth had she meant by that "vanity" remark when she was setting the table? That pretty things were evil? I certainly didn't agree with that. Trivial, frivolous perhaps, but not evil. And the idea that God would punish a child with deafness was not just misguided, but positively diabolical. No, darn it all, she needed to be set straight.

Maybe her mother didn't believe all this guff. Mrs. Beecham had seemed to think the heavy-handed religious training was all the father's doing, and now he was gone. Maybe her mother could guide her into a gentler sort of creed.

Maybe her mother killed her father. Very possibly she did. Gentle?

Despite the comforting warmth of my husband and two

cats, I tossed and turned in the bed and fell asleep only toward morning.

I was restless when I finally made myself get out of bed. The day after Thanksgiving, back in Indiana, was always a big Christmas-shopping day. There was no such tradition here, of course, and I didn't feel much like shopping, anyway. The house was clean and there were leftovers to last us several days; no need to cook. Alan, absorbed in the book of memoirs he'd begun to write, didn't need or particularly want my company. I'd given up my volunteer job at the Cathedral gift shop, but I felt at loose ends. Maybe I'd go over there and see if they needed any help. Even tidying up or restocking the shelves would help with the restlessness that possessed me.

The truth, of course, was that I didn't want to think about the Doyles, and I couldn't seem to think about anything else. That poor child. That poor woman. I wished I could help, somehow, but I barely knew either of them, and it would be foolish for me to become involved. Alan and I were too old to look after Miriam, and as for any other sort of help—well, the police were thoroughly competent to investigate a case that seemed all too simple. I refused even to think, this time, about poking my nose into the matter.

I changed from slacks into a sweater and skirt, to fit in with the Englishwomen at the Cathedral. Women in England still don't wear slacks much for any except the most informal occasions, a habit I find uncomfortable. But I conform, most of the time. I told Alan where I was going (I doubted he heard a word I said), put on my hat, and stepped out the door.

It was a beautiful day, more like October than nearly December. I'd do a little gardening when I came back from the Cathedral, I decided. My gardener, Bob Finch, had for the last couple of weeks been on one of his periodic alcoholic binges. I knew when he sobered up and came back to work he'd cluck over the state of my garden as if it were all my fault. Pulling a few weeds would make the place look better and me feel better. It is, I've found, very hard to be depressed when your knees and back are aching and there's dirt under your fingernails and sweat is dripping into your eyes.

My house is the last on my street, right up against the wall of the Cathedral Close, and it's by far the oldest in the neighborhood. It was built in the early 1600s, after the Cathedral (then the Abbey church) fell into private hands upon Henry VII's dissolution of the monasteries. The house was meant to be a gatehouse for the manor house that had been built on the Abbey grounds. As the wheel of history turned and the Abbey property came back into the possession of the church, the new Close was laid out, the new wall built, and the house that centuries later was to be mine was divorced once and for all from the Cathedral. But it is the nearest house in all the town to the great church, and the bells, sounding overhead at frequent intervals, have become so much a part of my life that I scarcely hear them unless I'm listening for them.

This day I listened. There was no mighty peal being rung, only the bells of the clock telling the hour, but there was comfort in the sound. The bells, some of them, have been there for longer than my house; the two oldest date from the fifteenth century. The chimes of the clock are nothing like that old, but somehow, when I hear them ring out, I hear also a hint of eternity. Age and tradition suggest continuity and permanence. In this uncertain, impermanent world, I find that a consolation.

I was already feeling better as I entered the side door and walked past tombs and chantries and memorials in stone and bronze. Even these reminders of mortality didn't depress me. They were, after all, reminders of immortality as well. I stopped in the little chapel set aside for private meditation and said a prayer for Mrs. Doyle and little Miriam, and a reluctant one for Mr. Doyle, and then went on to the gift shop.

It turned out they didn't need me there. It was a slow day. The manager, Mrs. Williamson, kindly let me putter around a bit, but it was busywork, and I soon tired of it. The Cathedral had done its work on my mood, anyway. I'd go home and get at those weeds.

I was on my knees and thoroughly grubby when my husband came to a stopping place in his work and strolled out to survey my progress. "Nearly time for a turkey sandwich, wouldn't you say, love?"

"Right. I'm starving. But I want to finish this corner first."

"Then I'll make the sandwiches. Oh, by the way, Derek called while you were out. They've let Mrs. Doyle go home."

"Somebody bailed her out?" I crawled forward another foot, careful not to crush any chrysanthemums.

"Posted bond, my dear. No, as a matter of fact. They found some evidence that cast considerable doubt on her guilt."

I sat back (to the ruination of several plants) and looked up at him. "Really! What evidence?"

"Don't get excited. It's nothing conclusive, and it won't be until the autopsy is completed, but it turns out that there was a good deal less blood on Mr. Doyle's clothing than one would have expected. So little, in fact, that they are now not sure the stabbing was the cause of death. That upsets the whole scenario, of course. So they're letting Mrs. Doyle go home, for the time being, at least. I imagine they'll put pressure on the medical examiner's office, try to get the autopsy rushed through."

I pulled another weed or two and thought about that. "It doesn't really help much, does it? Because even if she didn't stab him, she might have killed him some other way. Though why she would then stab him . . ."

"Precisely. She might have done. People will do almost anything. If I learned anything in nearly fifty years of police work, it was that. If she hated him enough, she might have wanted to make assurance doubly sure. But it seems a little unlikely."

"So she's home with Miriam?"

"For now. The forensics people have finished with the house, so they've let them back in."

"That was quick work."

"I imagine it was the thought of the little girl that hurried them. She'd have had no place to go."

So now they had a home, anyway. But Mrs. Doyle wasn't likely to go back to her teaching job for a while, I thought as I disposed of the last few pesky weeds. That wouldn't help the family financial situation. It gave me a practical way to help a little, though. I'd take some turkey and other leftovers to the house this afternoon. At least they wouldn't have to worry about food for a while.

I went in with a lighter heart to clean up and eat my lunch.

6

I HAD to stop at St. Stephen's to find out where the Doyles lived. Catherine wasn't in the office; the secretary told me she was taking Mrs. Doyle's class. I felt guilty that I hadn't even offered to substitute for another day. I also felt that if I didn't get out of there quickly, I might very well be roped in. I got the address and some directions from the secretary and hastened out the door.

The Doyles lived in a part of town I knew only by reputation, and I got lost getting there. Sherebury isn't a big place, but because the heart of town is medieval, and was at one time walled, the streets are narrow and winding, and even after several years here I can still get lost very easily. One might think that the newer areas, developed from the middle nineteenth through the late twentieth century, would have been laid out on a more rational grid, but not so. The streets are slightly wider, but they wind just as much. In a way it's actually harder to navigate in the new housing estates, because the buildings are all exactly alike, at least in the less expensive developments.

The Doyle home, when I finally found it, was in the least expensive area of all. Built in the 1980s (not a happy period in English domestic architecture), the skimpy two-up-and-two-down houses were of shoddy construction, and most of them were showing it badly. The pebbles that had originally covered up the exterior stucco had fallen off in haphazard patterns, giving the walls an odd moth-eaten look. Large cracks had appeared here and there. Rain gutters sagged, downspouts were missing. Roof tiles had been replaced, not with the original brown, but with any color that (one assumed) was on sale. Woodwork had been left unpainted for so long it was, in many places, beginning to rot. The small square houses must always have been ugly, but it would have been an austere, sterile ugliness when they were new. Now the majority of them were simply squalid.

The Doyles had done their best to make repairs and restore the house to its austere sterility. A fresh coat of stucco had been applied. The roof tiles all matched. The woodwork was painted a repellent shade of shiny gray. The tiny patches of ground on either side of the front walk were covered, not with flowers, but with grass that had, one felt, never been allowed to grow so much as an extra quarter of an inch before being efficiently mowed. High yew hedges, clipped to rigid rectangles, gave the house a dark, secretive look.

Never had I seen a house that so clearly shouted of cheerless duty relentlessly done.

I had expected to see several cars parked near the house, but there was only one, probably Mr. Doyle's. No friends and neighbors had come to call on the victims of tragedy? I checked the address to make sure I had the right house. This was 42 Wilbraham Crescent, all right.

Well, Catherine had said Mrs. Doyle had no friends except for Mrs. Beecham. I shrugged, got out of the car with my shopping bag full of food, and rang the bell.

I heard a key turn. The door opened two inches against the chain and Miriam peered around the edge.

"Hello, Miriam. I came to see you and your mother. May I come in?"

"Hello, Mrs. Martin. I'm sorry, but Mummy told me not to let anyone in."

"Is she out?" I asked in some alarm. Surely no woman would leave the child alone, under the circumstances.

"No. She's taking a nap. She's very tired."

"I'm sure she is, and I don't want to disturb her if she's able to get a little rest. Maybe I could just give you this?" I held up the bag. "We had so much food left over from dinner yesterday, and I thought your mother might not feel like cooking for a while, so I brought some of it to you."

"Well—Mummy said not to open the door, but p'raps it will be all right—I'll have to close it first, though—"

The door closed and I heard the chain rattle. Before Miriam could open the door again I heard Mrs. Doyle's voice sounding clearly through the thin walls. "Miriam? Who is it, darling? Remember, you mustn't let anyone in."

"It's just Mrs. Martin, Mummy. She brought us some food. And I'm hungry." The last was said in a near whisper. I wasn't intended to hear.

There was a pause and then the sound of footsteps on the stairs. When the door opened, halfway this time, it was an exhausted-looking Mrs. Doyle who stood there, a depressing bathrobe over her pajamas.

"It's kind of you to call, Mrs. Martin, and especially kind to think about food. I'm afraid I've been too put about to do any marketing. I don't suppose you have time to come in for a moment?"

She didn't want me there. That was perfectly plain from her tone of voice. Any polite person would have taken the hint. However, she had asked me in, and she and Miriam needed some lunch.

"Thank you, I have plenty of time, and I thought I'd just make you a cup of tea before I go." I moved forward. Mrs.

Doyle had little choice but to stand aside and open the door the rest of the way.

There was no need to ask the way to the kitchen. It, with a dining area, was to the right of the minute entrance hall. The living room was on the left. A steep flight of stairs led, presumably, to the bedrooms and bathroom. The house was very cold. I left my coat on and buttoned the top button.

"Really, I don't need any tea," said Mrs. Doyle, following me. "At least, I can make some myself."

"But so can I, my dear, and you look ready to drop, if you don't mind my saying so. You just sit there at the table and I'll have tea and sandwiches ready in no time. Miriam, dear, if you'll show me where things are?"

The habit of obedience was strong in both of them. The mother sat; the daughter got out the teapot, mugs, and plates while I sandwiched thick slices of turkey into leftover dinner rolls. There was no butter in the small refrigerator, but margarine would do, and I'd brought some lettuce. When the tea was brewed, I asked where the sugar was.

Miriam looked shocked. "We don't use sugar in tea. It's too expensive. Here's the saccharine."

"Never mind. This time you need sugar. Do you have some for baking?"

Miriam looked at her mother, who nodded wearily. The little girl got a pound box of sugar, about half empty, from the pantry. I measured two teaspoonsful into each mug, poured out the tea, and looked for the milk.

"We take our tea without milk, and I'm afraid there's none in the house at the moment," said Mrs. Doyle. "But if you'd like a cup taken black—"

"No, thank you, but I'll sit down for a moment if you don't mind." I sat without waiting for permission. I was being shockingly rude, but really this woman needed some help. She must have some acquaintances, at least, among the neighbors. It seemed inexcusable that none of them had come to offer assistance.

I took a deep breath. This wasn't going to be easy. "I don't quite know how to say this, but I can hardly sit here where—here in your kitchen, and act as if everything is normal. I'm sure you must be terribly shocked and worried over what's happened, and I'm upset that you seem to have no help in your time of trouble. I don't know either of you well, but if there's anything I can do, please tell me. I'd be glad to go to the store for milk, for instance. Or if you're afraid to stay here alone, I could easily—"

"Thank you, but we'll manage." Mrs. Doyle took a sip of tea and then set her mug down carefully. It clattered against the tabletop; a little tea slopped out. "Mrs. Martin, you've talked to Ruth Beecham. There's no need to pretend a grief I don't feel. You know that my husband was not an easy man to live with."

"He was wicked," said Miriam in the cool, precise way of a polite English child. "Everyone thought he was a righteous man, but he wasn't." She took a bite of her sandwich. "He pretended to be good, but he was a Judas."

Mrs. Doyle gasped, swallowed the wrong way, and coughed. I could understand why. I tried not to react, but I suppose my mobile face betrayed me. The woman across the table clasped her hands, hard, and leaned forward, looking at me with an expression of such intensity that I moved back involuntarily.

"You are shocked by what Miriam says. She is simply repeating what she has heard me say. You are surprised that no one has come to help us. I don't know that it's any of your business, to be frank, but since you've wondered, I'll tell you. It's because John made enemies of all our neighbors. He would complain to the police about barking dogs, and parties, and rubbish fallen out of the bins. He once stayed awake for three nights in a row to catch a neighbor dealing drugs. He enjoyed that sort of thing, showing up other people, making them pay for their wrongdoing."

"Your family—"

"I have no family," she said flatly.

"Well, then, surely your church—"

"John's church. Not mine. They will stay away because John convinced them that I was an unrepentant sinner, a worldly woman, an unfit mother for Miriam. No, we'll get no help from them, nor would I want any."

"Then I insist on doing what I can. I'll go pick up some milk right now, and any other food you might—"

Mrs. Doyle pushed herself back from the table and stood. "Mrs. Martin, you will help us most by leaving us alone. Since you ask what help we want, that is my answer. I instructed Miriam to let no one in because we prefer not to talk about John. Nor do we need anything from anyone." She put her hand on her daughter's shoulder.

Miriam finished her sandwich and leaned against her mother. "Daddy was a wicked man," she said again in her precise manner. "He deserved to die. I'm glad he did. We'll get on much better without him."

Mrs. Doyle looked down at Miriam, but not before I got a good look at the mother's face. All the blood seemed to have drained from it, and her eyes held the hunted look of sheer, stark terror.

7

I MUTTERED something about being sorry I had intruded and got out of there as fast as I could. Driving heedlessly, my knuckles white on the wheel, my mind racing, I found myself presently in a cul-de-sac somewhere in some development. I pulled up to a curb, turned off the ignition, and sat there shaking for a while.

I could not accept what I had seen back there in the Doyles' kitchen. It was impossible. Surely I was mistaken.

Did Mrs. Doyle really think Miriam had killed her father? Think? Or know?

Miriam. Polite little Miriam, product of a strict Christian home and a strict Christian school. Miriam who thought cats were dirty and anything pretty was "vanity." Miriam who rejected her father but appeared to embrace his cold, harsh religion. Miriam who hated her father and thought him so wicked he deserved to die.

Could that child have killed that man?

Well, of course she could. Children did kill, sometimes

spectacularly. There had been a famous case in England not so long ago, two boys who had killed a girl, apparently simply for kicks. As I recalled, they hadn't been much older than Miriam.

But those children were mentally and emotionally disturbed.

It was easy to see that after the fact, wasn't it? And who was to say that Miriam wasn't disturbed? She'd certainly been brought up oddly enough to disturb the balance of anyone's mind.

Could she have stabbed a full-grown man? I wondered how sharp the knife was, and then was struck with horror that I would even think about it. Anyway, Doyle had, perhaps, not been killed with the knife. It would be easy enough, one would think, for someone to stab a dead or dying man. It wouldn't take much strength. Even a child . . .

Nauseated, I pushed the picture out of my mind.

However sickening the image, though, I forced myself to consider the idea. Not the details, but the broad outline.

Doyle has been to a meeting at the church. What sort of meeting? Would that be what they called their services? Well, no. A worship service would hardly go on until after midnight, would it? Or would it?

Well, let it pass for now. He's been to a meeting. He comes home and lets himself in with his key. Maybe he's in a bad mood—not an unlikely supposition. He doesn't bother to be quiet, and he wakes Miriam, who is a light sleeper, according to her mother.

Then what? They quarrel? He scolds her for something, probably for being up at that hour, even though it's his fault. He rouses such childish rage and resentment that she takes a knife and . . .

No. He was probably killed some other way, remember. And it's hard to imagine Miriam, such a controlled child, in a rage. No, she takes everything he has to dish out, all the cold verbal abuse, all the sadistic torture a harsh parent can inflict on a helpless child. But this child has decided she isn't helpless. She makes him some tea and puts in some . . .

Some what? What does a child know of poisons?

A child with intelligent parents knows a lot about them. There's poison aplenty in every household, and children must be taught caution. Something common, more or less tasteless—anyway, she finds something and puts it in his tea, and waits.

It would have to be something without violent symptoms, no vomiting or . . . no, I don't know that, do I? Mama cleaned up the kitchen the next morning, don't forget. Still, it would be hard to clean all traces of vomit off the victim's clothing, and the police didn't mention finding any.

At any rate, she waits. When her father is dead, she arranges him nicely on the floor and stabs him.

And then goes quietly off to bed to leave her mother to discover him in the morning?

The fact was, I thought, sitting back with a sigh, that I didn't know one single thing about what had gone on. The mother could have been in on it, but then why that look of horror on her face? Well, let that go for the moment. Suppose she was involved. Together they could have cleaned up the scene and waited for morning to call the police. Everything Mrs. Doyle said could have been a lie. And as for Miriam, a child suffering under harsh, unreasonable discipline often learns to lie almost as a matter of course.

Miriam hadn't actually said much, had she? Silence can be the most effective lie of all, if one has the poise to carry it off. And Miriam had plenty of poise, and plenty of intelligence.

I let out a long, shuddering sigh. I was constructing an elaborate hypothesis on the basis of nothing more than a few words and a terrified expression on a face. But I was ready to swear that Amanda Doyle believed her daughter guilty of murder.

What was I going to do about it?

I started the car and slowly picked my way through the maze of streets, heading uphill whenever I had a choice, until I came to an overlook where I could see the city spread out at my feet. Then it was easy enough to use the Cathedral spire as a homing beacon.

I didn't go home, though. Not just yet. I drove down the hill, found a space in a car park near the Cathedral, and walked across the Close. I needed more time to think, and I can think better in the Cathedral than anyplace else.

The chimes in the tower struck a quarter to three as I entered the church by the south door. The late November afternoon was wearing on, and clouds were gathering. The more remote areas of the Cathedral were dim, though the choir stalls were lit; Evensong was about to begin. I heard a murmur of voices as the choir and clergy assembled. I didn't join them. Just now I wanted to deal with my anxiety in my own way. I dropped into a pew toward the back of the nave, behind a pillar where the vergers wouldn't easily spot me, and thought it out.

I had three options, I realized when my emotions had calmed enough that my reason could operate. I could do nothing at all. I could take my suspicions to the police and let them deal with the horrible possibilities. Or I could keep quiet and look into the matter myself.

I hated all three options.

How could I leave it alone? That clichéd idea about evil prevailing when "good men do nothing"—well, it got to be a cliché because it's so true. I've never been the "I don't want to get involved" sort.

The police. If I talked to them, they would take me seriously. I was, after all, the wife of the former chief constable. They would talk to Miriam, perhaps bring her in for questioning. They would take her fingerprints and ask her if she wanted legal representation. They would do it all with exquisite courtesy and the utmost regard for her tender age, and it would all be pure hell for her.

And if they found likelihood of her guilt, there would be a hearing and a trial and then—then, what? What did they do with juvenile murderers in England? Prison of some sort? An "approved school"?

And if she were not guilty, what then? What of the suspicion that would cling forever? What of the nightmare memories?

How could I set in motion such a juggernaut train of action?

Up beyond the choir screen, the boys' voices soared in that angelic sound that is the epitome of English church music. I couldn't hear the words and didn't know the tune. They were just children singing.

Did Miriam sing? Would she ever sing again?

I often found peace in the Cathedral, but this time it eluded me. I slipped out before Evensong was over and made my way drearily back to my car with a sense of duty hanging heavy over my head.

Almost four o'clock. Ruth Beecham would probably have left school. She might be at home, unless she had gone over to comfort the Doyles. Of course I didn't have her address. I drove to St. Stephen's, caught the secretary just as she was leaving, and persuaded her to go back inside and get me Mrs. Beecham's address. She was snippy about it, as she had every right to be. This seemed to be my day for offending people.

This time I found the house with no trouble. Mrs. Beecham lived at one end of the High Street in a charming Georgian house. She, too, was just coming out the door when I pulled up in front.

"Oh! It's you. I'm sorry, I'm just going to pop over to Amanda's and see what I can do for her."

"I just left there. Well, a little while ago. She told me she didn't need any help, but of course she doesn't know me."

"No, and she values her privacy. I'm sure you can understand, especially at a time like this."

"Yes, and I'm afraid I was a little pushy. I can't blame her for being annoyed with me. But I do know she needs milk, and her neighbors didn't seem to be exactly rallying 'round."

"No, they wouldn't. I do want to push off, so—"

"Yes, but can you tell me one thing, first? What family does Mrs. Doyle have?"

"None, for all practical purposes. They don't like her, or they didn't like him, or something. She didn't talk about it much, just said there were no ties anymore." She opened the door of a car at the curb.

"One more thing, then. What's the name of the church Mr. Doyle attended?"

"Oh, Lord, something outlandish. Let me think. No, the name's gone, but I know where the place is. A horrid, dingy pile of brown brick near the university. Left at the big round-about and then the second right; Thomas Street, it is."

"Thank you, I'll find it. Sorry to keep you waiting."

But she stood there, car keys in hand. "Why d'you want to know?"

I might have known she'd ask. Fortunately I had a reasonable answer. "I want to give them a piece of my mind for not doing anything to help the Doyles at a time like this!"

"Now there's a thought! Give them a piece of mine while you're there." She waved, got in the car, and drove off.

By this time it was nearly five. I wondered what sort of hours a nonconformist church secretary kept. In fact, I wondered if they even had a secretary. I really knew nothing about any churches in Sherebury except the Anglican ones (or Episcopal, as we would say in America). Some were large and prosperous and stayed open all day, with staff in evidence. Some were tiny and poor and were kept locked, with no one in evidence except during services.

Well, in America the fundamentalist sects were the same way; some small, some big and very rich. I supposed it might be the same here. At any rate it wouldn't hurt to try, and I thought I could get there without too many wrong turns.

I spotted the building, in fact, halfway down the street. It was easily the biggest one around, and the ugliest. It looked like 1920s vintage, and not a good year. I can't imagine what its original purpose was, but it was now clearly, indeed gaudily, identified as the CHAPEL OF THE ONE TRUE GOD. Two large, lighted signs, one on the roof and one over the front door, informed the world of the name, incidentally implying that if they worshiped elsewhere, they were misguided.

There was, of course, no place to park, but I squeezed the car into a half space at the front of a row, only partially on the double yellow line that indicated no parking. I probably wouldn't be long, and surely the police had better things to do than seek out parking misdemeanors.

I wasn't sure why I had felt obliged to come here. I wouldn't like these people, and they certainly wouldn't like me. And what might they have to tell me that could possibly advance my unpleasant quest?

Maybe nothing, but if all else failed, I could do as I'd told Mrs. Beecham I would. That at least would be satisfying.

The front door was unlocked. Trying to look braver than I felt, I pushed it open and went inside.

8

NSIDE, the place fully justified my expectations. Whoever had planned and executed the interior design had subscribed zealously to the creed that beauty was sinful. There was a small entrance hall, paneled in dark, narrow boards that made the space seem even smaller. A dangling lightbulb emitted about fifteen watts of illumination. There was no sound of human occupancy, but a coat hung from one of the bent, rusty hooks that, together with a tract rack, were the sole adornments of the walls. Maybe somebody was around, after all.

Double doors led out of the foyer into, I discovered, the main worship space of the church. At least I supposed it was. It resembled no church I'd ever seen. An assembly hall in some old and poverty-stricken school, perhaps. The walls, paneled in the same disgusting brown tongue and groove, rose to a high peaked ceiling painted prison beige. No pictures hung on the walls, no plaques commemorating pious or generous parishioners, no stained-glass windows, oh, no. The windows were narrow and plain, with the kind of knobbly glass found in bus-station rest rooms. Come to think of it, the place smelled like a public rest room, too—eau de Lysol. The odor of sanctity, perhaps.

There were a lot of plain wooden chairs, arranged in precise rows. At the far end of the room, a raised platform accommodated a few more chairs. And that was it. No altar, no candles, no flowers. No organ, not so much as a modest upright piano. Linoleum tile on the floor in a predictable brown and beige checkerboard. Industrial fluorescent fixtures hanging from the ceiling.

The One True God appeared to be a drab, dreary deity.

There were small doors on either side of the platform. In most churches they would have led to a robing room or sacristy on one side and perhaps a choir room on the other. In this odd establishment, I hated to think what might lie behind them, and I was reluctant to find out. Indeed, the place reminded me of the horrible mission church in a 1930s Hitchcock film, *The Man Who Knew Too Much,* and I was getting cold feet. Some very nasty things went on in that Hitchcock church.

My feet weren't the only cold parts of me. There was no sign of radiators in the room, and the longer I stood there, the colder I got, both literally and figuratively. I had to make up my mind. Go in search of someone to talk to, or turn tail and run.

My sneakers squeaking on the tiled floor, despite my earnest attempts at stealth, I edged along the wall toward the door to the right of the platform.

It opened. I thought for a moment I was going to scream. There was no creak of hinges, no sound of footsteps, but a woman appeared in the doorway.

She didn't really look like a Hitchcock housekeeper. It was just my imagination, or the dim light, that gave her a long black gown and black hair pulled back in a bun.

"What do you want?" was her cordial greeting. Hitch would have loved her chilly voice.

I moistened my dry lips. "I was looking for the church secretary, or the—er—pastor."

"I am in charge of the business affairs of the chapel. Mr. Rookwood, the elder, has left for the day, and I was about to do so when I heard a noise in here. Since no one should be in the meeting hall at this time of day, I naturally checked. So I ask again, what is it that you want?" She hadn't moved from the doorway. She was shouting and expecting me to shout back.

I was no longer afraid of her. Bad manners rouse my anger, which is always a galvanizing force. I drew myself up and moved closer to the platform. "My name is Dorothy Martin, and I'm here on behalf of one of your parishioners, Mrs. Doyle. And her daughter, Miriam."

"You are misinformed." Her voice had become positively glacial. "There are no followers of the One True God named Doyle."

"Mr. John Doyle—"

"Mr. Doyle is dead, at the hands of the woman you mention. This chapel has no interest in her, save to hope and trust that she will receive the punishment she so richly deserves. It is a pity that capital punishment has been abolished. Good day."

"Just a moment, Mrs.—"

She ignored me and started to step back.

"Wait! What is your name, please?"

"Mrs. Rookwood." She said it grudgingly, and her glare dared me to comment.

"Mrs. Rookwood, you should know that the police are not entirely convinced that the murder lies at Mrs. Doyle's feet. There is considerable doubt, and they are looking into other possibilities. Meanwhile, she and her daughter—who I believe attends your school—are in financial need, and in need of comfort, as well. Surely the church—the chapel—must have some sort of plan, some routine for bereaved—er—members."

"Madam, our faith tells us to shun the sinner and avoid the path of the evildoer. It is plain that you do not follow this commandment, but we in this chapel do. We have no communication with whited sepulchres."

She turned away and shut the door firmly behind her. I heard the snick of an efficient lock.

Yes, definitely my day to annoy people. I left the depressing place, got in my car (which by some miracle had not collected a parking ticket), and drove thoughtfully home.

I'd gone to the church to learn what I could about John Doyle. In a way I'd hit a blank wall, but in another way I'd learned quite a lot. Any man who could devote himself to such a religion and associate with people like Mrs. Rookwood was a man few normal people would like. I could easily believe he'd made enemies.

And if I intended to go through with this, to try to prove that neither his wife nor his daughter killed him, it behooved me to track down a few of those enemies.

I would come back to this travesty of a church and talk to as many of its members as possible before I got thrown out. Meanwhile, there were other paths to follow.

His job. Frictions often arose on the job. Where had Mrs. Beecham said he worked? A bank, wasn't it? That was unfortunate, because the weekend was upon us, and I'd have to wait until Monday.

On the other hand, the weekend was the perfect time to visit a church. I wished I'd taken a leaflet from that tract rack in the foyer, since it would presumably list service times. Never mind. I'd find out. And tomorrow I'd talk to some of the neighbors, find out if any of the animosities Mrs. Doyle had talked about had been serious enough to lead to murder.

The only thing was, what was I going to tell Alan?

I didn't want to tell him about Miriam. Alan was a kind man. His first wife, who had died some years ago, had presented him with children, and they with grandchildren, to all of whom he was devoted. He was also, however, a policeman.

He had a deeply ingrained respect for the laws and procedures under which he had operated for a lifetime. I was sure he wouldn't want to keep my terrible secret. He would argue, quite plausibly, that the officers in charge would take great care of the little girl, that there would be psychiatric help available if she needed it, that even if she were to be found guilty, some form of rehabilitation was far more likely than a prison sentence. And if she *were* guilty, then surely I, a responsible adult, didn't want her to go free, perhaps to kill again.

It would all sound reasonable. And I simply couldn't accept it.

If the police, acting by themselves, conceived a suspicion that Miriam might have murdered her father, I wouldn't do anything about it, but I would not take the responsibility for pointing them in her direction.

In fact, now that I thought of it, I was going to have to have a private talk with Mrs. Doyle. If she behaved with everyone the way she did with me, the police, who are not stupid, would soon draw the same conclusion I had. She was, somehow, going to have to polish up her act. Maybe she should send Miriam away. If the child weren't around to utter those chilling remarks about her father, people wouldn't notice the mother's nerves so much, or would attribute them to other causes. Goodness knows she had enough to be nervous about.

I was avoiding the real issue: what to tell Alan. And I had to make up my mind soon, because I was almost home.

In the end I decided to stick to a version of the truth. I was concerned about the Doyles, who seemed to have no friends. I wanted to do what I could to help, blah, blah, blah. He would accept that, I hoped, as a screen for my curiosity about the murder. I had something of a reputation for poking my nose into crime, and Alan had learned to be tolerant, so long as I kept myself out of danger and didn't get in the way of the police.

But I hated not telling him everything.

As it turned out, I didn't have to say much. He had just hung up the phone when I walked into the kitchen.

"Hello, love. I thought you'd fallen off the ends of the earth. How did you find Mrs. Doyle?"

"A good deal upset, and pretty prickly about accepting help. I spent the rest of the afternoon trying to talk someone from her church—or her husband's church—into offering a little support, but I might as well have talked to the bricks on the wall. They'd have been just as sympathetic."

"Well, I have some news for you. That was Derek on the phone. He did manage to push through the autopsy, over the usual bitter complaints about overwork and everyone always wanting everything yesterday."

"And?"

"They came up with a time of death, for one thing. Doyle died at some time after midnight Wednesday night. Thursday morning that would make it, officially. Between midnight and two, they think, and probably closer to midnight, though the doctor wouldn't commit himself to an exact time, naturally. They never will.

"The interesting thing is that it turns out they were quite right about the stab wound. It was made after death. Quite soon after, probably, because there was some blood, but not a lot. I'll spare you the details, but the kicker is that the man died of an overdose of some form of digitalis."

"Foxglove," I said automatically. In novels, when someone dies of digitalis poisoning, it's always because the bad guy has brewed up some foxglove tea.

"Not in this case, apparently. I didn't grasp the niceties of the medical explanation, but apparently he was bungful of ordinary medicinal digitalis, the kind given for certain kinds of heart trouble."

"Did he have heart trouble?"

"Don't know. Derek hasn't managed to reach his doctor yet. But he says there was no digitalis in the house when his men searched. No medicine of any kind; they noticed particularly. It's pretty unusual for a family not to have any aspirin around, or cold medicine, or that sort of thing, but there was nothing at all."

Well, that was a relief. "Then it looks as though Mrs. Doyle is out of it, after all."

"It's too soon to say that, Dorothy. But the likelihood has certainly been reduced. Derek phoned the woman and asked if she wanted police protection."

"Why—oh, because someone killed Doyle and might be a danger to the rest of the family, you mean?"

"That was the idea. But Mrs. Doyle rejected the offer quite flatly. Said she was perfectly capable of taking care of herself and her daughter. Rather a peculiar woman, is she?"

I took a moment over that one and answered with care. "Not so much peculiar, I think, as overwhelmed. Her husband's dead, and even though she didn't get along with him, it's a terrible shock. And she has suffered so long under his domination that I don't imagine she's able to cope very well by herself. It isn't that she's stupid. She's a teacher, after all, and a good one. It's just that he made the decisions all their married life, and she hasn't learned how, just as she hasn't learned how to make friends."

Alan smiled a little and shook his head. "I knew I'd hear it sooner or later."

"Hear what?"

"That tone of voice that means you're about to take another lame duck under your wing."

"Well—she does need someone with some common sense on her side. And I feel sorry for that poor little girl."

"My dear, you don't have to make excuses. Unlike Mr. Doyle, I don't presume to make your decisions for you. Except, as it's getting late and I'm getting peckish, suppose I make a unilateral decision that we're going out to dinner."

"That's one I'll never challenge. Shall I change into something nicer?"

"Not if a pub meal will do."

"Lead me to it."

We had a pleasant meal, but I was conscious, all the time, of an underlying feeling of guilt. Alan was being so nice about this, and all the time I was being devious with him.

And with splendid inconsistency, I also wondered, in between snatches of conversation, if there was any way Miriam Doyle could have known about the toxic properties of digitalis.

9

THE next morning I decided it was time to enlist some help, and there was only one person I could go to. I looked up Ruth Beecham's phone number and gave her a ring.

"Mrs. Beecham? This is Dorothy Martin. Look, I know I've been something of a pest lately, but there's something I need to talk to you about. Yes, about the Doyles. I'm sure you're frantically busy on weekends, I always was when I was teaching, but if you can spare me half an hour or so, I'd be grateful. Well, right now if that'll work."

Alan was busy with his book. I kissed the top of his head and told him to expect me when he saw me. He grunted something.

When I got to Mrs. Beecham's, she was alone, her husband and the kids out on various pursuits. "I hope you don't mind if I carry on with my shopping list," she said as she seated me, somewhat reluctantly, at the kitchen table.

I took the hint and got straight to the point.

"Mrs. Beecham, we don't really know each other, but I'm

going to trust you with something important. As far as I can see, you really are the only friend Mrs. Doyle has. I hope you'll believe that I want to be her friend, too. And I hope you'll understand my motives when I ask you if you've noticed something very odd about her attitude toward Miriam."

Mrs. Beecham, who had been fidgeting with pad and pencil, became suddenly still. "Odd how?"

"So you *have* seen it. You think, don't you, that she suspects Miriam of killing Mr. Doyle?"

After a pause she said, "You're very—direct, aren't you?"

"When polite fictions are inappropriate, yes, I am. I believe you're the same."

"Sometimes." She stood up suddenly. "Would you like some tea? I've just given up cigarettes, and I'm dying for one. Tea would help."

Seated again with a pot steeping on the table, she opened up. "Yes, you're right. I don't know how you saw it, not knowing Amanda, but I could tell right away that something was wrong, and when I saw the way she looked at Miriam—"

"That's it, you see. The look. I wouldn't have noticed anything if it hadn't been for that look. Of course it came after Miriam had said some extraordinary things about her father, how wicked he was, and that he had deserved to be killed."

"She didn't do it!"

"We don't know that, do we? Even her mother thinks she did, or might have."

Mrs. Beecham put down her teacup and looked at me, hard, for about five seconds—which is a long time to be under scrutiny. "I've been talking to people about you," she said slowly. "You've rather made murder your hobby, haven't you? And you're Alan Nesbitt's wife."

"A few crimes have come my way, yes," I said in a voice I had to work hard to keep steady. "And yes, I am married to a retired policeman. I don't know that I would call murder my hobby, precisely. And you might be interested to know that I have told neither my husband nor anyone else what I believe

Mrs. Doyle suspects. I came here hoping we could talk about what's best to do for both Mrs. Doyle and Miriam. If you don't want to trust me, I'll go away and we'll both forget this conversation ever took place. But I'd much rather have your help."

Our eyes met and held for a long beat. Then she shrugged. "Very well. I suppose it can't do any harm. If Amanda keeps on shying like a startled colt every time Miriam makes remarks, the police will catch on soon, anyway."

"Exactly! Just what I thought. Now, look, Mrs. Beecham—"

"If we're to be conspirators, or accessories after the fact, or whatever, you might as well call me Ruth," she said with the ghost of a smile.

"Good. And I'm Dorothy. What I was going to say was, what are the chances of Miriam going away for a while? It would calm Mrs. Doyle down and defuse the situation. Surely there must be *some* family she could go to, somewhere."

"I suppose there must, except Amanda never talks about them. Let me think, though. She mentioned a sister once, in—Canterbury, was it? If I remember properly, the sister wasn't quite as off-putting as the rest of her people."

"I don't suppose you remember her name?"

"Lord, no. I may even be wrong about the whole thing."

"Would Mrs. Doyle tell you?"

"You might as well stick to Amanda. She hates being called Doyle. I think she's planning to go back to her maiden name. As for telling me the name of the sister—I don't know. She's stubborn, you know."

"She's also extremely frightened, for her daughter and perhaps for herself as well. Could you convince her that Miriam would be much better off away from her for a while?"

Ruth groaned. "I don't even know if Miriam could be persuaded to go. They've always been close, she and her mother, but now! They cling. Miriam isn't going to school, even.

That'll come to a screeching halt soon; the authorities will see to it."

"That reminds me. Did you know that Miriam had been enrolled at St. Stephen's as of the beginning of next term? I heard Amanda talking about it to the school secretary."

"She told me. Quite calmly, too, as if she hadn't had major battles with John for years about that chapel school. Then one day she just coolly puts Miriam down for St. Stephen's. I don't know how she got the nerve."

I sighed. "That doesn't look good, you know."

"What do you mean?"

"She defies her husband's wishes, which she's never had the courage to do before. A day or two later he's dead. It doesn't take too much imagination to believe that she knew he was going to be dead."

Ruth winced. "You're a frightening person, Dorothy Martin. God, I wish I had a cigarette!"

I picked up my purse and rummaged in it. "Here, have a chocolate bar instead. Chocolate makes you produce a lot of that feel-good stuff, what do they call it? Endorphins, that's it."

"And puts on pounds and pounds." She reached out a hand.

"But to return to the subject—I do believe that somehow we've got to get Miriam out of town. I can try to approach Amanda, but you'd be much more likely to get results. Tell her we know what she suspects, if you have to. If that won't scare her into action, I don't know what will."

Ruth swallowed a large bite of chocolate. "Okay, I'll try. If I can't manage it by myself, I'll call you in for reinforcement. You can be a very persuasive lady." Her eyes strayed for a moment to her shopping list.

"All right. I said half an hour and I've been here an hour *and* given you extra work to do. I'll let you get on with your day if you'll tell me one more thing. Did Amanda ever tell you why she didn't show up to teach that day?"

"Not a word. I tried and tried to get it out of her, but she just kept on saying it was necessary and she was sorry to have been a nuisance."

"All right, once you've worked on her about Miriam, I'll tackle her about her absence without leave. I was the injured party, after all. Maybe I can play on her guilt."

I left then, but as I drove off I wished I hadn't used that particular word.

I also wished I had thought to ask where Amanda had been married. The record of that marriage would give her maiden name. That would be useful in tracing her family if she proved obdurate with Ruth.

Or perhaps—of course! How could I have forgotten? The very best source for information of any kind about anyone in town lived next door to me. I'd go and talk to Jane!

I went home, made lunch for Alan (whose mind, perhaps fortunately, was still on his book), petted two sleepy cats, and then set out across the backyard. Jane and I have been on a drop-in basis for years now.

Jane was washing her luncheon dishes, and her dogs, fortunately, were sleeping off their midday meal. Jane adores her bulldogs, whom she rather resembles, and spoils them. They're nice enough beasts, but there are a good many of them and they're pretty boisterous. Their welcomes can be overwhelming, especially to someone used to the restrained affection of cats.

Jane greeted me with raised eyebrows and a proffered coffeepot. "No, thanks," I said, and sat down. I've often wondered why Jane uses words as though there were a tax on every one she utters. But that's Jane, and I've gotten used to her style by now.

She poured herself a cup and sat down at the kitchen table. "Doyle?"

"Doyle. I seem to have gotten myself embroiled in the affair."

"Never thought you'd leave it alone. Here to pick my brains?"

"Something like that. What do you know about him, for a start?"

She snorted. It was eloquent, expressing every derogatory adjective in the thesaurus in one explosive sound.

"Well, I'd gotten that impression from other people, but can you give me any specifics?"

Forced into speech, Jane amplified. "Self-righteous prig. Bible-thumper. Killjoy. All-round troublemaker."

"I've heard he made some enemies along the way."

She snorted again. "Everyone he met, except those masterpieces at the chapel. All cut from the same cloth, that lot."

"But, Jane, it's one thing to be universally hated, and it's another to have enemies, real enemies. Did he make anyone mad enough to kill him?"

"Wouldn't be surprised. Small feuds everywhere. Reported another clerk at the bank because he was a pound short at the end of the day, twice in a row. Boy lost his job because Doyle made such a fuss about it."

"For *two pounds?* You've got to be kidding."

"Would've been overlooked if Doyle hadn't made such a stink about no smoke without fire, that sort of thing. Made it look as if the boy'd taken a lot over time. Only a kid, not even twenty."

"You knew him."

Jane nodded. "Son of a pupil of mine. She—the mother—came to me. Nothing I could do. Sure you won't have coffee?"

"I think I need some to take the taste of that story out of my mouth."

"Worse to come." Jane put the kettle on and spooned coffee into the French *cafetière*. "Heard about the neighbor he turned over to the police?"

"Drug dealing or something, wasn't it?"

"Just the point. It wasn't."

I raised my eyebrows. Two can play the game.

"Young man. Long hair, low-slung jeans, nose rings. Played in a band. Lived next to the Doyles. Not thought to be

respectable." The snort again. "Set great store by respectabil-
ity, Doyle did. So he took to watching the boy."

"How old was he? The young man, I mean."

A shrug. "Eighteen, nineteen. Young wife, baby. Not
much money. One night, some shady business. Parked cars,
something changing hands. Doyle called police. Found
money and marijuana in one of the cars, arrested everybody."

The coffee was ready. Jane poured out cups for both of us
before she went on.

"Boy'd been in trouble with the police before. Kept at the
station for quite a while. Had just landed a job. Doyle told the
boss he'd been arrested. Lost the job." She sipped her coffee
and continued, her voice no longer quite steady.

"Wife talked to me, weeks later. Said he'd been buying her
a diamond ring that night. Never been able to afford it before.
Thought it was maybe stolen, needed to be under the table.
Marijuana belonged to other man."

"But surely the boy was cleared of any drug charges?"

"He was. Too late. When he was sacked, went home and
stuck his head in the oven."

10

I was a long time before I could ask any more questions, but there were questions to be asked. I blew my nose and cleared my throat. "Did Doyle ever apologize?"

"Not he. Seemed to feel he'd done the right thing, and the boy was to blame for being so wicked as to take his own life."

I shuddered. "And the girl, and the baby?" There was a murder motive with bells on, I was thinking, for her or her family.

"Don't know. Left town. Went back to her parents, maybe. She was from the north somewhere."

I sipped at the fresh coffee Jane had provided, a little brandy in it this time, and pondered how often murder victims seemed to earn their fate. If I had had any doubt before, I had now come around fully to Miriam's opinion. Her father *had* deserved to die.

Then I shook my head. Maybe he had, but that was not a decision for any individual to make. Murder is never justified, as unattractive, as downright villainous even, as the victim may be. Killing in self-defense, yes. Killing in combat, maybe.

Execution? Well—maybe, sometimes, in cases of particularly heinous crimes when there is no doubt about the criminal's guilt.

But murder, never. So no matter how glad I was that John Doyle was dead, I felt I had to go on hunting for his murderer.

"So is that the worst?"

"That I know of," said Jane.

"Did *anybody* like the man?"

"Big man at the chapel. Well respected there. Says something for the rest."

"Indeed. I've met one of the denizens, the pastor's wife, and I must say I didn't care for her. But I think I need to talk to some more of them, little as the idea appeals to me. Do you know when they hold their services on a Sunday?"

"Never wanted to know." Jane lowered her head and looked at me over the tops of her glasses. "In your place, I'd stay away. Those people are dangerous. Not just crazy. Dangerous."

I was more shaken by her grammar than her words. When Jane uses a complete sentence, she is very serious indeed.

Nevertheless, the next morning I rose early and went to the first service at the Cathedral. I felt I needed some spiritual sustenance for my next chore of the day.

The early service has always been very moving for me. There is no music save the music of the lovely old words of the Eucharist. There are few tourists, few communicants at all, if it comes to that. The Cathedral is quiet and, in November, dim. One is free to give oneself up to the age-old words of faith and comfort.

The Eucharist was celebrated by one of the canons, but as I left the church and went out, blinking, into the chilly early-morning sunlight, I met the dean on his way in.

"Good morning, Mrs. Martin. A lovely morning, though winter is coming, I fear. You're up early."

"Yes, I have something to do later."

"Alas, even the Sabbath can seldom be devoted entirely to rest, more's the pity."

"Well, Dean, it's never your day of rest, is it?"

"It is a day of service," he said gently, "which can be exhausting, but brings its own rewards." He looked at me more closely. "You're looking tired, my dear. Not ill, I hope?"

"No, just a little—worried, I suppose."

"Ah. That would be the Doyle matter, I expect. I understand you're a friend of Mrs. Doyle?"

I have long since stopped expecting anything in Sherebury to escape the dean's notice. "Not a friend, exactly, though I feel very sorry for her."

"Yes, of course." He paused. "You will, I expect, be spending a good deal of time with her for a few days. It does you credit, but you must on no account neglect your own safety. We are sometimes called to walk into danger, but never blindly, you know. And if at any time I can be of help, you know you can always come to me. I shall pray for you, my dear." And having thus offered spiritual comfort and delicately warned me to keep an eye out for murderers, without mentioning anything so vulgar, he bade me good morning and went into the shadowy vastnesses of the Cathedral he so loved. I mentally contrasted him with Mrs. Rookwood and went home shaking my head.

When I found that Alan was still in bed, I left him a note saying that I'd be home for lunch, and with the utmost distaste made for the Chapel of the One True God.

I was early. The proceedings, according to the badly printed leaflet in the tract rack, would not begin until ten, and it wasn't even quite nine.

That was fine with me. The longer I could put off the evil hour, the happier I was. I hadn't had breakfast, so I walked in search of a cafe that was open on a Sunday morning. The university being across the street, and students living in the Victorian houses nearby, I didn't have too much trouble finding one. It was shabby and smoky, but the coffee smelled good and the doughnuts looked edible. I bought a jelly-filled one and a cup of coffee and sat down at a Formica table scarred with cigarette burns and coffee rings. No one paid the slightest attention to me.

What did I hope to accomplish at the chapel? It would be a pity to put myself through one of their services without a clear goal in mind. I was sure, remembering an experience in the church of a tiny American sect, that I had an excruciating morning ahead of me. Very well, what could I hope to gain from it? I pulled a paper napkin out of the metal holder on the table, found a pen in my purse, and began to make a list.

Well, first, I wanted to get a really clear idea of the theology of the place. One can learn quite a lot about a man by knowing what he believes, or in this case believed. That his creed was harsh and peculiar, I already knew, but the details might be enlightening.

Second, of course, I wanted to meet some of the people. Or perhaps that was the wrong way to put it. The one woman I had met there had not inspired in me the least desire for acquaintance with any more. However, if I could get some of them talking about John Doyle, it might give me some insight into the man. Like Hercule Poirot, I've always felt the character of the victim was often the key to finding the murderer.

Finally, I hoped I could talk to some of the teachers of the school run by the church, and learn a little more about Miriam. If nothing else, it would be an interesting experience to find out just what sort of people could have instilled the warped values she recited so glibly, and so horrifyingly.

That was about it, really. I might not accomplish anything, of course, but it seemed worth a try. I left my coffee, which had not tasted nearly as good as it had smelled, and went back to the repellent chapel.

The congregation nearly filled it. I've never understood the appeal of some of the more offbeat religions, but it's a fact that many of them seem to fill the pews. Even at my age, which is closer to seventy than I care to admit, I don't have more than a rudimentary understanding of human nature.

I won't go into details about the service. It seemed to go on forever and was as dreary and depressing as I had expected, consisting entirely of Scripture readings, testimony from the congregation, and a long, ranting sermon by (I presumed) Mr. Rookwood. The theme might have been taken straight from Jonathan Edwards, the terrifying eighteenth-century American cleric whose favorite topic was "sinners in the hands of an angry God." The readings, of the eye-for-an-eye variety, were all from the Old Testament. I tried to maintain an objective attitude, but I found myself becoming more and more angry. What right had these people, who presumably called themselves Christians, to ignore any hint of a gospel of loving kindness, forgiveness, and redemption? They preached a message of fear, of empty observances of rigid disciplines, of damnation for the mortal who strayed so much as an iota from the arbitrary path set before them, and set, moreover, by Mr. Rookwood. Myself, I preferred a higher authority.

No wonder John Doyle had hounded a man to his death and felt no remorse about it.

The proceedings finally ended, and as we filed out of the hall I realized I hadn't the least desire to talk to these people. I wasn't even sure I *could* talk to them. Our views of the world were so opposed, we could have but little common conversational ground. I was not, in any case, certain that I could keep my temper for more than five seconds if someone tried to convert me. However, I had suffered a great deal for this opportunity, and I would grit my teeth and do my damnedest.

The offering was taken at the door as we all left, by Mr. Rookwood and his wife. Typical, I thought with sardonic amusement. That way they could see exactly how much each person gave. No doubt they would find some way to punish those who kicked in too little. I would have given nothing, but something in the bleak eyes of the Rookwoods sent a little shiver of intimidation up my spine. I fumbled in my purse, produced a pound coin, and dropped it into the basket, where it shone dully among the pile of banknotes. They were certainly raking it in, weren't they? Amazing what some people will pay out of guilt.

I was somewhat surprised that they had a gathering after the meeting. I had hoped they would, but boiled coffee and squashed buns seemed wild dissipation for so austere a crowd. It made more sense when I realized that the dismal little meal constituted lunch for most of them. Sunday school, Bible study, and other small group meetings would take place immediately after they had refreshed themselves (if "refreshed" was the word). So I joined them in the building next door, ignored the food and drink, and sat down at a table. I immediately found myself, as a newcomer, the center of attention.

It wasn't congenial attention, either. People stopped talking as they approached my table and fixed me with hostile glares. They sat elsewhere as long as there were chairs elsewhere, but the last ones into the room were forced to sit with me.

No one said anything for a while. They stolidly drank their coffee and ate their buns while darting glances at me, glances that were immediately averted. They took in my makeup, minimal as it was, my clothes (a favorite suit in soft blue-and-purple tweed), my earrings (amethysts and sapphires, small but attractive), my hat (blue felt with purple feathers). I felt, irrationally, that they probably knew I had lace on my underwear. They were clad, men, women and children alike, in blacks and browns and grays, with neither jewelry nor makeup in evidence—nor hats.

Finally one woman cleared her throat. "You're a reporter, aren't you? Come to ask us questions about the death. Indecent, I call it! Coming here flaunting your gaudy clothes and your evil ways! Well, you're wasting your time. We don't talk to reporters."

"Actually, I'm a teacher. Retired." I took deep breaths and dug my fingernails into my palms.

"Oh, then you're a friend of That Woman."

The capital letters were plainly there. My temper rose a little higher. "If you are referring to Mrs. Doyle, I hardly know her. I understand her little girl goes to school here."

"*Went* to school here. She was always a troublemaker, asking questions and stirring up the other children. We wouldn't have her back now if she came crawling, not with a murderess for a mother."

"That's right," another woman chimed in, "and her father not the saint he pretended to be, either, or he wouldn't have married a woman like that."

I had to listen. They might say something important. I tried to put my emotions in another compartment of my mind, seal them away so I didn't react.

"Mr. Doyle was quite an important member of the church—of the chapel, wasn't he?"

"Not half so important as he thought he was," growled a man. "We're all equal sinners in the sight of God; all need to repent and undergo proper discipline. Why, he thought he knew more than Elder Rookwood. Such arrogance." The others nodded.

Their attitude, however nasty, was interesting. I was beginning almost to wish I had known John Doyle. He had managed to alienate even people of his own ugly stripe. Unless, of course, his death had somehow made him anathema. Yes, that could be it. By the sort of logic that prevailed in this crowd, the fact that he had been murdered could have proved that he was the sort of person to get himself murdered, therefore untouchable, and they were distancing themselves as far as possible.

I felt ill.

A couple of heads turned away from me, then a few more. I saw the preacher coming across the room, toward the table.

Toward me.

"I have been talking to my wife, madam," he said coldly. "You are not a sinner seeking to repent and be saved from the pit. You are a meddlesome outsider, and you are not welcome here."

"Elder Rookwood, I presume?" I was so angry now that I didn't care if I lost my temper.

"My name is of no concern to you."

"Oh, but it is. I want to tell people about you and your so-called religion." I stood up. The room had gone deadly quiet. Recklessly I continued. "I want this town to know what kind of people you are, people who would condemn an innocent woman without knowing a single one of the facts. I want them to know that your precious piety is nothing but self-righteous hypocrisy, mixed with a fair amount of sadism. I'd like to expose every one of you!"

And with that outburst I stormed out of the room.

11

I WAS shaking before I got outside, and in tears by the time I got to my car. Furiously I wiped my face and blew my nose and roared out of my parking place. It was lucky that no one else was on the street, for I never looked.

The adrenaline ran out about the time I got to the roundabout, and when I had negotiated it, I pulled into a side street and sat there and shook.

What on earth had I done? Jane's voice came back to me: *These people are dangerous.* And with one ill-considered speech I had infuriated every one of them.

Furthermore, I had learned very little. The people at the chapel had displayed hostility toward all the Doyles, even John, who had so recently been one of their leading lights. Perhaps my impression of his position in the group was overblown, but even so, it was remarkable that no one seemed to mourn him. Or it would have been remarkable in another kind of church, but with this crowd . . . I shivered a little and remembered the words of the Litany: *From envy, hatred, and malice, and all uncharitableness* . . . "Good Lord, deliver us," I said aloud.

Maybe I had just talked to the wrong people, I reflected, trying to be charitable myself. Maybe there were some good-hearted souls among those seeking the One True God.

If so, my bitter side retorted, Elder Rookwood was surely not among them.

Well, I'd expected the experience to be unpleasant, and I hadn't been disappointed. Fine. That was over. I'd learned more than I ever really wanted to know about these people, and with any luck at all, I'd never have to see any of them ever again.

Meanwhile, Sunday afternoon stretched out before me, and I was suddenly hungry. I headed back out into traffic (looking first, this time), and made for home.

Alan, who had just come back from church, looked at me quizzically when I walked into the house. "Taken to heathen ways after all these years?"

"You're not so far wrong," I said, hanging up my coat and hat. "I did go to early service, but I spent the rest of the morning at John Doyle's church, or chapel, or whatever it's called."

"I wouldn't have thought you'd find Mrs. Doyle there. Derek gave me to understand that she and her husband disagreed about religion."

"They did, and she wasn't there. I was just—oh, I suppose I was trying to get an idea of what kind of influence that church was for Miriam. Jane's been telling me some pretty disturbing things about Doyle, and I wondered if the church, and the church school, had been any comfort to that poor little mite. If I'm to get close to her and her mother, I think I need to know what they've been coping with."

"And did you learn anything?"

"Alan, it was appalling! Terrifying, really. How do people get that way? Bitter and malicious and—oh, just hateful!"

Alan cocked his head to one side and looked at me. "Perhaps they start by thinking they're better than other people."

"Ouch! All right, I deserved that, and I really will try to

keep an open mind. But when a pastor throws you out of his church—"

"You were thrown out?"

"I was told, not at all politely, to go. I'm afraid I lost my temper then and told them off. I didn't leave any friends behind me there, I'm sure of that."

"Then let's hope they're not quite as malicious as you suppose. And not to change the subject, but what were you thinking of doing about Sunday lunch?"

"A reprise of Thanksgiving dinner, unless you're sick to death of turkey by now."

"I like turkey," he said mildly.

We talked of other things over our meal. I don't think I could have eaten if I'd had to rehash details of the malevolence I'd faced that morning. But I couldn't get Miriam out of my mind. What a life that child must have led, facing her teachers by day and her father in the evenings and on weekends, all of them poisoned by that harsh, narrow creed. Doubtless her mother had tried to protect her, but Doyle had been a cruelly domineering tyrant.

I didn't believe, refused to believe, that Miriam had, in the end, taken the ultimate revenge against the tyrant. I believed that she was at bottom a sweet child. Look at the way she had behaved on Thanksgiving, when her world had been torn apart and she had been terrified for her mother. But she was too controlled, too quiet, too much under the influence of the pernicious doctrines her father had hammered into her. And her mother was, I thought, not the best person to cope with her, at least not just now. She, too, was under intolerable stress, not least because of her suspicions. It would be healthier for them both if Miriam could get away from the situation for a while, get to some haven where she would be treated with kindness and a dose of good, common sense. A favorite grandparent would be the ideal solution, but if Ruth Beecham was right, no such person existed.

That reminded me that I had never asked Jane about

Amanda's family. As soon as the dishes were washed and the kitchen put to rights, I went next door while Alan settled down to read the Sunday papers.

"Don't know much about her," was Jane's surprising answer to my question about Amanda's background. "Not from Belleshire. Hampshire, maybe? Just an idea. Don't know where I got it."

"Then she'd have no family around here," I said, disappointed.

"Not that I know of."

"Do you know where she was married? I could check records if I knew where to look."

"No idea. Ask her."

"I'm not sure she'd tell me. She's never told her friend Ruth anything about her background; why would she tell me?"

"Why're you so keen to know? What's it matter, anyway?"

"It's Miriam. She's behaving very unnaturally, it seems to me. Too quiet. And Amanda is ready to snap. It would be good for both of them if Miriam could go away for a while, but if there's no family, where's she to go?"

"Hmm. Best ask. She can only refuse to talk, and you're no worse off. She'll say, if she has any sense about the child at all."

"That's it, you see. I don't think she does have any sense about Miriam. She's been living under such strain for such a long time, trying to protect her daughter from her husband. I had no idea how bad it was until you told me all that about the people John Doyle had—had savaged. And then when I went to that church this morning and realized the kind of school Miriam's had to go to—well, I'm truly worried about the child's emotional health."

Jane nodded. "I'd take the little mite in myself, in a minute, but I'm the wrong person. Too old, too many dogs, and not far enough away."

"That's why Alan and I can't volunteer—barring the dogs. Alan is wonderful with his grandchildren, but they're a good deal older than Miriam. I, of course, have no more children than you, but like you I've taught a good many hundred. But that was years ago. I have to face it; I haven't the energy or the understanding to look after a troubled nine-year-old girl. And she needs to get away from here, out of this town with its unhappy memories." I didn't tell Jane the other reason why I wanted Miriam out of Sherebury. I was trying hard not to think about that one.

"You talk to Amanda Doyle, Dorothy. Make her see sense."

I doubted I could do that, and I doubted it even more that evening when I got a call from Ruth Beecham.

"Is anyone listening in?" she demanded when she had identified herself.

"Of course not!"

"You never know. Some husbands do, or there might be someone else in the house. My kids pick up the phone by accident sometimes, and I think they listen if there's anything interesting going on. They went out for pizza, though, so I'm safe here. Dorothy, I talked to Amanda today and it's no good, I'm afraid. She flatly refuses to let Miriam go anywhere, and she flatly refuses to discuss—what we think she thinks."

"Would she tell you about her family?"

"Not a word. I asked her about the sister, and she wouldn't talk about her. I think that means there is a sister, though. One thing about Amanda. She can be maddeningly stubborn, but she never lies. If she doesn't want to tell the truth, she goes all silent. She said hardly a word to me today, about anything. I don't know if she's just built up a wall around herself, or if there's so much she dares not say, she's decided not to talk at all. Or just possibly she's . . ."

Ruth fell silent on the other end of the phone.

"She's what?" I gently prodded.

"I wonder if she's going right 'round the bend, she and Miriam both. They're getting odder and odder, Dorothy. They didn't go to chapel today at all, for one thing, and for years they've gone to both services, every Sunday, without fail."

"I know. I mean I know they weren't there, because I was, in the morning at least. And with the way people were talking about them, I'm not surprised they didn't go. No sensible person would have, given any choice in the matter."

Ruth sighed. "Yes, well, Amanda gave me the impression that the place was pretty bad. And of course Amanda and Miriam are both terribly upset; one can't wonder that they haven't established a new routine yet. But what bothered me was the way Miriam acted about it. She couldn't seem to decide whether to be afraid of what would happen to them—a lightning bolt, or some such, I gather—or pleased as Punch that they needn't go any longer. And Amanda wasn't much better. I'm truly afraid they both might be losing their grip."

"I'm worried, too, especially about Miriam. Do you think it would do the slightest good for me to go and talk to them?"

"Honestly, I don't. I was walking on eggs myself, and I'm her best friend. I think she'd slam the door in your face."

"Me, too. In that case I'll have to be devious about it. Isn't there someplace in London where you can look up basic information about people? Births, deaths, marriages? It used to be Somerset House, but I think they've moved."

"Of course! Why didn't I think of that! Yes, those records have been moved more than once, I believe, and I'm not sure where they are now, but it's easier than that. I've heard there's a new commercial Web site that makes searches really easy. It's called—wait, it'll come to me—I think it's saintcatherines.com. That is—do you use a computer?"

"I do," I said with dignity. Then I laughed. "Okay, to be honest, I'm not terribly good with them. But we have one, and I know a real expert who can check this for me in about thirty seconds flat. I'll give him a ring this minute; I don't think this can wait. I'll keep in touch."

I disconnected, waited for another dial tone, and called Nigel Evans, my friendly computer guru. If the information was out there, Nigel would find it far faster than I could.

There was no answer. I tried again, thinking I'd dialed the wrong number, but still nothing.

"Drat!"

"What's the matter, love?"

"I'm trying to reach Nigel, to get him to look up something on the computer for me, and nobody's home."

"Ah. Nobody?"

"No, and the answering machine isn't picking up. Which is very odd. Nigel's so attached to his gadgets, I wouldn't think he'd ever forget to turn it on."

"Not," said Alan with a grin, "unless he was extremely distracted."

"Yes, and—oh! Do you think? How exciting!"

I called the Rose and Crown, our favorite pub, whose owners, Peter and Greta Endicott, are Inga's parents. An unfamiliar voice answered. "No, I'm afraid they're both out. I'm filling in. I'm not sure when they may be back."

"Is it—this is Dorothy Martin, an old friend—is it Inga's baby?"

The owner of the voice sounded as if he were smiling. "Yes, indeed, Mrs. Martin. This is Bill Bricknell. We've met. I serve at the bar sometimes?"

"Yes, of course, Bill. What's happening?"

"No word yet. It's only been about three hours, and of course first babies can take a long time, but Peter and Greta were off to the hospital like a rocket the moment Nigel rang up. We're all quite excited."

"Of course you are. So are we. Please let me know the moment you hear anything, will you?" I gave him my phone number and hung up.

"You heard that," I said to Alan. "I'm about to become a godmother!"

He smiled and kissed me on the cheek. "And you're going to have to do without your computer expert for a while."

"Oh, dear, yes. For ages, probably. He'll be busy with Inga and the baby once they come home."

"What did you want to look up, anyway? Can I help?"

"Ruth Beecham said that the records Somerset House used to keep are available on-line now. I'm trying to find Amanda's sister, but Amanda refuses to talk about her family at all."

"Hmm. I've never done that kind of research on-line, but it oughtn't to take long."

For Alan's writing, we had created a den out of a small room I had kept, before we were married, for the sewing machine I seldom used. He led me to his desk, sat me down at the keyboard, and gave me instructions. In no time I was looking at the Web site, a commercial one. I registered according to instructions, entered a credit-card number, and proceeded.

The first step was to establish Amanda's maiden name, and for that the logical place to look seemed to be the record of her marriage. The search could have taken forever, and probably would have, without the miracle of computers. I had only a man's name and a woman's first name, no location, and no exact date, though I could approximate one from Miriam's age. So I put in what little information I had, clicked the mouse, and waited anxiously.

12

I took a while. We tried various months of various years until we finally came up with a marriage that seemed likely. "Eureka!" I cried. Alan, sitting behind me, gave a low whistle. "So she's a Blake, is she? And from Arborfield Common."

He looked at me as if he expected recognition. I shook my head in mystification.

"You remember Arborfield Common, darling. Five miles or so from Bramshill?"

"Oh, of course. Now I do." We had spent a few months at Bramshill when Alan took over the leadership of the Police Staff College there as a temporary assignment, the last of his police career. I'd whiled away quite a few idle hours exploring the countryside on foot, and Alan and I had taken longer excursions together when his schedule allowed. "It wasn't much of a place, as I recall, but there was something—oh, Blake— of course! The member of Parliament!"

"The rising MP then, and even more so, now. You really should keep a closer eye on the political scene, love. Scarcely a day goes by that one doesn't read about Anthony Blake making a speech in the Commons, Anthony Blake commenting on the failings of the current policy on something or other, Anthony Blake meeting with the shadow cabinet, Anthony Blake attending a Conservative meeting somewhere. He was on television just a few nights ago, standing in front of the House holding forth on whatever it was. I didn't actually listen to what he said. The man bores me. I must say he looked impressive, though, with that silver hair of his, and Big Ben, all lighted up and looking inspirational in the background. I think he's all pose and pretense, but there's a very real possibility that Anthony Blake might be prime minister next time the Tories get in. At the very least, he'll have a place in the cabinet."

I stared at the screen, trying to wrest some answers from the bare facts before me. "But, Alan! With such a prominent father, why would she—no, wait. Maybe he isn't her father. Blake's quite a common name."

"Dorothy. Do you remember the size of Arborfield Common?"

I did. It wasn't more than a hamlet, really. Perhaps fifty families lived there. It was stretching coincidence pretty thin to imagine that two unrelated families named Blake might live there. "An uncle, then, maybe? Even so, you'd hardly think Amanda would pretend they didn't exist. For one thing, they're very well-to-do, aren't they?"

"Rolling. One of the wealthiest families in the county, or so local gossip had it. The liberal press is forever bringing it up, as well. There must have been a quarrel between Amanda and her family for her to cut off all ties in that extraordinary way."

"Let's see. They were married in April of—uh-oh! Alan, look at this." I pointed to the date on the screen. "They were married about nine and a half years ago. And Miriam's nine years old. I don't know when her birthday is, but she's enrolling in St. Stephen's with the current crop of nine-year-olds, so she couldn't be just barely nine. So—"

Alan looked at me and pulled a wry face. "The old story, eh? The first baby can come any time, as the saying goes, though the rest require nine months. Well, so Miriam was conceived a little early. That's somewhat unfortunate, but hardly a reason, nowadays, for a father to cast his daughter into outer darkness. Unless . . . wait, I'm trying to remember . . . yes. Yes, I think so. Oh, Lord, that could be it."

"What could be what?"

Alan sighed heavily. "Blake, my dear political ignoramus, rather goes in for causes, highly visible ones, you know. He campaigns on the hot issues of the day, the ones that can be guaranteed to generate more heat than light."

"Yes, dear, and neither of us cares much for that sort of politics, but what does that have to do with—"

"Wait. A few years ago, and I'd have to do some digging to find out exactly how long, one of the hot issues was teenage pregnancy. Anthony Blake was loud and fervent in his insistence that sex education, and the distribution of condoms, and abortion, and so on, were anathema. Abstinence was the only doctrine to be preached, the only way to solve the problem. Furthermore, parents were to be held squarely responsible for the actions of their youngsters. Teenage pregnancy was, he said, and I think this is almost a quote, 'a most flagrant example of the failure of parents to teach their children the proper standards.'"

"Oh, Lord," I echoed Alan. "And if this was about the time Amanda got pregnant . . .'"

"I'm almost sure it was. There was an election 'round then, if you recall."

"I wasn't living in England then, but I'll take your word for it. So that's it, then."

"Yes, I would say that was a pretty powerful reason for an ambitious politician to want his daughter's activities hushed up. Marry her off in a hurry and send her off to another part of the country."

I nodded, but that wasn't what I was thinking, or not all of it.

It was also, I thought unwillingly, a pretty powerful weapon for John Doyle to use on Amanda, especially if he was not the father of the child—and I was willing to bet he wasn't. They'd had no more children, after all. They didn't, in fact, sleep together. That wasn't proof of anything, of course, but for the moment assume he wasn't Miriam's father. He had, however, married Amanda, for some reason. Maybe Daddy had sweetened the deal somehow. Anyway, he'd married her. And then, every time some disagreement had come up, it could easily have been "Do as I say, or I'll not only let the whole world know that you are an immoral woman"—yes, Doyle would have thought of it that way—"and probably an unfit mother, but I'll reveal who your father is and bring his success crashing down around his ears. And never forget it will be your fault!"

Alan, sometimes unfortunately, can often read my mind. It's that mobile face of mine, I suppose. "Dorothy," he said gently, "you do realize I must tell Derek about this? Of course, he may already know. They'd do a background check as a matter of routine. He may have believed her when she said she had no family, so this information may not yet be in police hands, but it will be sooner or later. Sooner is better."

"Why? What does it matter to the police who her father is? I only wanted to know to trace her sister, to know if there was a place Miriam could go to be out of all this."

"It matters, as you very well know, because it provides further motive for Amanda Doyle to kill the man who knew about Miriam's illegitimacy."

"Well, but—no, look, there could be another explanation. Miriam could be adopted! Maybe—maybe Amanda knew, for some reason, that she could never have children, and she wanted a baby right away—well, it *could* be," I finished defensively. I was grasping at straws, and both of us knew it.

In reply Alan clicked the mouse a few more times, and the information appeared on the screen: Miriam Janet Doyle, born to Amanda Doyle (née Blake). The birth date was in July of the year the Doyles had been married. In April.

I sat back, defeated.

"Take heart, love. We're still a long way—that is, Derek is still a long way from accusing Amanda of murder. So far as I know, Derek hasn't traced the source of the digitalis. I don't know if he's been able to get at the man's medical records, even. The weekend makes things more difficult. But I agree that Miriam needs to be sent away, if at all possible, no matter what happens. Shall we look for the sister?"

That was reasonably easy. Alan found the page listing the birth dates of all the Blake children. In addition to Amanda, there was one brother and one sister, Gillian. She was two years older than Amanda. Next he checked for a marriage record for Gillian Blake. Knowing the county made it easier. He could find no record that she had ever married.

"So presumably there is a Gillian Blake living somewhere in England. That's a fairly easy search to do, in fact. Pity Blake is a common name, but Gillian isn't. Do we have an idea where?"

"Ruth Beecham said Canterbury, but she wasn't too sure."

We tried Canterbury without success and then opened the search to any locality. We got lucky. There was only one Gillian Blake, at least only one that the search engine could find, and she lived in London. The screen obligingly provided her telephone number.

"Do you think, after all this trouble," Alan asked, "that the sister will be of any help?"

"I have no idea," I said drearily. "I'll call Ruth and see what she thinks. I just hope we can talk Amanda into the idea of sending Miriam away. That's at least half the problem. I can see why Amanda might not want Miriam to go to her parents, but maybe the sister would be all right."

Alan stood. "Then you don't need me anymore. You mastered the telephone quite some time ago. But, love"—he hesitated—"you don't have to do this, you know. It's upsetting you, and you have no real connection with Miriam and her mother."

"Just call it my penance."

"For what?"

"All those uncharitable thoughts about John Doyle and his chapel buddies." I gave him a peck on the cheek and picked up the phone.

Ruth wasn't home. I gave a passing thought to calling Amanda, but discarded the idea. She probably wouldn't answer the phone. Ruth had given me the impression that Amanda had barricaded herself away from all comers.

No, I was, I thought, justified in taking direct action.

Sunday evening. Usually a good time to catch people at home. Before I could think about it too much and lose my nerve, I dialed the number and waited.

She answered on the fifth ring, and she sounded cross. "Yes?"

"Um—is this Gillian Blake?"

"Oh, for God's sake! Not on a Sunday night!"

"I beg your pardon? I'm trying to reach Gillian Blake, but if I have the wrong number—"

"Look, whatever you're selling, I'm not interested and I'm busy!"

"*Wait!* Don't hang up! It's about your sister."

There was a long pause. I could hear the snick of a lighter and a long drag on a cigarette. Finally, "Who is this and what do you want?"

"You don't know me. I live in Sherebury and I know your sister, Amanda Doyle. My name is Dorothy Martin, and I'm trying to help her."

"Do you belong to that so-called church?"

"No. Look, Ms. Blake, you may have read in the papers about the trouble your sister is in."

"I don't read the papers. What kind of trouble?"

I decided the only way to get through to her was to hit her between the eyes. "She's likely, very soon, to be accused of murder."

13

ANOTHER pause. Another long inhalation. When Gillian Blake spoke again, her voice had changed. "Well, well, well. So she's finally had the guts to do it, has she?"

I said nothing.

"Listen, Mrs. Whoever-You-Are. You are telling me Amanda's murdered that bastard she married, aren't you?"

"I'm telling you no such thing. Yes, Mr. Doyle has been murdered, but not by Amanda. I'm convinced of that, but the police may have other ideas. I'd very much like to talk to you about the whole situation."

"Who *are* you, anyway? You don't sound English. You're not a solicitor or something?"

"Certainly not! I'm American by birth, and I'm simply a friend—well, an acquaintance—of your sister. She *is* your sister, I take it?"

"She is. But why are my sister's affairs any of your business?"

"Strictly speaking, I suppose they're not," I snapped, stung. "I suppose it's none of my business if a man gets murdered and his widow is totally unable to cope. I suppose it's none of my business if a child is foundering in a sea of misery and confusion. I suppose I ought to pass by on the other side and forget about the whole thing and get on with my life. Certainly Amanda has made it quite clear that she doesn't want my assistance. I'd have thought you might consider her problems your business, since she's your sister, but obviously I was mistaken."

The temperature of my voice had been dropping steadily. For once, losing my temper seemed to help, because Ms. Blake's attitude changed.

"Okay, sorry, sorry. Look, I was busy when the phone rang, and I thought you were a telemarketer. We got off to a bad start. Let's begin again. Explain everything, including how you got into this and exactly what you think I can do about it."

Explaining everything took some little time, even omitting Amanda's suspicion of Miriam. I told Gillian about Amanda's uncharacteristic behavior both before and after the murder, the manner of Doyle's death, and, finally, Miriam. "She's acting very oddly, I think. She didn't like her father much, I gather, but even so, a murder in the family must be a terrible shock, and she seems much too controlled, too—oh, I don't know. I don't really know her, of course. You'd be a better judge than I."

"I have seen Miriam exactly once, Mrs.—Martin, is it? Amanda had to bring her to London for something, I forget what, dentist or school uniform or something. That was four or five years ago, and they popped in at the flat. They stayed for perhaps fifteen minutes. That is the sum total of the time I have spent with my only sister in the last nine years."

"I see." I sagged into my chair with the disappointment of it. "Then you wouldn't be interested in looking after Miriam for a while. I'm sorry I bothered you, but—"

"I didn't say that." I heard another cigarette being lit and inhaled greedily. "My sister is the world's biggest fool, but she *is* my sister. P'raps it's time to show a little family solidarity. Are there decent roads to that godforsaken place?"

I resented the description of Sherebury, which I consider one of England's loveliest little towns. However, this probably wasn't the time to say so. "The roads are very good, actually. You take the A twenty-one out of London, and then—"

"Never mind. I can find it. Where do you live?"

"In Monkswell Street, the house at the end, right up against the wall of the Close. You can't miss it; it's Jacobean and all the rest are Georgian."

"Sounds like something out of Trollope. Anthony or Joanna, take your pick. God help us! I'll be there in an hour."

"But, Ms. Blake, it's after nine. It can wait until tomorrow—" I broke off. I was talking to a buzz.

I sighed and went upstairs to clear the junk out of my tiny spare bedroom.

There was a lot of junk. I had barely finished making the room habitable, and had gone downstairs to tell Alan we were expecting a visitor, when the doorbell rang.

"Good grief, she must have flown all the way from London!" The bell rang twice more on my way to the door.

I don't know exactly what I expected, but the woman who stood on my little porch, her finger extended to press the bell once again, wasn't it.

She wasn't actually tall, but she gave that impression, being so thin. Her cheekbones were high, her eyes deep sunk, and the black poncho she wore didn't do much to hide her long, skeletal, black-clad arms and legs. Her spiky black hair completed the impression of something between Cher and a rather elegant spider. The inevitable cigarette dangled from her lips, which now curved into a half smile.

"You're exactly what I expected," she said. It didn't sound like a compliment.

Two could play that game. "You're not. Come in. That is, I take it you're Gillian Blake?"

"Just Gillian. I use only the one name." She stopped in my narrow hall and looked around. "Do you have an ashtray?"

"No. We don't smoke. And we'd actually rather that our visitors didn't, either."

"Yeah. Right." She stepped back outside the door, flipped the cigarette in a fiery little arc into the shrubbery, and came back looking hostile.

I led her into the parlor. I use that old-fashioned name for my living room because it seems appropriate. The house itself is roughly four hundred years old, and though I've made no attempt at "period" furniture, I've tried to use styles and fabrics that blend in. The effect is cozy and comfortable, especially with cats draped over the furniture here and there, but it'll never feature in *Architectural Digest*.

Gillian Blake—or simply "Gillian"—looked about as much at home in that setting as a Martian in Buckingham Palace.

Alan came into the room. He was wearing a shabby pair of old trousers, a stretched-out turtleneck sweater, and bedroom slippers. I introduced them and watched with interest. Alan's expression didn't change by so much as a flick of an eyelash from his usual reserved courtesy. Gillian, on the other hand, took in his conservative-old-fogey dress and rolled her eyes up as she accepted his proffered hand and sat down.

"Would you care for a drink, Gillian?" He'd gotten the name right the first time. I wasn't surprised, but she was.

"Whiskey, gin, vodka? Or of course white wine or sherry." She found her voice. "White wine. Please."

Well, the "please" was a start. Alan raised his eyebrows at me. I nodded. When he brought Gillian her wine, he also brought some Jack Daniel's for both of us. I felt I was going to need it.

"Cheers," said Gillian, and took a sip of the wine.

I cleared my throat, not sure how to begin this conversation. "I—um—I'm not sure what your situation is. Your daily schedule, and your—er—means—"

"All right, we'll cut to the chase. I write. For television. Soaps. It pays damn badly, but I manage. I live alone in a *very* small flat, and it would be pure hell to have a kid around making a row while I'm trying to get some work done. But there doesn't seem to be much choice, does there? Miriam needs to get away from this mess, and unless Mandy has made some good friends here, which I very much doubt, it's me or nobody."

"Your parents?" I said doubtfully.

She reached in her purse and took out a cigarette, then gave both of us a baleful look and put it back. She took a healthy swig of wine. "How much do you know?" she asked. "About our family, I mean. You found me, for a start. I'll give you long odds Amanda never told you about me, and I'm not all that eager to be found, so you must know something."

Alan responded to that one. "We know that your father is Anthony Blake, the prominent Conservative member of Parliament. We know that your sister became pregnant with Miriam before she was married. All the rest is supposition."

"Well, if you suppose that my father went up like a rocket when he found out Mandy had been and gone and done it, you suppose right. It wasn't quite never-darken-my-door-again, but he made it perfectly clear that she was a terrible embarrassment to him, and he wouldn't be shattered if she vanished from his life. I was still living at home then, and I'll never forget the row. He was all for sending her off to America to have the kid well out of his way, and put it up for adoption, but then he found out he'd have to pay a small fortune in hospital bills, what with no National Health over there. My dear papa is as tight with money as he is in other departments. And then, you see, Mandy didn't want to give the baby up for adoption, and she was stubborn about it. She sometimes has more guts than you'd think, to look at her.

"So then Father found this Doyle person, God knows where. I think he'd worked in a campaign once, or something. Anyway, he seemed to my father to be a 'Godly, righteous, and sober' person, and he had no family. No brothers or sisters, I mean, and his parents were dead. Well, of course, that pleased Father no end, because it meant that fewer people would know about the situation. So Doyle agreed—for a sum—to marry Mandy in some moldy old chapel. It was a thoroughly dim affair, notably minus champagne and 'The Voice That Breathed O'er Eden.' She was showing by then, but she wore shapeless clothes to cover it up, and if anybody in the constituency ever knew, there was never any talk."

"What did your mother have to say about all this?" I hated to interrupt, but I wanted to know. Maybe the mother could help in the current crisis.

Gillian finished her wine in a gulp. "Lydia Blake, perfect wife. That's the image Father projects. It's true, up to a point. She's gone along with everything my father wanted, and been a good politician's wife, and all that rot, but Mum's—well, she's a decent person at bottom. She tried to intervene when Mandy was in trouble, look after her, find her a place to live nearby. She wanted to get to know her grandchild, you see. This was the only one she was ever likely to have, after all, unless Mandy had more kids. She knew I never wanted marriage and a family; I have a career to think about."

"And your brother?"

"Jack's gay."

"Oh, dear. Your father—"

"Too bloody right. Thanks." This was to Alan, who had refilled her glass. "Yes, the dustup when Father found out about Jack was even worse than when he found out about Mandy. As far as Father is concerned, you see, his family is a total washout. Not only are we of no use to him politically, we're actually liabilities. And since politics comprise Father's entire life . . ." She took another swig of her wine.

"That's one reason I dropped the Blake a few years ago. The entertainment industry is among the many things Father disapproves of. He was on the news just last Wednesday fulminating about the trash one is offered on TV these days. Ironic, isn't it? The Beeb didn't dare not run it, even though he was ripping them to shreds. Anyway, I saw no reason to give him excuses for the diatribes he likes to deliver when his children displease or embarrass him. Besides, it's a highly competitive business and, his views being what they are, *he* was just as likely to embarrass *me* if our relationship was known. How *did* you find me, by the way?"

"Computers are wonderful. And your telephone is still listed under the name of Blake."

"Damn! What a slipup! I'll change that." She finished the wine and shook her head to Alan's interrogative look. "No, thanks. I need a clear head to tackle Amanda. We don't get on all that well. I think she's a wimp and she thinks I'm a terror. I admit to a few rough edges; the business does that to you. But Amanda's always tried to act the sweetness-and-light bit, and she thinks I'm crude."

"I don't know about that sweetness and light," I said a trifle grimly. "She's been fairly abrasive with me. Now that I know you a little better, I can tell you're sisters. However," I went on before she could react to that, "it's late by our standards. I imagine you keep odd hours, but in Sherebury we start rolling up the sidewalks about ten-thirty or eleven, and as it's nearly midnight, I'm sure Amanda's already in bed. I'm putting you in the guest room for the night."

She frowned. "I was expecting to stay with Amanda, so I didn't take time to pack. I knew she'd lend me something for the night."

"I've plenty of spare nightgowns, and if you don't have a toothbrush, I trust you can make do with floss and some mouthwash."

"I have one. I do draw the line at sharing some things."

"Good, then come on up. I'll show you which room it is, and then you can stay up as late as you like, but Alan and I are going to bed."

"You know," said Gillian, rising from her chair, "you're not quite what I expected, after all. A little more vinegar and a lot less sugar. Live and learn."

14

HAD expected Gillian to sleep very late Monday morning. Somehow she seemed like a night person, rather than morning, and I knew for a fact that her light had still been on at about two-thirty when I'd gone to the bathroom. But she appeared at the breakfast table a little after eight, attired in a nightgown of mine and a robe of Alan's, which she could have wrapped around herself twice. I wouldn't say she was exactly awake, but she sat silently and drank coffee while we had cereal and toast.

"Shall I go with you when you visit your sister?" I offered when she seemed to have ingested enough caffeine to be coherent. "It's not easy to find, and then, too, she's been in a sort of state of siege these last few days. I'm not sure what kind of welcome you'll get."

She yawned. "How hard can it be to find a street in a town this size? And I think Mandy'll talk more easily with only me there. She'll be all right, now that the bastard's dead. He was the one who caused the real trouble between us."

"I did wonder," I said frankly. "You seem to care for your sister, yet you've been estranged for years."

"That wasn't the way I wanted it. I went to London just after she got married. I knew I couldn't stick it at home without her. We didn't always get on well—I told you that—but we were close, all the same. Do you have sisters?"

"Just one left, now, and yes, I know what you mean. I used to fight with the other sister all the time, but we loved each other dearly, anyway. Go on."

"Well, it was just that without Mandy, there was nothing at home for me. And I had this job offer, a pretty dire job actually, and only part-time, but it was with the Beeb—sorry, the BBC—and I thought it could lead to great things."

"The BBC? In Canterbury?"

"Who said anything about Canterbury? In London, of course."

"Sorry. Amanda's good friend—she does have one—thought you lived in Canterbury."

Gillian shrugged. "If she let slip to somebody that I existed, she would have made up a location for me, because—well, I'll explain all that.

"So, anyway, I went to London, but for the first few weeks, I tried to stay in touch with Amanda. I wanted to be with her when the baby came, for one thing. I knew damn well Mum wouldn't be allowed to go, and there aren't any aunts or cousins or anyone.

"Well, so I rang her up every few days. At first it was all right. She sounded more or less normal. Oh, she was tired, and a bit fed up, but of course the whole situation was a mess. She had a husband she didn't care tuppence for, and her father had thrown her out, and she'd had to move house when she was seven months pregnant—all that. But she always seemed happy to talk to me, and of course she was excited about the baby. We never talked very long, but we made plans for me going down when the time came.

"And then one day I phoned a bit later than usual, and the

bastard answered. I asked for Amanda, and he said I couldn't talk to her. Of course I thought he meant she was having a bath, or something, so I asked when I should call back. And he said never."

"He said *what?*"

"He told me, quite coldly, that I was a 'bad influence on her,' that he was 'trying to reform her, save her from her life of sin,' and that 'she had no need for her wordly family.' Those were his exact words. He told me he would not allow her to see or talk to me anymore."

"How would he know, if you were careful to call only in the daytime?"

"You think that didn't occur to me? I phoned the next day. She hung up on me, and when I rang again, she didn't answer. Two days later I got a note in the mail saying he'd put a tape recorder of some kind on the phone, and I mustn't phone again, or even write, ever.

"That was the last I heard from her until she dropped in out of the blue that day in London. We didn't talk much then, as a matter of fact. When it's been years, there's too much to say, and not enough, all at the same time. And she was nervous as a cat the whole time. I really think she thought the bastard was going to find her there, somehow, and punish her."

"Do you think," I asked unwillingly, "that he ever actually beat her? Her good friend says not, but—"

"I asked her, that day when she came to visit. Miriam was out of the room for a minute, and I asked, straight out. I hadn't seen any bruises, but that wasn't why I believed her when she said not. There was something about the way she said it that was absolutely convincing. Almost as if she wished it were that simple."

I shivered.

"Right. Chilling, isn't it?"

"Utterly. I hope you'll find her happier now." It didn't take the heavy irony of Gillian's look to make me realize what a stupid idea that was. Happy, right. With a possible murder charge hovering in the background and nameless fears about her daughter, fears I thought I understood.

"Yes, well," I said meaninglessly. "I still think I'd better at least point you in the right direction for her house. When do you want to go?"

"I don't, if you want the truth. But the sooner I go, the sooner we can settle things. There's something we haven't talked about, though."

"If it's money," I said hastily, "I mean, if you need some help with Miriam's expenses, I imagine we can—"

"I said I was badly paid. I didn't say I was poor. Daddy dear is so happy to have me out of his life, and so eager to make sure I stay there, that he makes a contribution from time to time. I don't need money!"

So vehement was her tone and so fierce her glare that I was sure she *did* need money, but plainly she wasn't going to take any from us. "Sorry. What, then?"

"I don't know what I'm walking into, that's what. If Amanda didn't kill the bastard, who did? Is some maniac going to walk in the door and kill us all?"

I sighed deeply, and so did Alan. "We don't know, Gillian. Unless there's something the police haven't told us, there's literally not a clue."

"Why should the police tell you anything? I thought they never said a word to the public."

Drat. I'd had no intention of telling her about Alan, but now I'd put my foot in it. "Alan has special contacts. Before he retired, he was the chief constable."

"I see." Gillian's eyes narrowed; her voice hardened. All her suspicions, all her defenses were up again. "Oh, yes, I think I do see, finally. So that's what this is all in aid of, is it? The Good Samaritan gets the sister down from London, picks her brains, softens her up, gets her to talk to the murder suspect, to spy out the situation and then report back to the

Bill—is that the game? Sorry, I'm not playing." She pushed her chair back with a scrape and stood up.

"Gillian." Alan's deep voice stopped her. He was as angry as I, I could tell, but with him it comes out as steely control, and it's very intimidating. "I have no idea why you have leapt to these conclusions, but there is no basis for them, and no possible excuse for your rudeness. My wife has put herself to considerable trouble, and experienced considerable distress, in an attempt to help your sister. The least she can expect from you is simple courtesy."

She looked from one of us to the other. "So you're doing this out of pure, disinterested kindness, right? Is that what I'm expected to believe?"

"I don't know that I care what you believe, Ms. Blake," I said, using the name deliberately. "Nor do I greatly care what you do. I begin to think Miriam would be better off with her mother, after all. Your imagination has plainly been influenced by what you write, and your outlook on life, perhaps, by your father."

She gave me a look of pure hatred and pulled a cigarette out of her pocket.

I snapped. "Oh, for heaven's sake, smoke the thing if it'll put you in a better mood. Smoke five of them at once and die a year or two sooner, for all I care! But get it into your head that I am *not* a police spy, whatever that might be, and I want to get Miriam out of this town because she's a sweet little girl who's had as much as she can take. Furthermore, I've gotten involved in all this at least as much out of curiosity as kindness, and I admit it, so you can put *that* in your—your cigarette—and smoke it, too! I just hope you can cut down around Miriam. She doesn't need lung cancer along with everything else."

For a moment I thought I'd gone too far. Then Gillian shrugged, broke the cigarette in half, and dropped it into her coffee cup. "I've been trying to quit," she said mildly.

I waited, but there was nothing more, so I accepted the gesture as an apology and took a deep breath. "If you think we can spend ten minutes together in a car without tearing each other's hair out, I'm ready to go as soon as you are."

"Let's not chance it," she said with a trace of a grin. "I'll follow you."

She was dressed by the time I'd tidied up the kitchen, and we were off, she behind me in an old, battered, but evidently powerful Jaguar. It was a low-slung, sporty-looking model in British racing green, whose engine snarled impatiently at the slow pace I set.

It was the sort of day one often gets in an English December, not really cold but gray and damp, with the threat of rain any minute. Perhaps, I thought as I drove, it was partly the general gloom that had touched off Gillian. My moods are greatly affected by the weather; why not hers?

Or maybe she was just a prickly sort of person. Certainly her sister was, and I could imagine that growing up with the Honorable Mr. Blake might put a rough edge on anyone's temper.

My own temper hadn't been exactly serene, either, had it?

Ah, well, the situation was difficult. And if I had any insight into Amanda's mind at all, it was going to get worse before it got better. If I had any sense, I'd leave Gillian at the house and beat it out of there.

But then I wouldn't know what went on, and I very much wanted—needed, I corrected myself—to know. So far I had absolutely no ideas about who might have killed John Doyle, beyond the general suspicion of everyone who knew him.

Good grief! The thought hit me so suddenly that the car swerved. I nearly hit a bicycle that was parked by the side of the road, and a screech of brakes behind me told me Gillian had nearly hit me.

Could *she* be the one?

She had hated and resented the man, and she'd had good cause. He had caused her estrangement from her sister, and had bullied and tormented that sister. True, the estrangement had happened years ago, and Gillian'd had no contact with Doyle ever since, but she struck me as a good hater, one who could keep a grudge alive for a long time.

She lived in London, but London, as she had proved last night, was less than an hour away for someone who drove the way she did. She lived alone and worked at home. There would have been nothing to prevent her driving to Sherebury, murdering Doyle, and driving back again, getting to bed not much later than her usual time.

I got the car back under control and tried to do the same for my mind. Given the physical possibility of the thing, why would a resentment that had been simmering for years suddenly boil over? A person doesn't simply decide, one night, to kill someone she hardly knows, no matter what she may have against him. There has to be a catalyst, an incident, and since Gillian and Amanda hadn't been in touch with each other for years—

But I didn't know that, did I? I knew what Gillian had told me, but why did she have to be telling me the truth? I remembered the maxim practiced by Miss Marple, one of my favorite fictional sleuths: Never believe what anyone says. Like the detective she was admonishing at the time, I tend to be too trusting.

After all, I thought as I absentmindedly negotiated a small roundabout and turned off on the wrong street, Amanda Blake had been somewhere on that day she went AWOL. Why not London?

15

I took me a while to retrace my steps and get back on the right road to Amanda's house, but I did it eventually. Untangling the snarl of thoughts in my mind was harder. Of course I didn't really believe that Gillian was a murderer. On the other hand . . .

I wanted very much to see Amanda's face when she first saw her sister at the door. I wanted to know whether the visit was in fact a surprise. Surely I could tell from their greeting whether or not they had seen each other recently, made plans, perhaps made plots?

I was defeated by Amanda's paranoia about visitors. Once again it was Miriam who answered the door (after repeated rings and knocks), but when I attempted to talk to the little girl, Gillian took over.

"I suppose you're Miriam. You won't remember me, but I'm your aunt. We met once when you were about four. Let us in, there's a good girl."

"But I don't know you! Mummy said—"

"Gillian?" The voice from somewhere inside sounded just

as astonished as I might have expected if the speaker was greeting a long-lost sister. But I couldn't see the face, or the body language that sometimes tells a different story.

The door closed, then opened. Amanda stood in the doorway looking blank. Gillian stepped forward. "Surprise, surprise, Mandy! Here's your big, bad sister come to your aid in a crisis. Amazing, isn't it?"

There was no embrace. Amanda merely stood aside, an arm draped protectively around Miriam's shoulders. No one said anything.

Then the moment broke. Gillian said, in a too-high, too-bright voice, "So this is Miriam. She's changed."

"Children do in five years." Amanda's voice had as little expression as her face.

I stood there, uncomfortable. I had precipitated this situation. Was it up to me to do something about it?

Probably. I moistened my lips. "Amanda, may we sit down? There are some things to talk about."

Gillian directed a sharp glance at me. "There are things Mandy and I need to talk about. There's no need for you to stay, now you've got me here."

"*You* got her here?" Amanda's voice rose. "Why? How?"

"I thought you needed some help, and your sister was the obvious one—"

"How did you know I had a sister? How do you know anything about my family? Why are you prying into my affairs?"

"Mummy," said Miriam in a scared little voice. "Mummy, it's all right. Don't be upset. Things are all right now that Daddy's not here anymore. Please, Mummy, don't worry."

Something inside me tightened, clenched. "Mrs. Doyle, I simply felt that perhaps you needed some help with Miriam. She's under considerable strain, anyone can see that, and I thought—"

"*You* thought! *You* thought! Who are you to tell me what my daughter needs? What do you know about my kind of life? You push your way in here, knowing you're not wanted, pretending to help. You pry, you make us say things we don't mean. You find my sister, somehow, and force her back into my life. You think you have all the answers. Well, let me tell you something. You don't know a thing about what we've had to deal with, Miriam and I. Has anyone ever told you you were a worm, an unrepentant sinner, day after day after day? Has anyone ever taken everything you valued out of your life, everything that meant hope and happiness and comfort? Have you ever watched someone squeezing life and joy out of your child, month after endless month?"

She caught a ragged breath. "You don't know what hopelessness is. You don't know what it means to be caught like a rat in a cage, to try and try to think of a way out and know that there is none. You know nothing about it, you with your fine clothes and your fine food and your fine house. There's nothing you can do for us. There's nothing I want you to do for us. Leave us alone!"

Sobbing, she clasped Miriam to her fiercely.

Gillian said, "I told you not to come. I think you've done enough damage here. You'd better go."

I went.

I had planned, this morning, to visit the bank where John Doyle had worked. I knew the manager would tell me nothing. Bank managers are first cousins to oysters, even under normal circumstances. When a crime had been committed, I could imagine that they would try to pretend it hadn't happened. Things like murder could have no connection with *their* bank.

I had thought, however, that Doyle's fellow employees might be able to tell me something useful. I might learn, for example, whether anyone at the bank had particularly hated the man. There was probably no point in asking if he had any particular friends. I thought I knew the answer to that one.

Now, though, my heart wasn't in it. The police would already have questioned anybody who had close connections with Doyle. The police weren't stupid. They'd solve this murder eventually, and I could just stay out of it. Amanda didn't want my help. Maybe she would accept help from Gillian. Maybe not.

And if she didn't, what of the child? What of Miriam, nine years old and caught up in a nightmare?

"She isn't your responsibility!" I said, out loud.

Right. Pass by on the other side. You're a lot less likely to get hurt that way.

I pulled into my garage. I had some thinking to do, and it was time I let Alan help me. I'd played this alone long enough. Whatever the consequences, Alan had to know what I feared. "Tell the truth and shame the devil," as the old adage had it.

He was working at his computer, but when he looked up and saw my face, he shut the thing down immediately and stood. "What is it, love?"

"I've made a big mess of things, and I don't know what to do now."

"That sounds uncharacteristic. Shall we have some tea and talk about it?"

Tea. The English chicken soup. I almost smiled as I followed him into the kitchen.

"Now," he said when the tea was poured out, steaming, and we sat waiting for it to cool enough to drink. "I gather things did not go well with Mrs. Doyle?"

"They went even less well than I had feared. Amanda resented my being there and went into a tirade, in front of Miriam. I won't go into the whole thing. It's too painful. But she threw me out of the house."

"That's twice, now, isn't it?" Alan took an experimental sip and put the cup down. Still too hot. "And once at the chapel. So are you ready to give up, yet?"

"Almost. I really am almost ready to drop it, leave it to the police. But, Alan, there's one thing that keeps eating at me."

"The child."

Alan knows me rather well. "Yes, the child. I'm worried

about her, and I feel sorry for her. She's become the parent, here. You should have seen her just now, trying to calm her mother down. It was pathetic. But there's more." I sipped the tea myself. Too hot. Alan waited.

"Alan, I think that Amanda thinks Miriam did it." There. I'd said it. Now let the chips fall where they might.

"Yes," he said. "Ahh," he said, testing the tea again, "just right. Yes, I knew there was something you weren't telling me. I thought that might be it."

"You mean—you thought of Miriam—"

"My dear, she was there. I'm a policeman. I've seen nearly everything over the course of my career, and never rule out any possibility. Of course I thought of her."

"Then that means Derek—"

"Derek, too, has almost certainly thought of her. We haven't discussed it."

I tried to digest this. If the police suspected Miriam, as well as her mother . . . "They haven't done anything about it. Questioned Miriam, I mean, or anything like that."

"Oh, they've talked to her, of course. I doubt she knew she was being questioned. We *are* trained for this sort of thing, you know, love. A policewoman—they always use women with children—will have made conversation with Miriam, subtly extracted her story of what happened that night. Evidently they found nothing particularly alarming. Now suppose you tell me why you think she did it."

"I didn't say I think so. I said her mother thinks so."

"Very well. Tell me what evidence you have of the mother's belief."

Alan can, at times, sound very much like a police report. "It isn't anything that can be called evidence. A facial expression, a tone of voice—those aren't evidence. All I really know is that Amanda is terrified for Miriam. And it shows the most when Miriam goes around making remarks about how wicked Daddy was, and how much better off they are now that he's gone."

"I see." Alan pursed his lips and ran a hand down the back of his head. "That's why you've been so eager to get Miriam out of town."

I swallowed hard. Here was the really sticky point. I very much didn't want to admit to Alan that I was trying to hide things from the police, but if honesty was my new policy, I had to. "There are other reasons, but that's the main one, yes. I was afraid—"

"You were afraid the police would see what you have seen."

I nodded.

"And that they would then do what?"

I sipped tea, lukewarm by now. "Question Miriam, frighten her—oh, all right, arrest her, even. And she's only nine, and so—so—" My chin wobbled.

"Have you considered that Miriam might be acting the way she is, saying the things she is saying, because she, in turn, is afraid that her mother is the murderer?"

I poured out more tea, not because I wanted it, but to give me time to get my voice in order. "No, to be honest. I thought—if you'd seen them together—"

"One of the first things a good detective learns," said Alan, tenting his fingers in his lecturing position, "is that people under strain act in certain predictable ways. One is that they close their ranks. They tell unimportant lies in an attempt to protect others. Those lies muddy the water considerably, because although good policemen can tell when people are lying, they don't usually know what they're lying about, or whether the lies are material to the case. It isn't at all uncommon, for example, for a husband and wife to suspect each other of a crime, and lie to protect each other. Once the police get on to what's happening, of course, the two suspicions cancel each other out and we're back where we started."

"Then you think—what, exactly?"

"About who killed John Doyle? I have no idea. About your

problem? That it's probably less of a problem than it appears. You say Miriam has been trying to protect her mother, trying to calm her down? Why do you think she's doing that?"

"Well, because—oh. I see. You think it's because she wants to stop her mother from saying too much. And that means Miriam thinks Amanda did it. And that means Miriam didn't." It was all somewhat muddled, but Alan nodded.

"I think it's very possible."

"Then—then I'm completely confused. Where do I go from here? Give up the whole thing?"

"Do you want to? You're under no obligation, and you've been thoroughly snubbed by the whole Doyle family."

"I think they'd rather think of themselves as the Blake family. Or maybe not, come to think of it. Heavens, how awful it must be to have no family to belong to. Very lost and alone." I was dithering, I knew, stalling while I tried to come to a decision.

Or maybe not. Maybe the thought that had come unbidden to my mind, of how lost and alone Amanda must feel, was a part of the decision making.

"I think," I said after a pause, "that the first thing I am going to do is write Amanda a note. She won't let me in to talk to her, I'm sure, but I can drop a note in her mailbox and hope she reads it, or Gillian does. If you're right, there's a good deal of misunderstanding between Miriam and Amanda, and maybe I can help clear it up by spelling out what we've just talked about. And then, no matter what happens with Amanda, I think I'll go on talking to people and trying to help ferret out the truth. That little girl is terribly unhappy, and somebody sensible has to help her. I'll start with the bank where Doyle worked, I think."

"Good." Alan picked up his cup, looked at it with distaste, and put it down again. "Feel better now?"

"I always do when I've talked things over with you." I put my hand in his in an unspoken apology for my lack of trust, and he squeezed it in understanding.

There's an old joke about the man who, late one night, finds himself with a flat tire in the middle of nowhere. Rummaging in the trunk, he discovers that there's no jack. He remembers passing a farmhouse not too far back, so he sets out to borrow a jack. But as he walks down the dark, lonely road he gets to thinking. He'll have to begin by apologizing for waking the farmer at midnight. The man may well be surly about it. He might even demand a deposit for the jack. Maybe he has dogs, who won't be exactly happy about a caller at that hour. Gosh, the motorist thinks, I'll really have to be careful. Maybe this isn't worth it. The farmer might even think I'm a burglar, come to rob the place. Good grief, maybe he's the sort of man who'll come to the door with a shotgun, the sort who'll shoot first and ask questions later.

By the time the motorist reaches the farmhouse, he's so belligerent that he hammers angrily on the door with both fists. When the inoffensive, yawning farmer opens it, the motorist shakes his fist, yells, "Keep your damn jack!" and runs off.

Someday, I hoped, I might learn a lesson from that little story, and stop writing my own scenarios for nice, reasonable people like my husband.

16

JANE, my usual fount of Sherebury information, told me
that John Doyle had worked for the local branch of the
Westminster Bank. Alan and I do our banking at Bar-
clay's. That was unfortunate, in a way, because I had no easy
excuse for stopping in at the other bank. However, I could always be thinking about changing banks, couldn't I? Or opening a separate account in my own name, or something. I can
tell quite convincing lies in a good cause.

First, though, I had to write that note to Amanda, and I
had to write it carefully. It had to be direct and completely
clear, but tactful. That's not an easy combination. I went
through several drafts before I had one I thought would do,
and even then I wasn't completely satisfied. I read it over before putting it in an envelope.

> Dear Mrs. Doyle,
>   I'm truly sorry I've offended you, but I remain wor-
> ried about you and your daughter. If what I think I have
> observed is true, you and Miriam each believe the other
> might have had something to do with your husband's

death. This, of course, means that neither of you is culpable. I urge you to speak frankly to your daughter about this. She is an intelligent child and would, I think, react better to an open discussion of the matter than to any sort of secrecy.

I realize that you are not pleased with my efforts to be of help to you. Certainly I have not gone about these efforts in the best way, but please believe that my intentions are good, and my motive a real concern for Miriam's well-being. She's a sweet little girl.

I will respect your wishes and not intrude any further upon your privacy, but I hope that, if there is any way I may be of use to you or Miriam, you will allow me to do so.

I shook my head over it. It sounded stuffy and way too formal, but it would have to do. It said what needed to be said, and was the best I could come up with. I signed it, put it in an envelope, and wrote "Mrs. Doyle" on the outside. I didn't seal it. If Gillian saw it first and wanted to check it out before giving it to her sister, so much the better. I stood very low in both their opinions at this point, but I thought Gillian might be willing to give me a little more credit than Amanda would. Of course, if Gillian was the killer, then all bets were off, but I couldn't think of a way to cover that base, at least not right now. One thing at a time.

At any rate, I'd tried. I drove to Amanda's house and stuck the envelope through the letter slot without knocking, and then got back in the car rather quickly, feeling like a prankster. I didn't look to see if I was being observed from a window. I didn't want to know.

There was no point in trying to find a parking place near the bank. On a Monday morning, that was going to be next to impossible. I went home, told Alan where I was going, and put on a flowery hat before I set out to walk. I have found that when people see a gray-haired woman in a silly hat, they tend to dismiss her as a harmless crank. The image can be useful.

English banks differ in many respects from their American counterparts, or at least from the way things were in America when I lived there. The paperwork is somewhat more cumbersome, for one thing, and the atmosphere more intimidating. English banks still separate the tellers from the public with ceiling-high glass walls. One speaks into small holes or microphones, and the actual transactions take place in sliding metal drawers.

But banks in both countries share one problem. They pay their junior employees, tellers and the like, so little that the turnover is high. Fresh-faced children of around twenty appear at the windows of my bank, remain there for a few visits, and then are replaced by clones. There is a seemingly endless supply of them, even in a small town like Sherebury. Most of them are bored silly by the job, and they're gone so fast that it's impossible to develop a personal relationship with any of them.

That makes a spot of deception easier.

I walked into Westminster Bank. Westminster is one of those huge banks with branches all over England, and, for all I know, Scotland and Wales as well. Our branch was quite small, appropriately, given the size of the town. There were three visible employees when I walked in, one dealing with an impatient string of customers at his window, the others doing, at the two other windows, whatever mysterious things bank tellers do. When I'm waiting in line, I always assume they're doing busywork on purpose to avoid moving things along.

One of them was at the Bureau de Change window, which had no customers at the moment. We get our share, in Sherebury, of foreign tourists who need to buy pounds sterling with their dollars and yen and, now, Euros, but early December isn't high-tourist season. I stepped up brightly to the window. The clerk whipped his task away into a drawer (it looked suspiciously like the *Times* crossword puzzle) and said, "May I help you, madam?" His tone clearly indicated his devout hope that he wouldn't have to.

I put on my best American accent, which has faded some-what after my years of English residence, and said, "I sure hope so. I need to talk to somebody about a loan."

The clerk brightened, his hopes fulfilled. "I'm sorry, madam. This is the Bureau de Change."

"Oh. I thought it was a bank."

He smirked. "It *is* a bank, madam. This window is the Bu-reau—is where you would change your dollars for pounds. You'd need to speak with Mr. Johnson."

I beamed. "Oh, good. Can you show me where to find him? I get just scared stiff in banks, and especially English banks."

He made one more attempt. "I'm not actually certain he's in at the moment."

"That's okay. I can wait." I smiled again, propped my purse on the metal drawer at the bottom of the glass wall, and tried to look as if I was prepared to wait—right there—all day.

The clerk capitulated with a sigh. "I'll see whether he's in."

Mr. Johnson was, of course, in. I knew he would be. When does a bank ever open its doors without at least one loan officer present? He was away from his desk for a mo-ment, I was told, but he would be back straightaway. I was shown through a door into an inner sanctum and invited to sit at a desk. The clerk went back to his crossword puzzle.

When Mr. Johnson appeared, I knew I was unmasked.

He was one of the weekend volunteers at the Cathedral bookshop, a fussy little widower, but pleasant enough. John-son is such a common name I hadn't made the connection.

He smiled genially. "Well, Dorothy, how nice to see you. Lovely hat, by the way. Need a spot of extra cash, do you? I hadn't known you banked here."

I sighed. "I don't. You've caught me, Sam. A fair cop."

"Ah." He sat back. "Something in the sleuthing line, eh? You know I can't give away confidential information, if that's what you're after."

"No, it's more personal than that. John Doyle."

His smile faded. "Doyle. Yes, it would be, wouldn't it? Someone told me you knew his wife. Bad business, that."

"Doyle? Or his death?"

Sam Johnson looked around and lowered his voice. "Both, if you want the truth. I couldn't bear the man, nor could most of the staff here, but it's bad for the bank that he was murdered. A bank doesn't want scandal anywhere near it."

"Was there scandal associated with John Doyle? I must say I find that hard to believe. He was such an upright soul."

Sam snorted. "Self-righteous, you mean!" He lowered his voice still more and said, "Would it astonish you to know that he was meeting a woman in London not a week before he was killed?"

17

I T did astonish me. If Sam had intended to create a sensation, he had succeeded. I gaped at him for a moment, then gathered my wits and said, "Are you sure?"

"Saw him with my own eyes! A week ago today, it was. My bookseller in London had a copy of the *Canterbury Tales* he wanted me to see." Sam, I dimly recalled, had a passion for old books. "Not actually rare, you know. My means don't run to that sort of thing. But quite, quite beautiful, quarter bound in calf, with engravings by—but I mustn't bore you. He rang me up on Sunday evening to tell me about it, and I really couldn't wait to see it. So I phoned Mr. Hawkins, my manager, and asked for a day's holiday. Well, naturally, I've been here at the bank for a great many years, and I seldom take any holidays at all, so of course when I ask for one there's never any problem in getting it. So I went up to town on Monday. Caught the early train. It got me to town much earlier than I needed to be there, but I'm an early riser, and the later trains are so crowded.

"And who should I see, when we got into Victoria Station,

but John Doyle, getting out of the next carriage! I was surprised, of course, and not best pleased. This is a small branch, and there ought not to be two of the senior staff away at the same time. If I had known Doyle planned to go up on that day, I should not have asked permission to take the day off, and I doubt Mr. Hawkins would have granted it, in any case. Quite frankly, Dorothy, it occurred to me that the man had simply taken French leave! After all, I had spoken to Mr. Hawkins rather late on the Sunday, and he had said nothing about Doyle being away as well. Furthermore, I ought to have been informed. Doyle is not technically under my supervision, but I am always told when those junior to me are taking their holidays. Really, I was most annoyed!

"However, there was nothing to be done about it by that time, and I didn't wish to confront the man there at the station. I made my way to the taxi rank, rather slowly so as not to catch him up, and you can imagine my surprise when I saw Doyle walk, not to a taxi, but straight to the curb to get into a private car! *And* driven by a most attractive woman! Now what do you think of that?"

I was too confused to think anything at all. Doyle in London that day! And I had thought maybe Amanda . . . "What did she look like? The woman driving the car? And what kind of car was it?" The only woman I could think of was Gillian, and surely it couldn't have been her. For one thing, it would make no sense, and for another, a fuddy-duddy like Sam Johnson was most unlikely to find Gillian attractive.

Sam frowned, groping for words. "I can't tell one car from another. Black, I think, or possibly blue. Ordinary looking."

Definitely not Gillian, then. No one would have thought her car ordinary. Unless she'd borrowed one . . .

"And the woman," Sam went on, "well, I saw her for only a moment, when she got out to wave Doyle over to the car. She was—um—slender, I think. Though she had a coat on, of course."

"A hat?"

"My dear Dorothy, you are the only woman I've seen wear a hat these last twenty years, barring the Queen."

"Well, I thought maybe in winter—something woolly to keep her head warm—but anyway, you could see her hair?"

He frowned again. "Long, I think. Brown? Yes, light brown, I believe. It was her face I remember. She had a rather—I can't describe it, an ethereal face, perhaps. She reminded me," he said, turning somewhat pink, "of a Botticelli Venus. With clothes on, of course."

I tried to look suitably grave. "Of course. What kind of clothes?"

"Really, Dorothy! I am hardly an expert on women's apparel!"

"Yes, but you must have noticed *something*. Bright, drab, long skirt, short skirt, miniskirt, slacks?"

"I hope you don't think I'm the sort of man who makes a practice of studying women's legs!"

Long skirt or slacks, I concluded, never having known a man who was still breathing who didn't look at women's legs. If the skirt had been short, he'd have noticed.

"Colors?"

"She wore a coat, I told you. Black, or brown, or something. What does it matter, anyway? It was perfectly obvious that she was meeting him, and what business had a married man meeting a woman in that furtive fashion?"

"Furtive?"

"Well, he certainly looked as if he didn't want to be seen."

"It matters," I said patiently, "because the police will want to try to find this woman. Has it really never occurred to you that when a man does something odd on Monday and is murdered on Wednesday night, there might be some connection?"

Sam was affronted. "What has occurred to me is that, if his wife found out he was having an affair, it gives her a motive for killing him. However, you don't seem to take that view. I suppose, if you're a friend of hers—"

"Amanda Doyle is not particularly a friend of mine, but I don't think she killed her husband, and I feel very sorry for her and her daughter. And that reminds me: What's going to happen with their bank account? They must have banked here, since he worked here. I don't mean I want to know what's in the account. I know you're not supposed to tell me that. But when someone dies, are the accounts frozen? And if so, what is Amanda going to do for money?"

Sam put on a mulish expression. I added, "Sam, I wouldn't ask, but you're a financial expert. I know so little of banking laws in England, and estate law, and all that sort of thing."

The syrupy approach worked. He squared his shoulders and looked like a financial expert. "I suppose it would do no harm to tell you that there was no joint account. Doyle had a checking account here, and a small savings account. I believe he took charge of the family finances. Certainly that was only right and proper. He was a bookkeeper here, you know, so of course he knew the proper procedures."

Of course. He also wanted his hand, and his alone, holding the family purse strings. How characteristic.

"Well, I won't take up any more of your time, Sam. I appreciate this. You've given me a lot to think about, and I'm afraid some things to tell the police. They'll probably come around to talk to you."

"They've been," he said with a shudder. "And no matter how discreet they try to be, having the police in the bank is not good for business."

What an epitaph for John Doyle. His murder was not good for business. It was my turn to shudder. "Oh, well then, I suppose you told them all this."

"I did not. They didn't ask me about Doyle's movements, and I saw no reason to tell them and expose the bank to scandal."

"Then I'm sorry, but I must tell them myself." I rose and

turned to go, and then thought of one more thing. "Oh, by the way, *had* he asked permission to take that day off?"

"I did not feel free to ask Mr. Hawkins. However, when I taxed Doyle with taking a holiday when I was away, he was quite rude about it. As much as said that it wasn't my affair, and that he had had urgent business in London. Business, hah!"

"Did you tell him you'd seen him?"

"Certainly not. *That* was none of *his* affair."

"Oh, and did you buy the book?"

"I did." He relaxed. "You must come 'round to see it one day. It's quite, quite lovely."

"I'll do that," I said, knowing I wouldn't, and left.

Oh, my. Here was something real at last, something to get one's teeth into. Why on earth hadn't the silly little man told the police what he knew? Didn't he know that every change in routine was of interest when a crime had been committed? Had he never read a crime novel?

Well, no, probably not. He was too busy with Chaucer and Co.

I walked home slowly, having, as Hercule Poirot might have said, been given "furiously to think."

I went straight to Alan with the news. "I think you ought to tell Derek right away."

"I don't," said Alan. "I think you ought to tell him."

"But I'm not exactly official. Will he get into a snit about me talking to witnesses?"

"Trust me, darling. Derek will not be unbearably surprised that you are looking into Doyle's murder. And members of the public are always encouraged to give the police any information they may have. However they may have acquired it."

So I called the police station and told Inspector Morrison Mr. Johnson's story. He promised to get people out looking for the mysterious woman immediately.

Well, that was something the police could do much more efficiently than I, and even they were facing a massive task. Identifying one particular car with one particular woman in it, on a Monday morning at Victoria Station, made the proverbial needle in a haystack look like a snap. Although, I thought irrelevantly, if I were looking for that needle, I'd tear apart the haystack and then get a large, powerful magnet. Perhaps the police had similar techniques for the impossible job of combing London for a single individual.

Meanwhile, what was I to do?

Well, really, there wasn't much. I'd talked to the people at Doyle's church, and learned nothing except that they were a nasty group with a malicious attitude. I'd talked to Amanda's sister and learned nothing except that the Blakes were not a loving, unified family.

There was always the possibility that Gillian had killed Doyle, alone or with Amanda's help. I had no proof of that whatsoever, but if Amanda had gone to London that day . . .

Hmm. What if Amanda *had* gone to London, and had seen her husband up to something? I found it almost impossible to picture John Doyle involved in the kind of hanky-panky Sam Johnson imagined, but there are other kinds. Let's see, what would a self-righteous prig with an extremist religion do in London?

Of course. He would do what he always did. He would get someone into trouble. Probably that "attractive woman." Attractive women sometimes have a lot to hide.

And if Amanda had seen him, and had jumped to the same conclusion Sam Johnson had . . .

No, that didn't really work, did it? Amanda hated her husband. She would most likely have been delighted to think he was giving her grounds for divorce.

Anyway, she probably wouldn't have jumped to those conclusions. She knew Doyle's real passion was not for women, but for what he no doubt thought of as exposing the truth.

And why would Amanda have gone to London in the first place, if not to see Gillian?

My mind was running in unproductive circles. It was time I gave it up for a while. I went back to Alan's study. "How would you feel about going out to lunch, love? Somewhere out of town. Maybe that little pub on the way to Brighton, what's it called?"

"The Pig and Whistle. How could you forget?"

"How, indeed?" I laughed. "Let's go."

18

WAS not feeling any clearer in my mind when we got back from lunch. Less so, indeed, since the bitter at the Pig and Whistle was particularly good and I'd had a pint, unusual for me at lunchtime. I was ready for a nap when we got home, but there were two calls on the answering machine. The first one woke me up in a hurry. Derek had left a message for Alan, simply asking him to return the call.

"Good heavens, you don't suppose they've found the mysterious woman already?" I asked, excited.

"Stranger things have happened, but I very much doubt it."

The second message was from Amanda. It, too, was very brief. "Mrs. Martin, I should like to talk to you. Please ring me up." She gave her phone number.

"Détente, perhaps?" commented Alan.

"Stranger things have happened. But call Derek first. I'm excited about his call, and I need all my wits in order before I talk to Amanda."

When Alan got through to Derek, he put the call on the

speakerphone so I could listen in. As we had suspected, Derek's men had not found the woman who had met John Doyle in London. That search had barely begun and was expected to take days or weeks. Rather, Derek had called to tell Alan of a development at the medical end of the case.

"It turns out Doyle had a heart problem for which Lanoxin, a proprietary name for a form of digitalis, was prescribed. According to his doctor, he'd been taking it for some time. As you know, my people found no medicine in the house. We assumed at first that he had simply run out and hadn't bothered to refill the prescription, but we talked again to Mrs. Doyle after we heard about the heart trouble. She claims she knew nothing of any health problems her husband might have had, and had never seen him take medicine or bring any home. We checked with chemists and found the one that dispensed the prescription, the big Boots in the High Street. Their records show he had refilled the prescription a week before he died."

"Ah. There would have been enough, then, to cause death?"

"Several times over, according to both Doyle's doctor and ours. The dosage was one tablet, point-two-five milligrams, per day. Thirty tablets were dispensed. If he'd started taking them the day he got the new prescription—which is by no means certain, most people get refills before they've quite run out—he'd have had twenty-three left. That many would have stopped his heart."

"So the questions, of course, are where he kept that medicine and where it is now."

"If we could find it, or even an empty bottle, we'd be far closer to getting a handle on this mess. I'll swear it wasn't in the house, though. My men are properly trained. They do a thorough job, even when the cause of death is obscure at first. They went through that house like a dose of salts, rubbish bins and all. They found no medicine, and no empty containers."

"Perhaps he kept it in his desk at the bank. Some men are

sensitive about taking medicine. They feel it's a weakness. He might not have wanted to admit to his family that he needed it."

"That's possible, of course, though one would have thought he'd be equally loath to let his coworkers see him with medicine, especially a heart medicine."

"Well, thank you for telling me all this, Derek. I appreciate being kept in the loop, so to speak, and if I get any brilliant ideas, I'll ring. Don't hold your breath. Wait a moment, Dorothy wants to ask you something."

"Derek, I'm sure you asked Mrs. Doyle what she was doing on that day she wasn't at school. Can you tell me what she said, or is that privileged information?"

"She *said* she needed to buy some clothes for Miriam, and there was never a chance to do it evenings and weekends, when her husband was around, because he wouldn't let her spend the money."

"I see. Did you believe her?"

"My people looked through the child's room. There were a few things that looked new, a skirt, some underthings. It didn't look like a day's shopping to them. So no, we didn't believe her, or not entirely, but she stuck to her story."

"I see. I think I may try to worm a little more out of her, if that's all right with you."

"Be my guest. At the moment we know nothing at all, and time is passing."

"Right. I'll let you know the minute I find out anything."

My need for a nap had disappeared. I punched in the number Amanda had given me. Rather expecting either Miriam or Gillian to answer, I was somewhat surprised when Amanda picked up the phone.

"Three-six-seven-four-two-eight."

"Amanda? Dorothy Martin."

"Oh, yes, Mrs. Martin."

Was that relief I was hearing? Surely not.

There was a pause and a long breath. Then, "I believe I owe you an apology, Mrs. Martin, and there are several things

I'd like to talk to you about. Would it be convenient for me to come 'round?"

"Of course, or I could come there. Which is easier for you?"

"I hate to put you to the trouble, but perhaps if you wouldn't mind coming here? I'm afraid the press are rather dogging my heels just now."

"Oh, dear. I wondered when that would begin."

"They've just got hold of who my father is, you see."

"That's unfortunate, but it was bound to happen sooner or later, I suppose."

"I was naive enough to hope not. However, Gillian managed to spirit Miriam away when the first reporter arrived, before the rest turned up. That's one good thing. But there are hordes of them here now, I'm afraid. They simply won't go away! I don't know how you're to get inside."

I thought about that for a moment. "Mrs. Doyle, do you have a lawyer?"

"No." Her voice was suddenly sharp with fear. "Why would you ask that?"

"It's all right, I don't mean a criminal lawyer, a—what do you call them?—a barrister. Just an ordinary solicitor, who can issue some sort of noncommittal statement to the press and make them go away."

"Oh, I see. No, there's no one like that, either. John didn't believe in any sort of legal proceedings."

"Don't you have a will?"

"No. He didn't, either. He said neither of us had anything to leave, and he saw no need to spend money for a meaningless piece of paper."

"Well, then, I'll call our solicitor. He's a pleasant man, but he can be forceful when necessary. If he's free, I expect he'll come with me. That should get me in the house, anyway. Shall I call you back and say when we'll be there?"

"Yes, please. The only thing is, I don't know quite when Gillian will bring Miriam back . . ."

She let the thought trail off, but I understood. There were things to discuss that shouldn't be talked about in front of a child. "I'll come right away then, lawyer or no lawyer. Don't forget, I used to be a teacher, and I, too, can be forceful when I have to be. I'll come to the back door if I can manage it."

I really wasn't sure how I'd bully my way through "hordes" of reporters, so I was relieved when our lawyer, Mr. Carstairs, said he'd be right over. He sounded quite pleased, actually. Maybe business was slow, or maybe he was just bored and thought a confrontation sounded interesting. At any rate, he was on my doorstop in something under five minutes. I briefed him quickly as I drove to Amanda's house.

"You probably don't want to get into the Blake connection," I finished. "All you really need to do is give them some sort of statement and tell them she will say nothing more, on your advice. That should keep them at bay for a little while. I realize that this is out of your usual run of business, but do you think you can manage?"

"Any attorney," he said with a smile, "has considerable practice in saying nothing, at great and tedious length. I'm sure I can keep them occupied long enough for you to get in the house. I rather think stealth is in order, don't you?"

That settled the question of his feelings. He was enjoying this.

I had deliberately come out plainly dressed and bareheaded. I usually enjoy the attention my hats draw, but this time I wanted to be inconspicuous. We had to park some distance away because of all the cars and TV and radio vans near the house. I stayed in the car while Mr. Carstairs got out and drew the crowd of microphones and cameras and notepads to himself. While their owners were all shouting questions, I slipped out the door on the street side of the car, walked to the end of the street and around the corner, and then went down the alleyway that ran behind the minute back gardens of the drab little houses. Most of the gardens were little more than waste ground, "yards," in the English sense, for garbage cans and junk in general. They were backed by high, ugly board fences. Amanda's fence was in decent repair and had recently been painted brown. Here, too, John's meticulous, depressing care was evident. The remains of what had been a flourishing vegetable garden, though, showed what I thought was Amanda's hand. In the early December rain, the garden looked straggly and forlorn. That, too, reminded me of Amanda. But the Brussels sprouts were still bravely green.

Once I had let myself through the back gate, the fence screened me nicely from any further observation. Amanda was waiting for me at the door, and there was, for the first time, a hint of color in her face, a trace of a sparkle in her eye. "I saw you," she said in a whisper, "but I don't think anyone else did. Do you mind coming upstairs? One of them was peeking in the windows a little while ago."

We went up the steep, narrow stairs to Amanda's bedroom. It had originally been small. Now, with the back half partitioned off to make a room for Miriam, it was tiny. There was a twin bed with a prim white spread, a chair, a small wardrobe of wood-grained metal, and a low two-drawer chest with a plain, old-fashioned windup alarm clock on it. No bedside table, no reading lamp, no ornaments, no mirror. Except for the clock, it might have been the cell of a medieval nun.

"Please sit down," she said, gesturing at the chair. She sat on the bed, which sagged under her weight, slightly built though she was.

The room was cold. I left my coat on and wished I had worn a hat, after all. Through the ill-fitting windows came a substantial draft and the drone of Mr. Carstairs's voice.

Amanda sat twisting her fingers. "I hardly know how to begin. You were right. There's been too much misunderstanding. But for you, Miriam and I might have been left to wallow in fear and suspicion. After I read your note, it took only a few minutes to realize how dreadfully wrong we'd both been. And I've also misunderstood you. I said unforgivable things. I hope you—I can't tell you how much—"

I decided she needed help. "For a start, you can forget the apology. I've been intrusive and I know it. I am, sometimes. I hope it was from the best of motives, but I also admit to curiosity. I have a hard time leaving puzzles alone, and my first puzzle is where you were that day you decamped from St. Stephen's. You caused considerable consternation, you know."

"Yes, and inconvenience, especially for you. At least let me apologize for that. It really isn't the kind of thing I do. I wouldn't want you to think I'm that sort of person. But I had to do it. It was for Miriam's sake, you see, and of course I couldn't tell anyone while John was alive. Now that he's gone, I suppose it doesn't matter so much for her."

I gulped. Was I about to hear a confession? Perhaps of conspiracy to murder? *Had* she, after all, gone to London to see Gillian and plan John Doyle's murder?

"I told the police I went shopping for Miriam's clothes, and that was true, as far as it went. I did buy her a few things, all I could afford. I—I have my own bank account. John didn't know about it. I always turned my salary over to him, of course, but sometimes I could save a bit out of the housekeeping money. Or in summer, if the garden did well, I'd sell some of the extra vegetables at the Women's Institute market. There was never much money, but it was all I had that was my own."

I was as shocked by this grim little picture of penury, I think, as by anything I'd heard about John Doyle. "Amanda, forgive me for intruding again. But was there nothing your father could or would do to make your situation easier? He's quite well-to-do, isn't he?"

"He made quite a generous settlement when I married. I'm sure he felt at the time—probably still feels—that it was more than adequate. It was paid to John, of course. You must understand, Mrs. Martin, that I have had no contact with my father since my marriage. That's the way we both want it." She sounded bleakly matter-of-fact.

"I understand." I thought I did, too. Years of bitterness on both sides had widened the rift with her father until it was now an unbridgeable chasm. How sad. "But I'm sorry. I interrupted. You were saying you bought Miriam some clothes . . ."

"Yes, but only at the end of the day. You see, I knew John was in London that day."

"You did? That is, he told you he was—"

"He said he had business there. I was to meet his train and have tea ready for him."

She waited for any further questions I might have, but I shook my head. Questions could wait until later. We were getting to the heart of the problem.

"So I had the whole day, and I went a little mad, I think. I had the chance and I took it."

"The chance to do what?" I wasn't sure I wanted to hear the answer.

"To visit Miriam's school, of course."

19

AN anticlimax can feel like that extra step one sometimes takes at the top of a dark flight of stairs. The foot comes down with a thump and one is jolted to the top of the head. I must have looked peculiar, because Amanda frowned and said, "Are you all right, Mrs. Martin?"

Fortunately I didn't have to say what I'd been thinking, because there was a knock at the front door. I looked out the window. "It's all right," I said. "The reporters are gone. It must be Mr. Carstairs. Shall I let him in?"

"Please. But no one else!"

It was indeed the lawyer. When I opened the door, he stood looking pink cheeked and very pleased with himself.

"Mission accomplished, I think." He all but dusted his hands together.

"And well done, too! Will they be back, do you think?"

"Not, I believe, if they think I'll be here. I treated them to several pages of legal precedent, quoted verbatim and with citations. None of it meant anything, but those who weren't intimidated away seemed to decide it was time for a nap."

"If I didn't think Alan would find out, I'd kiss you, Mr. Carstairs. Would you like to come in?"

"Unless you think I can be of further assistance, I must, alas, go back to the office. I have an appointment. My secretary rang me up on the mobile; she's on her way to fetch me. But please call on me anytime."

"I'll do that." I'd pay his bill, too. It was worth every penny to be allowed to talk to Amanda in peace.

I closed and locked the door, just in case, and called up to Amanda, "You can come down. They've gone away, and Mr. Carstairs doesn't think they'll be back." I thought about going to the kitchen and putting the kettle on, but I'd done enough high-handed tea making in Amanda's house. I would let her make the suggestion.

And it was, in fact, the first thing she mentioned. I wished I'd brought something in the way of food. Not that I needed anything to eat. It was early for afternoon tea, and I'd had a big lunch. But I doubted she'd eaten much, if anything, and there was no telling what was in the house.

I squelched that idea, too. Stop interfering, Dorothy. Everybody in the world doesn't need you to run their lives for them.

She settled me in the frigid lounge and went to make the tea. I looked around. The room was scrupulously neat and almost antiseptically clean. The floor was covered with linoleum that was meant to look like wood, but didn't. The furniture, a "suite" of sofa and two chairs, was covered in a scratchy fabric in a depressing shade somewhere between brown and gray. It looked as if it would, unfortunately, never wear out. Skimpy brown curtains hung limply beside the two small windows. The room, like the bedroom, had no ornaments, no pictures on the walls, no books. A lightbulb shielded by a small tan paper shade dangled on a cord from the middle of the ceiling.

If ever the grim questions of Amanda's life were settled, and I was able to establish a friendly relationship with her and Miriam, I was going to buy her a cushion for that room. Or maybe two. In the brightest canary yellow I could find.

When Amanda brought in the tea, the tray held a pitcher of milk, along with the tea things and a plate of biscuits. She'd been to the store, then. I hoped she hadn't spent every cent she had, but it wasn't, I kept telling myself forcefully, really my business.

Extracting as much information as I could *was* my business. I made small talk while the tea brewed and drank some as soon as it was cool enough. Then I got down to brass tacks.

"So you went to Miriam's school. There must have been some special reason. Is she doing badly?"

She looked at me over her teacup, an odd smile on her face. "I imagine when you say that, Mrs. Martin, you mean poor marks."

"Well—or a behavior problem, I suppose, although I find that hard to imagine with Miriam."

"No. She's a quiet child, isn't she?"

"Almost too quiet, perhaps." I studied Amanda's face to see if I'd gone too far, but she nodded.

"Precisely. Too quiet, too obedient, too pale. Frightened, in fact. Wouldn't you say?"

"Well, perhaps, but she's had a good deal to be frightened of, lately."

"But she's been that way for a long time. I should have done something much earlier, but I thought perhaps it was only because our household was—not quite an ordinary one."

"Your husband was somewhat—" How should I put this? Repressive, difficult, inflexible? I took a sip of tea and tried to think of the right word.

"My husband," said Amanda Doyle in her usual quiet, controlled manner, "was a bloody tyrant and a damnable hypocrite, and even if they put me in prison for the rest of my life for killing him, I will be freer than I ever was as his wife."

I carefully put my cup down. "You—um—you did kill him, then?"

"No, of course not. But the police think I did, and I'm not a fool, Mrs. Martin. Or not that kind, at any rate. I know I'm apt to be arrested. I did things when I found his body that the police don't like at all. How was I to know I oughtn't to clean up the mess? I couldn't let Miriam see her father like that, could I?"

"But you ought to have known, from crime novels, or television—"

"I have never read a crime novel. John didn't allow frivolous reading. We don't have a television set, and Father, when I lived at home, devoted the television to his interests, news and social commentary. The police told me that one is supposed to leave everything at a crime scene exactly as it is, and I understand why, now, but I didn't know until they told me."

"I see." I did, too, but I wasn't at all sure the police would. Really, the basics of forensic procedure seem like something you'd think everyone would know, but this woman had apparently lived as much out of the world as any nun. Or no, nuns these days were often very savvy women. A more apt comparison might be with the Amish communities near my Indiana home. Like them, Amanda had some contacts with the outside world, through her teaching, but her home life was so circumscribed as to be almost medieval.

"But let me tell you about Miriam. It's important that you understand. I ought to have seen how unhappy she was long ago, you see, but I didn't. Not until this year. Because this year she was the same age as the children I was teaching."

"And you began to see the differences."

"Yes. I've always thought the children at St. Stephen's were oversophisticated, too old for their age. But this year I began to compare Miriam with them. The way they dress. Their games. Their interests. Their speech. Oh, in every way, they are simply more *alive* than she is. And I began to see that it wasn't that my schoolchildren were too noisy and naughty, but that Miriam was too quiet and obedient."

"In America we have a saying: 'Everyone's out of step but John.'"

"That's it. I had thought everyone was out of step but Miriam, and then I saw it was she who was different, was wrong somehow. And I began to worry, and to wonder why."

"Did you try to talk to her about it?"

"Of course, but it was almost impossible. This is a small house, with no privacy. Even when John wasn't in the room, he might have been able to hear us, and of course she wouldn't say anything with him listening."

"She was that frightened of him?"

"We both were. He never struck us, you know. Never once did he lay a hand on either of us. I don't expect you to understand. Miriam says your husband is a kind man. You wouldn't know how words can hurt, and cold disapproval, and hatred. He hated us. And we him."

I felt cold to my bones. I must have shivered, for Amanda said, "Shall I make more tea?"

"Please." I would have liked to suggest that she turn up the heat. There was an electric radiator in the room, but electricity costs money, and Amanda had little to spare. I drew my coat closer around me and hoped she wouldn't notice.

She did, though, when she came back with a fresh pot. "Why, you're cold," she said in a surprised tone, as if she'd just become aware of it. "Why didn't you say something? I thought it was only me. I've been cold for years." She said it matter-of-factly, as she turned on the radiator, and I wondered how much of her discomfort had been physical and how much a reflection of the emotional temperature in the Doyle household.

"So you tried to talk to Miriam, but without much success," I prompted.

Amanda nodded. "Even when John was out, she would say very little. It was as if she was afraid even to think things he shouldn't know. And she grew paler and paler, and thinner and thinner, and sometimes at night I would look in on her, and there would be tears drying on her face. And I knew I had to do something."

"Were you thinking of leaving your husband?"

"Oh, no, I couldn't do that."

"Because of your father, I suppose?"

She sighed. "I worried so much, over the years, about keeping the great secret. I don't know why I cared anymore, honestly. Perhaps it was habit, perhaps it was for Miriam's sake. It's not pleasant to be known as illegitimate. Perhaps it was because I was afraid of losing my job if it were known. But I knew John would tell, and there would be consequences. And then, of course, I had no money. So no, I couldn't leave him."

"What then?"

"I didn't know, not then. But something had to be done. For myself, I could stand it. I had made my bed, as John never tired of telling me, and I could lie in it. But I could not stand by and watch my daughter suffer. So when John told me he would be away for a day, I decided to go to her school and see what her situation was there."

"To talk to her teachers, you mean?"

"Oh, no. I knew I couldn't talk to any of them. I didn't dare even let them know who I was."

"But surely they'd recognize you! They all go to your church, don't they?"

"Chapel. And it is not mine. It was John's. Yes, they are all of that faith, but I had no close contact with them. They despised me because they knew I was not really one of them. And of course they knew about Miriam. John had made sure they knew of all my sins. That made them despise me even more, and her, too."

"But the teachers would know you from other school visits, wouldn't they? I always used to know the parents of most of my pupils."

"I had never visited the school."

"But—but an involved parent is—"

"Don't you think I know that? John wouldn't allow it."

I could think of nothing to say.

"You don't know what he was like, Mrs. Martin. Don't judge me too harshly. You don't know."

"I'm beginning to," I said grimly. "Go on."

"It's hard to talk about it. I was so afraid, you see. Not for myself, but if anyone had recognized me and told John, Miriam would have suffered. And I had so little time to think about it. John told me only that morning, the Monday morning. He got up very early, and woke me and Miriam, and said we must breakfast early, because he had to catch the six thirty-four to London. Business, he said. I couldn't ask, of course. He never told me anything. But I thought it must be chapel business of some sort, because his job at the bank wouldn't take him to London. So all I could think of was that I could go to Miriam's school without his knowing."

"But why didn't you call Catherine and tell her you needed a personal day? The faculty must get a certain amount of time off for that sort of thing."

"I suppose we do," she said vaguely. "I've almost never taken any leave. But in any case I couldn't tell anyone, anyone at all, or it might have got back to John. I was sorry about letting Catherine down, but this was for Miriam. I'd never have had the courage to do it otherwise.

"I took John to the station. I can drive, you know; I simply never do, because John takes—took the car. Then I took Miriam to school and dropped her off. I was careful to hide my face, so no one would see. Then I went home and sat down and thought hard about what I had to do. And as soon as the shops were open, I withdrew some money from the bank and went to Oxfam and bought a wig."

"A wig. How clever of you! Nothing disguises a woman like a wig."

"It was a cheap one, of course, and very ugly, but that didn't matter. I didn't dare buy anything blond, or red, although that would have made more difference. But my hair is long and brown, so I found something short and black and hoped it would be different enough. And I bought a gray coat—I've worn a brown one for years—and a gray scarf. I never wear scarves. And I got a pair of glasses. I couldn't see terribly well with them, but that didn't matter. Glasses change a person's appearance a lot, too."

"I think you did extremely well on the spur of the moment. And then you went to the school?"

"Yes. I had to take the glasses off when I drove, of course. But I parked two or three streets away and walked the rest of the way. I could see quite well enough for that. And when I got there I walked into the school office and asked to see Mrs. Rookwood."

20

THAT startled me considerably. "Mrs. Rookwood! But she's the church secretary!"

"How do you know that?"

"I went there yesterday. I wanted to know all I could about the place. I soon learned more than enough. Never mind. Go ahead."

"You know, then, that Mrs. Rookwood is the wife of Elder Rookwood. She has a finger in all the pies. She is the secretary of the church, and of the school, and runs the Sunday school and the Mothers' League and any number of other groups. She's a terrifying woman."

"I know." I grimaced at the memory of Mrs. Rookwood and took a sip of my tepid tea.

"You can understand, then, why I was more afraid of her than of any of the others. But she didn't seem to know who I was. I told her I was new in town and had heard about the school, and that I was looking for both a place to worship and a school for my son. I didn't want to give her any idea that I had a daughter, you see."

"Very wise."

"I didn't actually lie, of course, but I let her think that I had rather a lot of money. The coat had been a good one, and it still looked nearly new. I hated to burn it afterward."

"Burn it—oh, yes, of course. You would have had to do that. And the wig."

"Yes, only it wouldn't burn. It melted into a horrid mess. However. Mrs. Rookwood thought I was wealthy enough to pay the school fees. They charge rather a lot, you see. So she said that it would be necessary for me to join the chapel, that they accepted only children of members, and I said that would be all right, but could I see the school first? And she took me 'round."

She fell silent. I looked at her, and she shook her head. I waited.

There were no tears, no sobs. She bit her lip and took several deep breaths, and when she spoke again, her voice was perfectly steady, but very quiet.

"It was appalling. I have never before seen children treated that way, and I hope I never do again. It—I try not to remember, not to think that I let Miriam live in that horror for years. If I don't think about it, perhaps someday I can forgive myself." She took a deep breath, steeled herself to go on. "The children—there was no noise, Mrs. Martin. None at all except for the teachers' voices. The children didn't stir. They sat in their chairs with their hands folded on their desks and listened. In one room they were copying lines from the blackboard. One child dropped a pencil, and the fear I saw in his eyes, in the whole room—"

Her own face was white, as were her knuckles.

"Don't say any more. I understand."

She ignored me. "I saw Miriam. She was just like the others. A—a frozen child. A little ice statue." Tears were rolling down her face now. "And she saw me. She tried not to let it show on her face, but she turned pale, even paler than she usually is. I thought she was going to be sick. And there was nothing I could do to help her, nothing I could say . . ."

I handed her some tissues. She blotted her cheeks, blew her nose.

"I'm sorry." She made an ambiguous gesture that might have been an apology for her display of emotion, or her failure as a parent, or her existence, or all of those things.

"Nonsense. Would you like some more tea? I can make some, if you—"

"No, thank you. I'm sure Gillian and Miriam will be home soon." She looked around nervously. "What time is it?"

She wore no watch, and there was no clock in the room. I consulted my watch. "Goodness. After four."

"I thought so. It's beginning to look late. Gillian said they'd certainly be home in time for tea, and there's more I need to tell you before they get back."

"Yes. Did anything happen at the school? Did anyone recognize you, I mean?"

"No, no one except Miriam, and she was so—controlled. I'm sure no one noticed."

"So then—?"

"I told Mrs. Rookwood that I was very interested in the school and would bring my son in later in the week to enroll him. She wanted a deposit on the fees, so I told her I didn't have a check with me and would be back. Then I went to Braithwaite's and bought a few things for Miriam, since I had some money left and she needed them, and then I went home and made a fire in the back garden, to burn the coat and the other things, and while they burned I made up my mind."

"To do what?"

"To defy my husband."

She said it in a rush, as though the thought still terrified her. I processed what she'd said. The light dawned. "You decided to enroll Miriam in St. Stephen's."

"Yes."

"Did you tell her?"

"Yes, I did. I thought about it for a long time, wondering if it was wise, if she could keep it to herself."

"You didn't intend to tell your husband?"

"Certainly not!" She looked at me as if she thought me moronic. Well, it had been a stupid remark, hadn't it?

"I knew I would have to tell him eventually, of course. But not until Miriam was actually out of the old school. That wouldn't be until after Christmas, and I wasn't sure Miriam could stay quiet about it that long. But she'd been so self-possessed when she'd seen me at school, I decided she would be able to keep the secret. And I thought perhaps, if she knew she wouldn't have to bear the school very much longer, it would make things a little easier for her. So I told her as soon as I picked her up that day."

"What did she say?"

"That was strange, and rather frightening. She said so little. I tried to lead up to it gradually, because I knew it would be rather a shock. So I told her I knew she had seen me at school, and that I had visited because I was worried about her. Then I asked her if she liked school, if she had good friends, if she liked her teachers. They were foolish questions. I could see quite plainly that she hated it all, but I wanted her to tell me that. She didn't want to answer, but I pressed her and she said it was all right. Just that: 'It's all right.' So I asked her if she would like to go to my school instead."

Amanda pushed her heavy hair back with a weary gesture. "She looked at me, and just for a moment I saw something like hope in her eyes. Then she said, 'Daddy won't let me,' and wouldn't say another word all the way home."

"I've heard," I said slowly, "that if an animal is caged all its life, sometimes when it is rescued and the door opens and it can go free, it cowers inside, afraid and unsure. It doesn't know what to do with freedom."

"That's just what she looked like. A caged animal. I talked to her some more at home, before I went to the station for John. I said that it was our secret, that we wouldn't tell Daddy, and that it would be all right. Really, I don't think I believed it myself. But Miriam—oh, I wasn't sure I'd done the

146 ◆ JEANNE M. DAMS

right thing in telling her. For the next two days, she seemed more miserable and frightened than ever, and I couldn't get her to talk to me. I had no idea what was going on in her mind, and that frightened me more than anything."

I was beginning to comprehend the depths of the hell Amanda had been living in, and even though the room had warmed, I shivered. "And then when you found him that morning, you must have thought . . ."

"I couldn't think at all. I was almost out of my mind. I couldn't seem to catch my breath, and the room kept spinning. I cleaned up, I think now, just to pretend things were normal. Or no, that's not it, exactly—I don't know."

"I expect you were in shock. Literally, I mean, physically and emotionally both. I've never had to go through anything as awful as that, but I've had a few unpleasant experiences in my life. The worst of them was my first husband's heart attack, and I remember sitting in the hospital waiting room, while he was in the emergency room, tidying up my purse as if it were the most important thing in the world to get it neat. It's an escape. The mind focuses desperately on something else to keep from thinking about the unthinkable."

Amanda nodded. Her fingers were slowly shredding a paper napkin, and when she spoke it was in a thin whisper. "I couldn't let myself think that maybe Miriam . . . oh, I knew she couldn't have stabbed her own father, no matter what, I *knew* that, but . . ."

It was time to get back to reality, to abandon the nightmare world of might-have-been. I risked a hard question. "Amanda, I hope you don't mind my asking, but did you really hear nothing that night, or did you just tell the police that because you heard something that you thought implicated Miriam?"

"I really didn't hear anything." She folded her hands in her lap. "It was the night of prayer meeting, but John let me stay home because I'd worried myself into a frightful headache, and even he could see I was ill. He said there was another meeting after that, and he'd be late. So I went to bed, and I—I took a sleeping pill." She said it as though she had just confessed a long-standing addiction to one of the more disreputable street drugs. "I'd never done such a thing before, but I hadn't been sleeping, and I'd got to the point I was forgetting things and could hardly teach. I'd bought them that afternoon, though of course I'd had to hide them from him. I thought just one wouldn't hurt, and maybe I'd get a good night's sleep."

"Uh-oh. If you're not used to those things, even the over-the-counter ones can pack a real wallop. I expect you were still groggy in the morning."

"I could hardly wake up. I don't know how long the alarm rang before I shut it off, and then, oh, how I wanted to stay in bed. I felt slow and stupid, and then I was so afraid John would notice and make me tell him about the pill, I went downstairs to make tea before waking Miriam."

"And you were in that state when you saw him! No wonder you behaved a trifle—er—irrationally."

"I behaved like a fool. I see that now. But what can I—oh, here's Miriam back!"

There were noises from the back of the house and then Miriam walked into the room, followed by Gillian. The love and warmth that suffused Amanda's pale, pinched face twisted my heart. What lay ahead for those two? What would happen to them if they were separated, if Amanda were imprisoned? Surely such a thing couldn't happen. Not in England, where the police were so efficient, so thorough.

"Look, Mummy! Auntie Gillian bought me a new coat and hat! And she took me to have my hair cut, and we had ice cream, and went to feed the ducks, and I petted the sweetest little dog in the park, it licked my hand and wagged its tail. May we have a puppy, Mummy? Auntie Gillian says they're nice, and not really dirty at all if you bathe them often enough, and I promise I'd take care of it and feed it and brush it all the time and take it for walks. Do you think we might, Mummy?"

For the first time in our acquaintance, Miriam was looking and acting like a child. Her hair, which she had worn scraped back into a tight ponytail, had been cut in short layers. Freed from its confinement, it curled attractively next to her cheeks, which were pink with excitement. She wore a bright red coat and matching hat, a couple of years out of style—Oxfam, I thought—but warm and attractive and infinitely preferable to anything I had seen on her before. She kept chattering, and I smiled at her. Perhaps she was too excited, too shrill, but there seemed some hope that she was beginning to heal. It would, I thought sadly, take a long time before the scars were obliterated, if indeed they ever were.

While Miriam chattered on, Gillian reached in her coat pocket, pulled something out, and held it up in her gloved hand. It was a brown plastic prescription bottle. "What on earth was this doing in your rubbish bin, Mandy?" she said, interrupting Miriam. "It blew out just as we drove up in back. I thought nobody ever took medicine in this house."

She was close enough that I could read the label. "Lanoxin," it read, with John Doyle's name and dosage instructions, and a late-November date.

It was empty.

21

M Y throat went dry, but for perhaps the first time in this whole crisis, I managed to keep my head. As Amanda reached for the vial, I stepped forward and got in first, though I had to swallow twice before I could speak. "May I see it, Gillian?"

I had snatched up a paper napkin from the tea tray. "Goodness, it's a bit grubby, isn't it?" I said in what I hoped was the right casual tone as Gillian dropped the vial from her gloved hand into the napkin. Had I told anyone about the way John Doyle really died? Would any of them smell a rat? Gillian was no fool, and unlike Amanda, she had probably read detective stories. Would she see the real significance of the paper napkin? Would she wonder what my interest was?

"What on earth do you want with it?"

The question came quick and sharp—exactly the question I'd been afraid of. I thought fast. "I have a young friend whose passion is her dollhouse. You remember Jemima, Miriam. You met her at my house. She likes to use these little bottles to make things for the house, or to store those tiny hinges and doorknobs and things like that."

I studied Miriam's face, but I saw no fear, indeed no interest. Her mind was apparently still on the possibility of a dog. Amanda's face, too, was blank, but it was too late to catch her first reaction. I'd been too busy rescuing the precious bit of evidence to watch her.

At this stage, Gillian was the one to watch out for. She persisted. "Mandy, it has John's name on it. You told me once he never took drugs, didn't approve of them."

"What is it, cold medicine or something?" Amanda didn't sound very interested, but again she held out her hand.

I kept the vial and pretended to study the label. "'Lanoxin,' it says. Anybody know what that is?"

"It's digitalis," said Gillian in that dry voice of hers. "It's for heart trouble. Did John have heart trouble, Mandy?"

"And exactly how do you think I would know that? He never told me anything, but I've never seen him take medicine of any kind. He didn't approve of medicine."

"Or anything else," muttered Gillian.

"Oh, for heaven's sake take the bottle, Dorothy, and welcome to it. Gillian, you must be longing for some tea. I know, I'll make scones. Would you like that, darling, just as a little treat?"

Miriam grinned. "We can have treats now, can't we, Mummy? Will you teach me to make scones? Do you think a puppy would like scones?"

If there was guilt behind the facade of either mother or daughter, Miriam was the best child actress since Shirley Temple, and Amanda wasn't far behind. I gave up on the psychology of the thing and decided to be content with the physical evidence. It might not be much, but it was something. There was only a slim chance of fingerprints, but the real point was that, once the police had their hands on the vial, they'd be in a much better position to trace who put it there. Of course, they'd be around to question everyone, and at that point I was going to be as popular in Amanda's household as a skunk at a picnic.

Should I stay and try to make a little more hay in the brief period of sunshine left to me? Or should I get out while the getting was good?

Discretion is the better part of valor. I couldn't remember who'd said that, but it seemed at the moment to be the epitome of wisdom. "Well," I said brightly, dropping the pill bottle into my coat pocket, "you don't need me to carry on the puppy discussion. I'm more of a cat person, though I do think puppies are sweet. I'll just—"

"Just a moment." Gillian's voice was as cold and sharp as chilled steel. "I think I'll have that bit of rubbish back, if you don't mind."

"Gill!" Amanda sounded shocked. "There's nothing in it, you said so. You surely don't think Dorothy's stealing something, do you?"

Gillian moved so that she could look me full in the face, and paid no attention to Amanda. "Exactly what did John die of, Dorothy?"

"Gill, I really can't have this! Miriam, darling, put your coat away and wash your hands and face, and then come back and we'll make scones."

Miriam, all the animation wiped from her face as though by a sponge, moved away silently.

"I'd have thought you'd have better sense!" said Amanda, her voice low but full of anger. "Talking about it in front of—"

"Well?" said Gillian, interrupting. "Is someone going to tell me? And are you going to give that vial back to me?"

"He was stabbed," said Amanda in fury. "I had to come down in the morning, half awake, and find my husband lying on the kitchen floor with a knife in his back. I didn't tell you because the thought still makes me sick and I don't want to talk about it. Now are you happy?"

"And was that what killed him?" Gillian was still talking to me, and her voice never wavered.

"No." I was tired of it, suddenly. "No, it wasn't. I'm sorry, Amanda. I didn't tell you, because I wasn't sure I should, but your husband was already dead when he was stabbed. He died of an overdose of digitalis, probably from the vial I have in my pocket. And no, I'm not going to give it back to you, Gillian. I'm going to give it to the police. They may be able to trace the murderer with it. And before you go into a screaming tantrum, either of you, let me remind you that I do *not* believe either you, Amanda, or your daughter had anything to do with the murder."

"I notice you left me off your little list." Gillian stood between me and the doorway of the room.

"Yes, I did, didn't I? Excuse me."

She stood still for a moment, and then moved aside and let me pass.

I made for the back door in case any reporters had come back. Miriam was in the kitchen, looking like a pale little ghost.

"Oh, sweetheart, it'll be all right! Really, it will. You see if you can't talk your mother into that puppy. It would do you both a world of good."

She said nothing, and after a moment's indecision, I let myself out and trudged to my car.

I went straight to the police station with my story and my bottle. Derek wasn't there, so I had to talk to one of the lower orders, an impassive woman who didn't know me. She wasn't impressed.

"Thank you, Mrs. Martin," she said in a bored tone when I had finished talking and had handed over the little brown vial. "I'm sure we're grateful for your trouble, though of course you know it would have been better to leave this where you found it."

"I didn't find it. I just told you. Ms. Blake found it, and if I'd left it with her, she would either have thrown it away or covered it with her own fingerprints, or both."

"Yes, I'm sure you did what you thought was best."

She sounded soothing and complacent, as if she'd been to nanny school and was practicing her lesson on a difficult toddler. I was nettled. "You will tell Chief Inspector Morrison the minute he gets in? It's important that he send someone to talk to the family right away, because—"

"I will deal with it, rest assured, Mrs. Martin."

With that I had to be satisfied, if not content. There is a certain level of English officialdom, in no matter what business or agency, that delights in condescension. It was the same in America, of course, or had been when I'd lived there. In America, though, the rudeness wasn't disguised as courtesy. "Okay, okay, lady," would have been the response from a bored cop in my hometown.

I thought it might have been easier to take. You can get mad at people when they're overtly rude.

I went home and told Alan all about it. "And I'll bet I'd have been treated better if you were still in charge!"

"Well, yes. You'd have been the wife of the boss, wouldn't you?"

"I mean—"

"I know what you mean, but I'm afraid the supercilious, like the poor, we have always with us. They usually either learn better or leave the force, though I've known a few senior officers . . ." He shook his head.

"Well, it's infuriating. That miserable little piece of plastic cost me all the headway I'd made with Amanda. The police might at least have acted grateful."

"I'm sure Derek will be ecstatic when he finds out about it."

"If he finds out about it."

"Oh, he will. The woman you talked to—sergeant?"

"Just a constable, I think."

"In any case, she'd know better than to make a mistake in a major investigation. She'll see he gets the report, however much she might resent being told what to do by the wife of a retired CC."

"Oh. Yes, I suppose that was part of it. She'd know who I am, you think?"

"Yes, my dear. *Gloria mundi* may *transit*, but not quite that quickly, not in a small town. Yes, everyone on the police is quite aware that you are my wife."

"She didn't act as if she knew."

"Of course not. She would have had to act deferential, and it didn't suit her. Now, what are you going to do while you wait for Derek to call and heap laurels on your head?"

I stuck my tongue out at him. "I don't quite know. I had planned to ask Amanda if she had any idea, herself, who might have murdered her husband. Yes, I know the police will have asked her, but she might open up more to me. Might have before all this, I mean. Now—I think I'm at a loose end."

"In that case, why don't we pop 'round to the hospital?"

"The hospital? What for? You're not feeling—oh! The baby?"

"The baby. A little boy, Nigel Peter. Mother and child doing splendidly. Born late last night, but no one got around to telling us till this afternoon."

"Oh, that's exactly what I need to take my mind off everything else! Yes, let's go. Right away, before visiting hours are over for the day."

There was a time in my life when I, an achingly childless woman, found it hard to visit a maternity ward. All those babies, when I had none. Fortunately, I'd eventually outgrown the oversensitivity. We stopped to buy flowers and thoroughly enjoyed seeing Inga (weary but beautiful), Nigel (haggard, with a bristly five o'clock shadow, but bursting with pride), and small Nigel Peter (red of face, black of hair, and roaring lustily).

We didn't stay long. Everyone concerned needed rest, and so did I. Though I absolutely hate admitting it, I'm not as young as I once was, and both physical and emotional exertion tire me more than they used to. I wanted to go home, thaw out something for supper, and put my feet up while I considered what role, if any, I could continue to play in the Doyle drama.

The phone rang when I was staring into the freezer, searching for inspiration. Alan answered it in his study and came padding slipper shod into the kitchen a couple of minutes later.

"You were right, love. Derek got your message, but not until he'd been back at the station for some time. He was livid about the delay, by the way. I think that young woman will have her ears pinned back. Anyway, he decided to go to the Doyle house himself, because he was quite certain that there had been no medicine vial in the rubbish bin, or anywhere else, when the house was first searched. And he was too late. The birds have flown."

22

No one was there?" I said stupidly.

"They were not only not there, but they left behind every indication of urgent flight. They forgot even to lock the door, so Derek had a bit of a look 'round. Drawers not quite pushed in, that sort of thing. The wardrobes are all half empty, the toothbrushes are gone, and so is Gillian's car. They've decamped."

I pulled out a kitchen chair and sat down. Alan closed the freezer door and sat, too.

"They've gone to London," I said finally. "Gillian's taken them both. Drat the woman! She doesn't trust me and she doesn't trust the police, but you'd think she'd be smart enough to see that the innocent are better off sitting tight."

"Or the guilty, if it comes to that. No, don't glare at me. I've no desire to find either of the Doyles guilty of murder, though I'm keeping a more open mind about it than you are. But I doubt they've gone to Gillian's flat."

"Too obvious? I suppose. Where, then? Surely not home to Daddy."

"It's not impossible, though I admit it's unlikely. One can imagine the sort of welcome they'd get. No, I would imagine it's London or Birmingham. Perhaps Manchester, though that's rather far afield."

"Not for Gillian, not the way she drives. A big city where they can get lost, then?"

"It's where people usually go when they're trying to run away. Unless they skip the country altogether. But that takes a little money, especially with three people, and apparently there isn't much money to spare in this case."

"Mmm. Daddy might have been willing to spring for some airfares, though, to get his troublesome family even farther out of the way. I suppose Derek will have notified the ports."

"Routine, my dear. Not that it does much good these days, when anyone can hop aboard a Chunnel train and be in France before you can look up the schedule."

"The *idiots!* When they could perfectly well have sat it out here. It'll work itself out in time, I know it will. Things always do."

Alan said nothing with such heavy emphasis that I sighed. "All right, all right. Not always. And if they really did do it, one or all of them, I suppose they were sensible to try and get away. But I don't believe for a moment that they're murderers—though I could cheerfully murder Gillian myself right now—and I intend to find out who *is* responsible."

It was Alan's turn to sigh and pick up the telephone as he rummaged through our take-out menus. "Indian or Chinese?"

I thawed out some meat loaf instead, and after supper sat in front of the parlor fire and did some serious thinking. I would have liked to go charging off in all directions, but I was truly too tired, and it wouldn't have done me any more good than it did Don Quixote.

No, it was time to make some lists. I make lists for everything. "Shopping," "Things to Remember" (that one gets longer and more vital with every passing year), "Things to Do."

The lists I began that evening were headed "Things I Know," "Things I Need to Know," and "People to Talk To."

The whole thing was more than a little daunting, now that I sat down to look at it logically. The first two lists could have been disposed of quickly with entries of "Almost nothing" and "Everything." However, as the high school teacher told the sophomore who wanted the topic of his required essay to be "Life," perhaps I could break it down a little and make it easier.

Very well, then, what *did* I know?

Start with the basics. I thought back over the past few days, as the complex pattern of personalities and circumstances had begun to unfold for me, and wrote down everything I could remember:

> John Doyle was a cold, harsh, self-righteous prig who bullied his family and delighted in causing trouble. He cost one man his job, another his life. He cut Amanda off from her only family support, her sister. He worked at a bank. He also ran the family finances.

> Amanda Doyle was forced to marry when she became pregnant, perhaps by another man. Her father, a prominent MP, didn't (and presumably doesn't) want the circumstances of Amanda's marriage known, and John held that over Amanda's head. Amanda hated John but was afraid to leave him.

> Miriam was taught that animals are dirty and that misfortunes are a result of wickedness, a punishment for sin. She was profoundly unhappy both at school and at home and was very much afraid of her father.

So much for background on the principals. Now for facts about the case:

> John Doyle died of an overdose of a digitalis preparation. He was stabbed after death. Both doors to the house were locked when Amanda found him the next morning.

The digitalis container was found today, empty, on the Doyle property.

John Doyle was in London two days before he was found dead. On that same day, Amanda played hooky from school and went to visit Miriam's school. The next day she enrolled Miriam at St. Stephen's.

John was at a church meeting, after the regular prayer meeting, the night he died.

I looked over what I'd written. Some things were open to question, of course, things I "knew" only by hearsay. However, it seemed to me I could accept most of it. I was not bound, as the police are, by the provable.

On to the list of questions:

Where are the Doyles and Gillian?
What did John Doyle do that day in London?
Is Amanda telling the truth about her AWOL day?
Where has the pill bottle been all this time?
What about that church meeting?
What does Gillian have to do with all this?

I studied the list with some dissatisfaction. That last entry was nebulous in the extreme, and as for the others, well, the police were far better equipped than I to find the answers to most of them. However . . . perhaps I could nose around and talk to people and find out a little more about a few things.

That led me to the third list, and there I stuck. I'd already talked to everyone I could think of. There were useful questions I could still put to the Doyles, and to Gillian, if I could find them. But that was the problem, wasn't it? Their neighbors, perhaps, but I couldn't feel very hopeful about that idea. His coworkers, others besides Sam Johnson? Maybe, but what was the point? The police would already have talked them into exhaustion, and they wouldn't be apt to greet me with open arms and a ready tongue.

Really, there was just one group I hadn't explored adequately. The people John Doyle went to church with. The followers of the One True God. The reason, I admitted reluctantly, was sheer cowardice. I feared and disliked everything they stood for. Extreme fundamentalism in religion, any religion, had always struck me as simplistic and therefore dangerous, and the worst fundamentalists of all were those who followed a creed of hatred. I wanted nothing further to do with those people. It was plain they felt the same way about me.

Wait, though. Did they? All of them? I had talked to only a few, hadn't I? I had, myself, never gone to a church where everybody believed the same thing, even though we all got up every Sunday morning and recited the same Nicene Creed. There were degrees of belief, shades of commitment, ranging all the way from the young husbands who really didn't believe anything much except that going to church was respectable and good for business, and Sunday school was a good influence on the children, to the devout elderly women who were pillars of the Altar Guild and turned up for every Saint's Day and Holy Day of Obligation and probably knew the Book of Common Prayer by heart.

Why should the Chapel of the One True God be any different? True, their rigid doctrines were light years removed from the warm and gently tolerant Anglican beliefs, but was I to think that every single parishioner, or whatever they called themselves, swallowed the dogma whole? Amanda used to attend, after all, and she wasn't a true believer. Surely there were others who were dragged along by a spouse, who didn't subscribe entirely, or at all, to the dark tenets espoused by Elder Rookwood and his dragon of a wife.

How was I going to find those straying sheep and talk to them?

Rapidly I ran through my list of sources. Jane was out. She knew everything that went on in Cathedral circles, most things about schools and schoolchildren, and the general run of Sherebury gossip, but the stranger nonconformist sects were beyond her ken. The Endicotts, as innkeepers, knew a lot of people, but I somehow couldn't see any of Elder Rookwood's flock bending a cheery elbow at the Rose and Crown of an evening. My entrée to university gossip, dear old Dr. Temple, was nearly housebound now with arthritis, and again, knew little of people outside his academic world.

The dean of the Cathedral?

Ordinarily he was the first person I'd turn to about anything ecclesiastic. A devout priest, he was also, as any administrative clergyman must be these days, an excellent politician. He kept up ties with the Baptists and Methodists, I knew, and the Roman Catholics, of course.

Rookwood's bunch? It didn't seem likely, but the dean *had* said I could call on him any time, if I needed help.

Or, no. Margaret, of course! The dean's wife was the one who kept her finger on the religious pulse of the town. If any outsider knew anything about dissension in the ranks of the One True God (really, it was impossible even to think of them without sounding blasphemous), it would be Margaret.

I looked at my watch. Nearly ten. That was far too late to call the poor woman with anything but a genuine life-or-death emergency. Besides, I was exhausted myself. It had been a long and troubling day. But I'd go to Matins tomorrow, without fail, and enlist Margaret's aid.

I tidied up the parlor, checked to make sure the fire was safe to leave for the night, and went to Alan's study where he was watching the news.

"There's Blake," he said, pointing to the screen.

He was an impressive figure, his silver hair gleaming like a halo in the glare of television lighting. Behind him that lovable symbol of the nation, the clock tower that housed Big Ben, towered straight and reliable, the lighted face of the clock indicating that Parliament was sitting.

". . . will see that Her Majesty's loyal opposition hold the day on this vital issue. The moral fabric of our nation cannot withstand such constant attack, and I and my colleagues intend to stop the blitz of pornography entering our living rooms every night. Wholesome entertainment . . ."

"I'm going to bed, love. Sufficient unto the day. Are you coming up soon?"

"I thought you'd never ask," he replied in what he fondly imagined to be a W. C. Fields voice. He snapped off the television. "Speaking of pornography . . . shall we indulge in a little X-rated activity ourselves, my little chickadee?"

The day ended far more pleasantly than it had begun.

23

MATINS was about as well attended as it usually was on a Tuesday in early December, which was to say that the clergy and choir combined easily outnumbered the congregation. It's a lovely little service, though. I've often wondered why more people don't come. You'd think there'd be enough music lovers in town that they'd fill the place just to hear the choir. Oh, well, perhaps Anglican chant isn't to everyone's taste these days.

As the last of the procession trailed out, I contemplated the probable reaction to more modern music at Matins. Rock? Rap? I shuddered and turned to Margaret Allenby, who had sat next to me. "Margaret, I need to pick your brain."

"It's at your disposal, such as it is. Shall we go to Alderney's for coffee?"

"I think maybe not, thanks. The trouble with Alderney's is that I never stick to coffee, and I'd gained three pounds the last time I dared step on a scale."

"Come to the Deanery, then. I overslept this morning and

haven't had my daily dose of caffeine yet. It's a miracle I didn't start snoring during the Te Deum."

"It was a rather long setting this morning, wasn't it? But beautiful. I sometimes wonder if Jeremy and the boys don't get discouraged, working so hard on such lovely music, only to have it heard by so few people."

"Oh, they do it for love, you know," said Margaret, leading the way across the Close to the beautiful little sixteenth-century house she called home. The morning was clear and still, but very chilly. Our breath formed little clouds as we talked. "Love of the music, and perhaps now and then love of God."

"Who is always listening."

"I'm sure Jeremy hopes not on those lamentable occasions when the trebles don't quite reach the high notes. But alas, I fear He probably always is."

Margaret makes wonderful coffee, and she casually set out some scones ("left over from yesterday's tea; I do hope they're not too dry and horrid"), so I ended up eating as much as if I'd gone to the tea shop. I waited until Margaret had absorbed a due quantity of caffeine before broaching my question.

"The Chapel of the One True God," she repeated thoughtfully. "Ah, yes. Rather an audacious thing to call one's organization, I'd have thought. Still, if anyone would make the claim, it would be Mr. Rookwood."

"It's his invention, then? I thought I'd never heard of it before."

"His brain child entirely, as I understand it, though it was established a good long time before Kenneth and I came to Sherebury."

"Margaret, what draws people to a church like that? There doesn't seem to be one iota of hope or comfort or peace in the things they preach."

"No, but some people aren't looking for those things, Dorothy. They're full of anger, and they're looking for justification, or for revenge. It pleases them, in a perverse sort of way, to be able to ascribe their own feelings and motives to God."

"You wouldn't think there'd be enough people like that to fill a church, though, and keep it going for years."

"Well, of course, not all of them are genuine zealots. Some are in it for the thrill—there's a nasty thrill in really virulent hatred, you know—and some go along for the ride. Some like the feeling of power they get from denouncing other people in public."

"That was John Doyle, wasn't it? From what I've heard, he loved making people squirm, and worse. Ruining their lives, sometimes."

"Yes, and feeling righteous about it all the time. I can't say so when Kenneth is around, and I probably ought not even to think such a thing, but I can't help being grateful that man is dead. He was pure poison."

"Especially for his family, I suspect. I know Amanda Doyle hated everything about the chapel. She went only because John forced her to. Are there others like that, do you think?"

"Oh, I'm sure there are. Though of course when you get a man like Rookwood, who rules through fear, very few people are brave enough to say what they really think. They simply leave when they can't bear it any longer."

"Yes, that's what I really wanted to ask you about, Margaret. I need to talk to some people like that, some of the ones who don't really subscribe to the party line. I need to know what John Doyle was up to the last few days of his life, and I can't ask Amanda. She's left town."

Margaret nodded. "I heard. She might well not have known, anyway."

"She said she didn't, but I thought if I pressed her, she might remember some little thing that would help. Anyway, I can't, because the little idiot's flown the coop. So I thought I'd better talk to someone at the church, but it'll have to be one of the disaffected. The others think I'm anathema."

"That puts you in excellent company, my dear. One gathers they don't think too highly of Jesus Christ, either. Now, let me see. There was the Collins family—no, they moved to Leeds. And I don't know what became of poor little Tony Prichard. He had a speech impediment, and they used to taunt him, say it was the work of the devil. Shameful, it was."

She ticked off a few more people mentally, and I marveled not only at her memory, but at her concern for these people who weren't even of her faith. Sherebury's a small town, but Margaret's wide-spread kindness is remarkable, even so.

"Ah! I think I have it. Miss Simmons. I don't know her Christian name. I doubt anyone has ever called her anything but Miss Simmons. She's an old maid, and quite a character. Not a spinster, or an unmarried lady. Quite definitely an old maid. Her father involved her in the chapel, and she went out of deference to him, though I gather she sometimes spoke her mind even then. She may be the only person in Sherebury who isn't afraid of the Rookwoods."

"Except you."

"My dear, they terrify me! That's why I've made friends with so many of their disgruntled parishioners, I expect. Anyway, old Mr. Simmons finally died, aged something like a hundred and ten, and as soon as Miss Simmons could do as she liked, she left and joined the Baptists. She told me she would have come to us, but she liked the Baptists' hymns better. After years of no music in church at all, she said, she wanted to lift up her voice. And my dear, she's ninety if she's a day, and her voice sounds like a cross between a creaky gate and a Siamese cat!"

"More power to the Baptists, then, if they can make her happy and put up with her singing. She sounds like exactly the person I need, if she didn't leave the chapel too long ago to know anything about current affairs there."

"She keeps up with some of the people, I think. She'll know a lot, still, and she'll know who you can safely ask about anything she can't tell you. She's a remarkable woman, a true original. You'll enjoy her. Give her my love, and here—take the rest of these scones with you. They won't last another day, and she likes her little treat."

Margaret gave me the address and precise instructions for how to get there (she knows me and my phobias well), and I sped off laden with scones, good wishes, and questions.

Miss Simmons's house, when I found it (without a hitch), was one of those anonymous semidetached Victorian things, neither beautiful enough nor ugly enough to distinguish itself from its fellows. I had hoped to get some idea of her personality from her front garden. Gardens tell a lot about people, I think.

Hers was gravel.

She was at the front door before I could ring the bell. She was less than five feet tall and certainly didn't weigh as much as ninety pounds. She wore gray slacks tucked into yellow Wellington boots, an Aran Isles cardigan three sizes too big over a soft rose sweater in what looked like cashmere, and a belligerent expression. Her gray hair, still abundant, looked as though it had been styled with an egg beater, and a cigarette was tucked into the corner of her mouth.

"Well?"

"Miss Simmons?"

"Nobody else living here."

"My name is Dorothy Martin. Margaret Allenby sent me with her love and a plate of scones."

The wrinkles of her weatherbeaten face crinkled into a grin. "Come in, then, why don't you? Too cold to stand here passing the time of day."

She showed me into the front parlor. It was densely populated with old-fashioned furniture, lace antimacassars, and ornaments of the present-from-Brighton sort. In the grate a coal fire literally roared. I'd never heard a fire make so much noise, nor endured one that produced so much heat. I estimated the temperature of the room at close to ninety.

"You'll be too hot in that coat. Take it off. Take off that hat, which is the silliest thing I've seen in years. Take off anything you can, down to decency level. I'm old and I like it warm, but you youngsters can never take the heat."

My seventieth birthday wasn't all that far away, and I hadn't been called a youngster in at least thirty years. I forgave her about the hat (which was a perfectly respectable black velvet with only one huge red rose) and obeyed her, stripping down to silk blouse and wool skirt and wishing I had a bathing suit on underneath.

"Now. I don't propose to offer you tea, because it isn't teatime, and if you've come from Margaret, you're bungful of tea or coffee anyway. The loo's through there, when you need it." She gestured vaguely. "And I'm not going to offer you these scones, because she sent them for me. She'll have told you I'm a frightfully rude old woman, so it won't come as a surprise."

"She said you were remarkable."

"At my age, that means I'm breathing. Never mind. I'm young yet, by my family's standards. That doesn't mean I have time to waste, though. I might break the average and pop off any time. So speak your piece."

"I—uh—"

"Margaret sent you here for some reason besides delivering scones. Don't be stupid, woman! Tell me what she wants, or what you want."

I began to believe that Miss Simmons was not afraid of the Rookwoods. It might, indeed, be the other way around.

However, I was determined not to be intimidated. "First I'd like a glass of water. With ice, if there is any."

Miss Simmons cackled. "American, aren't you? Ice water, pooh! How about some good English beer? I've chilled lager, if you must have it cold."

The time was a little after nine-thirty in the morning. I accepted the lager. "I'll get it, if you—"

"I've still the use of my limbs, young woman. Sit. I think that chair can take your weight." She pointed to a Morris chair sort of contraption that looked hideously uncomfortable, all wood and cracked leather arranged at odd angles. The seat was covered with perhaps a week's supply of newspapers, a knitted tea cozy in shades of magenta and bilious green, and a dented, blackened tea tray that looked as if it might once have been priceless Georgian silver. I scooped the collection off onto the floor and sat, wondering if I'd ever be able to get out of the chair's clutches.

24

M iss Simmons brought in the beer, mine in a thick, dimpled glass mug like the kind they once used in pubs, hers in a lidded pewter one dating back much farther.

"Cheers," she said, lifting her mug and draining off perhaps half its contents. "Aaah. Guinness is good for you. I know who you are."

"You do?" I had swallowed my sip of beer, or I might have choked on it.

"You're that American woman who keeps poking into crimes, and who stole the most eligible widower in town right out from under our noses."

"That's me. And he's a treasure, let me tell you."

Again the cackle. "I do like a person who isn't touchy. Can't abide people who get their feelings hurt."

"I should imagine you know quite a few people who do get their feelings hurt." I put down a healthy swig of beer. The room was, if possible, getting even hotter.

"No guts, that's their trouble. Can't take the truth. You're here about the Doyles."

If I kept on being surprised by what this woman said, I'd waste a lot of energy. "I am. Second sight, or did someone tell you?"

"Common sense. You fancy yourself some sort of sleuth. You've come to me. Only people I know who've got themselves mixed up in murder are the Doyles. Q.E.D."

"You wouldn't make a bad detective yourself. So you knew the Doyles?"

She finished her beer and put the mug down on the floor, the only available flat surface. "Want another?"

"I'm still working on this one, thank you."

"Hmph." She lit a cigarette.

I couldn't tell if her disgust was directed at my wimpy speed of consumption, or my implied criticism of her more robust drinking habits. I smiled.

"The Doyles. She's a mouse, he was a bastard. The child's peculiar. What else do you want to know?"

"Ultimately I want to know who killed him, but—"

"Why?"

"Why what? You lost me."

"Why d'you want to know whodunit? To put 'em in quod? Or give 'em a medal?"

"He wasn't a nice man," I said. "But I don't approve of murder." I sounded prim even to myself.

"Hmph! Milk and water, like all C of E people."

"You prefer the militancy of the Chapel of the One True God?"

"All right, all right, no need to get nasty. I went to that place for years because my dear papa went, and dear Papa may have been the crotchetiest old fool in England, but he also had money. I didn't want him to go and do something stupid with it, did I? I know which side my bread is buttered on." She looked around the crowded, stifling room with complacency. "I've this house now, and plenty of money to last me the rest of my life, even if I live to some damn-fool age like Papa. So it was worth all that ranting and raving and hellfire. Not that I didn't give them some of their own back every now and then." She smiled reminiscently.

We seemed to have wandered rather far from the subject. "The Doyles?" I prompted.

"What about them?"

"What I really need to know is what John Doyle was doing two days before he died, and that evening. He—"

"Can't tell you that. Hadn't laid eyes on the man in better than a year. Glory be to God."

"I agree with you about that. I'm grateful I never had to meet him. But what I was about to say was that he did a couple of odd things those last few days. He went to London, for one thing, on a working day, and told a colleague at the bank that it was on business. Would you have any idea what kind of business?"

"Other people's business, no doubt. That's what Doyle poked into. Liked to catch people out. Reveled in it. One thing for sure, it was chapel business. He did a lot for that chapel. Kept the books, for one thing, or audited them, or some such."

"Was he paid for doing that?"

She snorted while drawing on her cigarette and set off a coughing fit that lasted so long I was alarmed. I tried to struggle out of the chair, but she waved me back.

"Don't fuss," she said when she could speak again. "I don't need a nursemaid. But don't ask me again about old Rookwood paying anybody to do anything, or I might have a fit of apoplexy and die on the spot."

"Doyle did the work as a volunteer, then?"

"He did it," said the old woman, emphasizing her words with little jabs of her cigarette, "so he'd be in the know. There's a lot to learn from a set of ledgers if you know how to read between the lines, and Doyle knew, of that you can be certain. He might find out something discreditable about someone, you see? Something he could use to hound them. And if you want my opinion, which I gather you do or you wouldn't be here listening to an old woman natter on, that's what he was doing in London. Chasing something down, somehow, something he could use against someone. And if you're not going to strike a medal for the man who killed him, you just find out who it was, and I'll take care of the reward." She sat back and lit another cigarette from the stub of the last one. The air was growing thick with smoke, and I was dizzy from the heat, but I was learning things.

I persevered. "Hmm. That's a new thought, and a useful one. I can figure out a way to follow up on that. Tell me something else. A man I know thought Doyle was meeting a woman in London. Is that likely?"

"Having an affair, you mean? Never knew an Anglican yet who could call a spade a spade. I'd say it was about as likely as a hurricane in the desert. John Doyle got off on power, not sex. He despised women even more than he did men, and if a tart had offered him a free session, I expect he'd have spent it preaching to her about her sinful ways."

"All right, one more. The night he died, he was out very late. His wife went to bed at midnight and he wasn't home yet. He said he was going to a church meeting, but that doesn't sound very likely to me. I've never known any church meeting to go on that late, even among us Church of England types, and we're pretty sociable. Obviously, you don't think he was out indulging in an orgy." (There, was that spadelike enough for her?) "What's your best guess?"

But she shook her head. "Don't know. Not got a clue. This wasn't the Wednesday prayer meeting?"

"After that, Amanda said he told her."

"Well, then—unless he was spying on someone. That might have been it. He did that once, a boy who lived nearby, who—"

"Yes, I've heard that story, and it was painful enough the

first time. Any more and you'll have me rethinking that medal. Just one more question and then I'll leave you to your own affairs."

"Leave me and my smoke-filled house, you mean. I can see you sitting there thinking thoughts about lung cancer and trying not to cough."

"Indeed. But at your age, you've made your choices and don't need me to preach at you. And I expect I won't die from an hour of secondhand smoke. But I do have some questions that I need answered by someone who's still a member of Rookwood's chapel. Can you give me the name of anyone who doesn't think he's the cat's pajamas, and who wouldn't mind talking to me?"

"Do you ever go to pubs, or are you too afraid of smoke?"

"I like pubs. I prefer them not to resemble one of Dante's inner circles, if possible. Why?"

"Do you know the Bell, down by the river?"

"I know where it is. I've never been in it."

"Go. The publican is a man called Bell, if you believe it. Samuel Bell. Sam and his wife are Scots, and they joined the chapel when they moved down south because they thought it sounded like good old John Knox's brand of religion. By the time they found out what it really was, they were involved, but they don't like it. They'll give you an earful if you go at a time when they're not too busy. Not lunchtime. They do you a good lunch, but they're run off their feet then." She looked at the mantel clock, a Victorian horror of black marble and gilt cupids. "Now would be as good a time as any, if you think you can drink another beer at this hour without ruining your reputation."

"Right." With some difficulty I wriggled out of the chair and stood up. "Would you like to come with me? I'll stand you a Guinness."

"Lord save you, I've been drinking milk. That's why I put it in the pewter pot, so you wouldn't see. Just having you on, m'dear. This old stomach can't take the good stuff anymore. Have to drink milk. Pah!"

"Well, I must say! You are an unprincipled old woman, and the Baptists are welcome to you. May I come and see you again sometime? In summer, perhaps," I added hastily, "when we can sit outside?"

"You and that handsome husband of yours can take me rowing on the river. I'll criticize his rowing technique and eat all the picnic lunch."

"It's a deal. I'll see myself out."

"Not that far to the door, is it? Mind you come, after you've found out all about it, and tell me."

"I'll even bring you all the malicious gossip I can dig up."

"You be careful, young woman, or you'll be just as wicked as I am one day!"

I had, I thought as I walked down the front path to the gate, been told that the true English eccentric was dying out. If it was so, I'd surely had a rare privilege that morning in meeting one of the best of the breed.

25

SAMUEL Bell was a man in his fifties, at a guess. He didn't look at all like my idea of a publican. He was pale and lean, rather than round and rubicund, and looked very much like someone who would approve of John Knox's austere precepts. The perfect dour Scotsman, one would have thought. I wondered how he had ended up in the beer business, until his wife entered carrying a tray of glasses.

"I've polished them, Sam. That machine has got to be repaired. It leaves them all streaky." She spoke with a lovely burr. It matched her face, for Mrs. Bell was a bonnie lass indeed. Younger than her husband, she had roses in her cheeks that would have sent Robert Burns into ecstasies of comparison. Her hair was still black and lustrous, her figure buxom without being in the least blowsy.

Samuel's face lighted up when he saw her. They had been married—how long, I wondered?—and he looked like a honeymooner.

I had just come in and was the only customer in the pub. Appetizing smells hinted that lunch was being prepared, but the only edibles on display at the moment were packets of crisps and a tray of Scotch eggs in a glass-fronted cooler.

"Now, then, what can I get you, dear?"

"Some mineral water, please, and a Scotch egg. I've just come from a visit to a friend of yours, and she plied me with beer at nine-thirty in the morning. I need something to absorb it."

"Ah, that'll be Miss Simmons. She will have her little joke with visitors. Fizzy or plain?"

"Fizzy, with ice and lime, please."

"How do you know Miss Simmons?" asked Mrs. Bell as she uncapped a bottle of water and poured it into a glass, adding a wedge of lime and the single small ice cube that is standard issue in England. She put a Scotch egg on a small saucer and put saucer and glass on the bar in front of me.

"I don't know her, not really. I met her just this morning, sent by Mrs. Allenby. Are you acquainted with her? Her husband's dean of the Cathedral."

"Aye, we know her." Samuel sounded unexpectedly pleasant. "A good woman. As is Miss Simmons, if a wee bit unconventional."

Mrs. Bell laughed, the rich, full-bodied laugh of a woman who enjoys life. "A shocking old sinner, she is, but we love her. She's well, I hope? You said Mrs. Allenby 'sent' you."

"Miss Simmons is in roaring good health and spirits and will probably outlive us all. I went there, not to look after her, but to seek some information. And she sent me to you two. My name is Dorothy Martin, by the way, and I'm a friend of Amanda Doyle." That was stretching a point, but I thought of myself as her friend, even if she might not agree.

"I see." Samuel looked thoughtful. "I'm Samuel Bell, as you doubtless know, and this is my wife, Jean."

"Bonnie Jean," I said. "Or do you know *Brigadoon?*"

"That song I know," he said, and gave his wife another of those adoring looks before turning back to me. "You're helping Mrs. Doyle, then? I think I saw you in chapel on Sunday, and you looked—um—a mite out of place, with the hat and all." He eyed today's hat, but unlike Miss Simmons, forbore to comment. "Was that why you were there, on Mrs. Doyle's behalf? It's a shocking thing has happened to her."

"It is, and I'm trying to help all I can. I'm helping the police, in fact."

"Oh, aye. You'd be the chief constable's new wife, would you no'?"

"I would." I fought to keep the accent and lilt out of my own speech. It's contagious. "The former chief constable, that is. At any rate, I've looked into one or two matters for the police in the past, and I'm involved in this one because I feel very sorry for Mrs. Doyle, and worried as well."

"I've heard they've no suspects for the murder," said Jean, giving the r's their full due. "And in that case . . ."

"Yes, well, there you have it. I don't think Amanda Doyle is any more capable of murder than my cats. Less, in fact. The cats dispatch small rodents with great enjoyment, but I can't imagine Amanda killing even a mouse. I fear for her, all the same, and for her little girl. So I'm trying to find out what her husband did the week he was killed. He told Amanda he was at a church meeting that Wednesday night. Would you know anything about that?"

"Prayer meeting," both the Bells said in unison. Jean made a face and added, "I went, but it's the last time. The business is enough of an excuse, and I hate the meeting anyway. Sheer hypocrisy, the greater part of it. They stand and pray aloud, you know, and ask the Lord to forgive others for their terrible sins. Naming the people and listing the sins, you understand."

"I know about the prayer meetings, and though I didn't know exactly what went on, I can't say I'm surprised. This meeting was after that. Mr. Doyle hadn't come home by midnight."

"But that's not possible, Mrs. Martin." Jean shook her head decisively. "The prayer meeting was over before eight,

and the Rookwoods always lock up the chapel afterward. I remember Mrs. Rookwood standing there, jingling the keys,
hustling us out."

"Hmm. Maybe Mr. Doyle stayed on in the church and let
himself and whoever he was meeting with out when they
were finished."

"The doors lock with a key, and the Rookwoods have the
only set. And besides, he wasn't there."

I blinked, confused.

"John Doyle wasn't there," Jean repeated patiently. "I noticed particularly because he always came to prayer meeting.
Everyone commented about it. Later, when we heard about
the murder, I thought he must have been dead already."

This was news with a vengeance. "He wasn't, though," I
said slowly. "Amanda didn't go to bed till after midnight, and
he wasn't home by then. I suppose he could have been killed
somewhere else—but that doesn't make sense—and the
police—" I shut up abruptly. I had been thinking about the official time of death, but the autopsy report was not public information, and I had no business spreading it around, no
matter how befuddled I was.

If John Doyle hadn't been at the chapel at all that night,
where had he been, and what had he been doing? Was Sam
Johnson going to be right, after all? Had John Doyle been
having an affair?

I shook my head. "I can't make any sense out of it at all,
but it's very useful information. I'll think about it, and maybe
I can come up with something coherent. Now, the other thing
is, he—Mr. Doyle—went to London on the Monday before.
Took a day off from work and went to the city. He told
Amanda it was business, but no one sees how it could have
been banking business. Do you have any ideas about that?"

Samuel shook his head in bewilderment. "He never said
anything about it on the Sunday."

"He did, though, Sam," said Jean slowly. "I'd forgotten. I
wasn't meant to hear, but I had to go to the office for some

paper for the Sunday school class, and I heard him in Elder Rookwood's office. I think he was using the telephone, for I heard no other voices. I heard him say something about 'legal advice' and then 'Victoria Station, eight at the latest.' I thought perhaps he was making an appointment for Elder Rookwood, though Mrs. Rookwood usually does that sort of thing. But I couldn't think why else he'd be using the church's phone."

"Legal advice," said Samuel, still confused. "He couldn't have been making an appointment with a solicitor, not on a Sunday."

I could make nothing of any of it, but it was fascinating, all the same. I finished my Scotch egg and thought about all the contradictions while the Bells busied themselves with preparations for the brisk lunch trade. There must be some other things I needed to ask, but I couldn't think what. My mind was too busy trying to arrange what I'd learned into some kind of pattern.

When more customers came in, a group of men who seemed to be regulars, I gave up. "How much?" I asked Jean as she was drawing beers for the men.

"On the house, dear. You're a friend of Amanda's, and she needs a friend just now."

"How on earth," I said impulsively, "did nice people like you get mixed up with that awful chapel?"

She rolled her eyes and lowered her voice. "The Lord alone knows. I'm weaning Samuel away. He likes his religion the way he likes his whiskey, good and strong, but it's got to be too much even for him. We'll find another chapel. Any place would be better than that one."

"You're right about that, I think. Well, thanks for the refreshment and the information. I'm sorry I took up so much of your time."

"Not to worry, dear. Come back, won't you?"

She smiled, a smile guaranteed to set male hearts thumping, and hurried away with six foaming glasses of beer.

I drove home, my mind so far removed from my driving that I got lost twice.

Had Amanda been lying all along about when John came home? But no, the police doctor had said he died after midnight. He could have been at home all that time, I supposed, but why would he have been? It would have taken something really important to keep him away from the prayer meeting. That nasty little exercise in innuendo and accusation veiled as piety sounded right up his alley.

How much of this, I wondered, did the police know? They would of course have been trying to trace John's movements that evening. Was I simply duplicating their efforts?

Well, even if I was, I was enjoying myself. I wouldn't have missed meeting Miss Simmons and the Bells for anything. And one good way to find out whether the police already knew everything I had learned was to go and talk to them.

This time, fortunately, Derek was in, and I was shown into his office right away.

"Derek, I've been asking nosy questions again. I hope you don't mind."

He made a face. "Much good it would do if I did. I've got used to you and your ways, Dorothy, though I still pray every Sunday that you won't get yourself in serious trouble someday. Alan would have my guts for garters if you ever got hurt while messing about in a murder inquiry. All right, what do you have for me?"

"Two things that you may know already. One is that John Doyle was apparently seeing a solicitor in London that Monday, and the other is that he never went near the church Wednesday evening, the night he was killed."

His startled expression told me all I needed to know. I sat back with some little satisfaction and gave him the details.

When I had finished he swore under his breath. "I'm sorry, Dorothy, but both the Rookwoods told me flat out that Doyle was there that evening. They said he left when everyone else did and they didn't see him again. And they never mentioned him making a phone call from the church."

"They might not have known about that. But they certainly knew he wasn't at the prayer meeting. Unless the Bells are lying, and I don't know why they would."

"They're responsible people," Derek said with a sigh. "We keep a pretty close watch on pubs and publicans, you know, and there's never any trouble at the Bell. I have no reason to doubt them, but we'll get the names of some of the other chapel members and ask them, just to be sure."

"Why would the Rookwoods lie about it, though? You'd have thought they'd want to distance themselves as far as they could from a man who'd been murdered. On the very night he'd been murdered."

"I begin to think," said Derek grimly, "that the Rookwoods will bear some very close investigation. I'll go and talk to them myself, and this time I'll get the truth out of them."

I thought about suggesting he take Miss Simmons along, but he was in no mood for levity.

I was getting up to leave when a sudden thought occurred to me. "You might get someone to look at their account books," I said. "The chapel's, I mean. That place takes in a good deal of money, and where there's money, there's temptation. If John Doyle found some irregularity in the books, he'd have been on it like a hound after a fox, and I can't imagine the Rookwoods would like that much."

"You know, I had the same idea. I'm taking along an accountant."

26

THAT could explain a lot," Alan agreed as we sat finishing a cottage pie for lunch. "He could have gone up to London to ask a solicitor about what he'd found."

"He was the overseer, auditor, whatever, for the church books," I said, "though I gather Mrs. Rookwood actually makes the entries. If something was wrong, if she was cooking the books, he might have been worried about whether he'd get into some kind of trouble for not catching it sooner. I'm sure he'd look out for his own hide first."

"Sounds like his approach," said Alan. "But it's all speculative at this point, and there are lots of holes. What London solicitor could he have been phoning on a Sunday morning? Or meeting before eight on a Monday morning, come to that? Solicitors don't rise at dawn, as a rule. And why go to town so early, anyway? Why spend the whole day in London? You said he didn't get home until teatime."

"That's what Amanda said. I'm only taking her word for it, and for a lot of other things, too."

"True, but we have Sam Johnson's testimony on when

Doyle arrived in London, and it was very early. Surely he was
planning something else for the day."

"Maybe he was having lunch with his distinguished
father-in-law," I said with a straight face.

"Or the Queen," Alan said, nodding. "Well, if the lovely
lady in the car was the solicitor in question, the police
shouldn't have too much trouble finding her. Solicitors are
thick on the ground in London, but attractive female ones are
a little rarer. And I have an idea, love. Why don't you pop over
to see Carstairs this afternoon and ask him if he knows of
anyone fitting that description? You know he's pining to get
back into the act. Most excitement he's had in years, I
shouldn't wonder."

"Now that is a useful suggestion. It won't tell me anything
about John Doyle's mysterious whereabouts Wednesday
evening, though."

"One thing at a time. Shall we toss for the washing up?"

He lost, and I left him with his hands in dishwater while
I walked across the Close to the High Street and the elegant
little Georgian house where Mr. Carstairs kept his office.

The day was still sunny, but growing colder by the minute.
A wind had sprung up and clouds were beginning to form. I
was reminded that winter was nearly upon us. My cheeks
grew stiff with the cold, and were doubtless turning bright
red, but I was glad I had walked. The cobwebs in my head
needed clearing out.

Had I taken Amanda too much on faith? Had she made
up the whole story about how she had spent that Wednesday
evening? Papers to mark and sleeping pills and all?

No. I hadn't spent nearly seventy years on this planet
without learning a few things about people. Ruth Beecham
had said that Amanda never lied, except by omission. Well,
one of the things I had learned was that anyone will lie, if the
stakes are high enough. Some people will lie about anything,
just for the fun of it. But to tell repeated, consistent lies, and

be convincing, requires practice and a certain kind of personality.

Amanda Doyle simply didn't have that kind of personality. She might lie to protect Miriam—probably had, to John—but I was prepared to accept Ruth's conviction that those lies would have consisted of leaving things out, of not telling the whole story, rather than making things up. So when Amanda told me a long, detailed story about not being able to sleep and taking pills and so on, I believed her.

Anyhow, if I had to believe either her or her late unlamented husband, there was no doubt which I'd pick.

The law office, all white stone and green woodwork and brass fittings, gleamed in the brilliant sunshine. Entering, I was temporarily blind in the dimness of the hallway.

"Mrs. Martin! What a pleasant surprise. Do come in. Be careful of that rug; it trips me up every time. Really, we need to do something about the lighting in here."

Mr. Carstairs tactfully guided me into his office, a refuge of oak paneling and Persian rugs and velvet draperies pulled aside from sparkling, wavy old windows. The very essence of the English legal profession, I thought, and wondered momentarily what it would be like to spend one's life in that stable, comfortable, cushioned world.

Then I looked, in the improved light, at the expression on Mr. Carstairs's face and realized that the idyllic life bored him to desperation.

"Have you news for me? Oh, I know I shouldn't pry, and perhaps you can't talk about some matters, but . . ." He trailed off on a hopeful note.

"Actually, I am making some progress, even though I haven't very much to report. I'm here to ask you for some help, since you were so kind yesterday."

"The press again?"

"No, this time I want you to help me find a mysterious lady lawyer."

"*Cherchez la femme?*" he asked in an atrocious accent.

"Something like that. I doubt she's involved in an amorous role, however. More probably simply as a solicitor, but she's proving extremely elusive, and Alan thought you might be able to point us in the right direction. You know so many people."

"Tell me about it."

I did so, as succinctly as possible, bearing in mind what lawyers charge by the minute. "And I don't," I wailed, "have any idea who the woman is, or how Doyle managed to reach her on a Sunday, or why he arranged to meet her so early, or *anything.*"

"An attractive female solicitor, in London. Hmm. How old?"

"I don't know with any certainty. Sam Johnson isn't good at description. When pressed, he thought she had brown hair. She reminded him of the Botticelli Venus, he said. Really, I wouldn't have thought he had so much imagination! Anyway, that would seem to say she was young, or youngish at least, unless his memory was wildly colored by his daydreams."

Mr. Carstairs chuckled. "No, I would say his description was quite accurate."

"You know the lady, then?" I said eagerly.

"There is only one solicitor in London, perhaps in the whole of England, who could possibly remind even the most romantic man of the Botticelli Venus. Her name is Vanessa Thompson, and she is quite, quite lovely. Better men than Sam Johnson have dreamed about her, I daresay."

"Mr. Carstairs, you are a treasure! I should have thought to come to you ages ago. What else can you tell me about Ms. Thompson? I can't imagine how a man like John Doyle would have met someone like that."

"Ah, now, that's where the story gets really interesting. Ms. Thompson is not just a pretty face, she is also an extremely competent lawyer, indeed rather famous in the profession. She's in her forties, though one wouldn't think it to look at her. She is particularly expert in constitutional law and in finance, and those specialities have led her to a profound interest in politics." He sat back in his chair, pushed his glasses back on his nose, and looked at me encouragingly.

It was exactly the way I used to wait for an answer from a promising pupil who hadn't quite figured it out yet. I thought for a moment and then smacked my hand on the desk. "Politics! Of course! You're telling me that Ms. Thompson works with Anthony Blake."

"For a good many years, now. They're from the same part of the world, and I believe she began working with his campaigns when he was an anonymous backbencher. Now she's a trusted aide, or so I am told."

"And that, of course, is how she met John Doyle. He was a campaign worker at least once. Amanda's sister told me. So if Doyle wanted to consult a good lawyer, someone who knew a lot about finance, and wanted to be cagey about it, he would think of Ms. Thompson. Not only good, but in London, and with the family connection, he could probably get her services free. Oh, he was a sly one, was John Doyle."

"The family connection may also explain why he went up to town so early. He might well have wanted to spend some time with the Honorable Mr. Blake."

"I said he might have planned lunch with his father-in-law, but I thought I was kidding. How do you happen to know about that family connection, by the way? It isn't exactly advertised."

Mr. Carstairs smiled gently. "Pure happenstance. I'm interested in family histories. I was looking up Blake one day on the Internet, the other Blake, you know—"

"William? 'Tyger, tyger' et cetera?"

"Exactly. I came across Anthony and followed it up."

"I wish I'd known. I'd have come to you first, instead of navigating the shoals of cyberspace myself. Well, you could just be right about Doyle's intentions that day, though I can't imagine Blake would have relished a meeting with him. Doyle

188 ✦ JEANNE M. DAMS

would have been too powerful a reminder of an episode Blake
has tried his best to forget."

"Ah, but Doyle hadn't forgotten, had he? I think he would
have welcomed an opportunity to remind his esteemed rela-
tive by marriage of just how much he, Blake, owed Doyle. I'm
not suggesting blackmail, mind you."

"No, I think the righteous Mr. Doyle would have found
blackmail beneath him. There's never been any hint that he
was extorting money from Blake, beyond that first payment
Gillian said her father made when John married Amanda. And
that could well have been just enough to get them set up in
modest housekeeping. Certainly the Doyles aren't rich. Or
Amanda isn't, anyway. I suppose John could have been squir-
reling away money for some nefarious purpose or other."

"Don't you think he might have donated a fair amount of
money to the chapel?"

"Oh, of course. Silly of me not to think of that. And if he
did, he would have been even more upset if he discovered
that there was something rotten in that particular state of
Denmark."

"As you say."

Mr. Carstairs's clerk appeared in the doorway. "I'm so
sorry to interrupt, but Miss Simmons is on the telephone.
She wants to change her will again."

"Heavens, I mustn't keep you from Miss Simmons! I
didn't know she was a client of yours. I met her just this
morning. Amazing, isn't she?"

"Ab-so-lute-ly unique. And an extremely impatient lady.
You must excuse me, Mrs. Martin, but you will keep me informed, will you not?"

He waved me genially out the door and picked up the
phone.

27

THE police station was only a few steps away, and I thought I'd better stop in and give Derek my new information. It was important that they talk to the lovely Ms. Thompson as soon as possible. We were, it seemed to me, much closer to solving at least one mystery, the secret of what John Doyle had done in London two days before he was murdered.

Derek wasn't in; I was directed to a functionary I hadn't met. When I introduced myself and asked if Derek was still talking to the Rookwoods, I was given a bland smile. "I couldn't say, I'm sure, madam."

"When will he be back?"

"Ah, now, as to that, I'm not quite certain. I'd be happy to take a message, or is there someone else who can help you?"

I'd had enough of leaving messages that were delivered too late to do any good. I had also had enough of being obsequious. "Ask him to call me the moment he gets in. I have information he badly wants and needs, and I will give it to no one but him. You should understand that he will be seriously displeased if you delay in giving him this message. Have I made myself clear?"

"Madam, I assure you there are other competent officers who—"

"My name, as I have told you and you certainly knew already, is Mrs. Martin. I dislike being called madam. You doubtless also know that my husband's name is Alan Nesbitt. I am reasonably familiar with the workings of the Sherebury police force. I am also at least twice your age, and I prefer to do things my own way. Good afternoon."

I swept away before I could lose my nerve and start apologizing. If rude and dictatorial worked for Miss Simmons, why not for me?

I fumed all the way home and started talking the moment I got in the door. "Alan, I've found out who the woman in London is, and I tried to tell Derek, but he's out and the idiots wouldn't tell me where he is, so I lost my temper and did some name-dropping. Alan, where are you? Alan?"

The note was on the kitchen table. "I've gone to the barber. Derek called. You were right about the chapel books. The Rookwoods are being detained for questioning. Derek has a promising lead on the Doyles in Reading and has gone to check on it. Looks as though they may have headed for the family after all. I have some errands to run, but home for tea."

I sank down into my chair. Of all the luck! I had real news and there was no one to tell, no one to do anything about it. Alan wouldn't be home for hours. "Tea" at our house could mean anything from an austere cup of tea and a biscuit at four-thirty or so, to high tea, what I always called supper in Indiana, at somewhere around six. The later it got, the more substantial the meal. And Alan always takes forever running errands. He knows at least half the population of Sherebury, and they all want to stop and talk.

Meanwhile, Vanessa Thompson, busily efficient in London, might be walking around with valuable information.

I looked at the kitchen clock. Two-thirty. The next train to London left in fifteen minutes. If Alan hadn't taken the car . . .

He hadn't. I checked to make sure.

It was ridiculous for me to go running off to London in search of a well-known solicitor. I wouldn't get there until nearly four o'clock. Even if I could find her, she wouldn't see me. She wouldn't answer my questions anyway. Lawyers, except for dear old-fashioned ones like Mr. Carstairs, are close-mouthed. The whole thing was out of the question.

I picked up a pencil and scribbled on Alan's note, "Gone to London. Back around eight."

Then I picked up the keys and sprinted for the car.

If the train had been on time, I wouldn't have made it. However, trains are notoriously late in the UK, even more so since British Rail was broken up into privately owned regional lines. I've stopped listening to the excuses offered over the tinny PA systems in the stations. This time it was only five minutes late, and I was three minutes late getting to the station, so we meshed nicely.

It was a fool's errand, I thought as I settled into my seat. All right, that was established. Now, forget about it and decide what to do.

The first thing, obviously, was to find Ms. Thompson. I checked the supply of change in my purse. I had plenty; good. That meant I could spend all the time I wanted on a pay phone in Victoria Station. Of course, there was the cell phone in my purse, but my thrifty Hoosier soul can't get used to the idea of using it for anything but an emergency. I seldom even turn it on. However, in case Alan wanted to reach me, perhaps I'd better turn it on now.

That done, I took another look at what folding money I had. Not much, and taxi fares can eat up a lot of cash quickly. I'd have to stop at an ATM, which the English call cash points, but the area around Victoria is thick with them. Not a problem.

Now. What story was I going to tell the person who guarded Ms. Thompson's phone, no doubt with terrifying competence? Let's see. The lady's interests were constitutional law, finance, and politics.

Putting together something reasonable that touched on those interests occupied me the rest of the way in to town.

I found a pay phone in a reasonably quiet corner and got a number from Directory Enquiries. That part was easy. I took a deep breath, picked up the phone again, and punched in the number I had been given.

The phone was answered almost immediately with a rapid-fire list of names in an accent so "refained" as to be unintelligible. I didn't care. The name of Ms. Thompson's law firm was of no interest to me.

"This is Susie Smithfield, of the *Atlanta Daily Herald,* and I'd like to speak to Vanessa Thompson, please."

"Ms. Thompson is not available at this time. *Whom* did you say was calling?"

No, dear. It's "who," and you'd better not let Vanessa catch you making a mistake in English. Good Tory secretaries talk proper. "Susie Smithfield, from Atlanta, Georgia," I said sweetly, trying my best to sound as southern as all get out. "I'm a reporter with the *Atlanta Herald,* and they sent me all the way to England to do a feature article on Ms. Thompson. We're all just so impressed with her and the *wonderful* things she's done, 'specially with Mr. Blake's causes. We think Mr. Blake is just *marvelous.* You know, family values are very, very important to us in America, and Mr. Blake has really put his finger on some big problems. You-all must just be so proud of him!"

"Eoh. Quayte." There was a slightly stunned silence.

"And what's your name, honey?"

Another little silence. "Er—Hart. Elizabeth Hart."

"Well, Ms. Hart, what I was wondering was, if I could just see Ms. Thompson for just a tiny little minute this afternoon. I just got here this morning, y'see, and I had to take a nap the *minute* I got to the hotel. That jet lag is just *awful*, isn't it? But as soon as I woke up I thought, I'll just call her up and see if we can get together right away. Just to set up something for later?"

"Yes. Well, Ay'm not quayte sure—"

"I've heard," I said in a confidential tone, "that you-all might be havin' another election over here pretty soon, and that Mr. Blake might just be the next prime minister. That's so *excitin'*! We'd want to feature that in the article, if it's true."

"Ay kennot confirm any such rumor. However . . ." She hesitated again and then made up her mind. "Ms. Thompson is at the House this efternoon. You mayte tray to reach her there."

"At home?"

The secretary was condescendingly amused, as I'd hoped. "No, no. The House. Parliament, you know." She gave me a phone number.

I thanked her effusively, hung up, and raised my fist in solitary salute. Yes! I'd done it. The drawbridge was lowered, the portcullis was up, and I was ready to storm the castle just as soon as I made sure there would be no boiling oil. I called the number and dropped the phoney accent.

"My name is Dorothy Martin. I was told by Ms. Hart that I might reach Ms. Thompson here. I'd like to see her for a moment this afternoon, if I may. It's about a man she knows slightly named John Doyle."

"Just a moment, please." This one was far less concerned with her image, and probably more formidable. I might have to embroider my story here, too.

I was thinking about how to do that when another voice came on the line. "This is Vanessa Thompson. You're inquiring about a Mr. Doyle?"

Ah. "I am, and you can't imagine how glad I am to talk to you. You're very well protected."

"I need to be. I'm a very busy person. What is this about, Ms. Martin?"

"I realize you're busy, and I'm sorry to impose, but I'm looking into John Doyle's death, and I would very much like to see you for five minutes. I'm at Victoria Station, and I can be with you in twenty minutes. Well, perhaps fifteen if I take the tube. Traffic's probably pretty awful this time of day."

"Yes. Very well, Ms. Martin. I doubt I can be of any use to you, but I can see you, very briefly, in about half an hour. Do you know your way about Parliament Square?"

"More or less."

"There's a pub in Little George Street, the Grenadier. It's tiny, but pleasant. Suppose I meet you there. How will I know you?"

"I'm wearing a black hat with a red rose, but I'll know you." That should keep her guessing. "Thank you so much. I can't tell you what this means to me. I'll see you in—"

But she had already hung up.

I had time for the taxi, and I indulged myself. A London taxi is one of my favorite little luxuries. They're big enough that an arthritic lady of a certain age can get in and out. They're comfortable, sit high enough that you can see everything, and have drivers that are often chatty. They've come in colors for some time, which I don't approve of, and I certainly don't like the ones painted like newspapers, but I managed to snag a good old black one from the taxi rank at the station, and sat back with a sigh. "Parliament, and you don't have to hurry. I don't have to be there for almost half an hour."

"It'll take that, nearly, this time o' day. Traffic's somethin' shockin', innit?"

"It seems to get worse every time I come to town."

"Canadian, are ya then?"

"American, but I've lived in England for a few years now. Sherebury, down in Belleshire."

"Oh, well, then, 'ave to mind me *p*s 'n' *q*s, won't I? Can't get by wi' the tales I tell the or'nary tourists."

I grinned. This was the kind of Londoner I loved.

I also love the Houses of Parliament. The driver would

have taken me straight to the pub in Little George Street, just off Parliament Square, but I told him to let me down next to Big Ben. I had time, and I wanted to feast my eyes once more on that huge building. Critics can say what they want about pseudo-Gothicism and Victorian excess, but I think it's beautiful. I also love the concept that gave birth to the building and the ones that preceded it. This, for me, this set of buildings, always represents the cradle of our own American democracy, and I never fail to get teary eyed when I see it.

All right, so I'm sentimental.

28

I FOUND the pub without any trouble and Ms. Thompson with no more. I think my mind had subconsciously clothed her in something clinging and diaphanous, but even in a well-cut black suit she was unmistakable. Oh, she was slimmer than the model Botticelli had used. The ideal of feminine beauty then was a good deal more realistic than it is now.

But her hair, worn without artifice, was of that same indescribable color, neither brown nor auburn, but vibrantly alive. It waved softly around a face that any artist, of any century, would have found perfect. If you've seen the painting, you know what I mean. If not, I can only say that Vanessa Thompson was a classic beauty, timeless, changeless. The tiny lines that age was beginning to add to her face only enhanced her beauty. This was a woman who was doubtless enchanting as a child and ravishing at twenty, but she would still be the most beautiful woman in England when she was eighty.

It was in fact the first thing I said to her. "I had been told you were beautiful. It was an understatement."

She smiled somewhat wearily. I suppose when your beauty is as remarkable as hers, compliments cease to become a delight and become instead almost a burden. "That's very kind of you, but you didn't come here to see what I looked like."

Her voice was as lovely as her face and figure, warm and soft but at the moment very businesslike. I became businesslike as well. "No. I came to ask you a few questions, very brief, I promise you. I know John Doyle came to see you a little over a week ago, shortly before he died. I suspect he came to discuss irregularities in the accounts of the chapel he attended. May I ask you to verify that, if true, and tell me anything else you may know about his movements that day?"

She regarded me coolly. "I presume you are not connected with the police, Mrs. Martin, or you would have presented me with some identification. What, then, is your interest in John Doyle?"

Observant, wasn't she? She'd noted my wedding ring, put it together with my age and general appearance, and changed "Ms." to "Mrs." One could see why she was good in politics. I'd have to watch my step with her. No lies, I decided, not even teeny white ones. "I'm worried about Mr. Doyle's widow and daughter. I live in Sherebury and have become acquainted with them, and I very much fear Mrs. Doyle may be detained in connection with her husband's murder. I am convinced of her innocence, but the police, I believe, are not quite so convinced. I suppose you could call me a private detective, but not in any professional sense. I'm simply looking into the case in the interests of justice."

"May I ask how you learned of Mr. Doyle's visit to me?"

"Through a series of conversations that I could detail for you, if you wish, but it would take some time. Does it matter?"

"Perhaps not. You understand that he consulted me professionally, although we do have an acquaintance that dates back several years. He paid me for my time, and I am not at liberty to reveal what we discussed, except to legitimate authority with the proper court orders."

"Of course not. I wouldn't expect you to. The police will be asking, anyway, and I don't need to know. It was about the chapel, though? I should tell you that the police have discovered the irregularities for themselves, and have taken the chapel authorities in for questioning."

"In that case, I can say that yes, it was about the chapel. I will not tell you what advice I gave him."

"No. Can you tell me what he did after he left you? I wondered if he perhaps visited Mr. Blake."

"Since that does not fall within the sphere of my professional relationship with Mr. Doyle, I can say that I believe such was his intent. I have no idea whether he was successful. Mr. Blake is a very busy man and was, that day, preparing an important position paper. You may have seen him discussing it on television a night or two later. He had very little time to spare."

"I see. I don't suppose there's the slightest chance I could talk to Mr. Blake for just a moment and ask him."

"Not the slightest, I'm afraid. As there are no important divisions expected in the House in the next few days, he has been in Edinburgh since Sunday, and then he travels to Washington to confer with some of your more prominent conservative leaders."

She'd even identified my accent under the English accretions of the last few years. A formidable woman, indeed. "Actually, I'm English now, by virtue of marriage. I understand I may one day have the pleasure of voting for Mr. Blake as prime minister?"

"No, Mrs. Martin. You're confusing English elections with American ones. Here we do not vote for prime ministers. We vote in a general election for members of Parliament, and the majority party then selects its leader, who becomes prime minister. It is certainly possible, one day, that . . . but I mustn't speculate."

Well, I was allowed one slight pretence of ignorance, wasn't I? I find it never hurts to have one's intelligence underestimated. And people do so enjoy explaining things to ignorant foreigners.

"Yes, of course. I had forgotten."

She looked at her watch and pulled a slim appointment book from a side pocket of her slim designer handbag, dislodging a few pieces of paper as she did so. I helped her retrieve them. "Thank you. I loathe carrying large bags, but I'm afraid this one never has quite enough room for all the impedimenta one collects."

"Mine either. I clean out my purse every day or two, and it's amazing the amount of junk I find."

She consulted the book. "I'm afraid, Mrs. Martin, that I have an appointment."

I stood. "I asked you for five minutes, Ms. Thompson, and you've given me seven. You've been very gracious, and I thank you. And I wish you the best in your own political career."

She simply smiled. I suppose she was as used to that assumption as to comments about her beauty.

I thought about taking the Underground back to Victoria. The nearest tube station wasn't far away, just across Parliament Square, right where Big Ben could look down on it. But the chill rain that had threatened for some time was now falling, and I'd left home in too much of a hurry to remember my umbrella. I hailed a taxi. It took longer, with rush-hour traffic building by the minute, but I was in no hurry. I didn't even mind missing a train by five minutes. Victoria Station is well equipped with shops and restaurants. I sat sipping cappuccino and eating an almond croissant that I didn't in the least need, and watching the world go by.

I hadn't, I mused as my train finally pulled out of the station and began humming and clicking its way back home, actually learned very much. I had confirmed part of what I suspected, that was all. I had also prepared Ms. Thompson for the arrival of the police, which they might not appreciate, but she was not a person who would be easy to catch off guard in any case. It might be useful to Derek to know where Anthony Blake was, though. Derek and his minions would certainly want to talk to the man.

I had completely forgotten that my cell phone was turned on, so it was startling to hear my purse buzz. I found the phone, right at the bottom, and answered it just in time. It was Alan, of course, the only person who knew the number.

"Where are you, Dorothy?"

"You sound upset. I'm on my way home—are you still there?"

The train had gone through a tunnel and severed the connection. I waited and the phone buzzed again.

"I'm on the train," I said hastily before another tunnel interfered. "About half an hour away."

"Good, because there's been a development. Rather a serious one, I'm afraid. The Doyles have been involved in . . ."

The signal broke up and disappeared again. I waited, and then tried to call Alan, but nothing happened. I looked at the phone closely then and realized the battery had died.

So I had to wait until I reached home to learn that Amanda and Miriam, and Gillian, too, had been in an automobile accident.

"Where? How? How bad is it?"

"Pretty bad. Gillian was driving, and she's not so badly hurt. A few broken bones, a good deal of pain, but nothing that won't heal given time. Amanda has a concussion and is still unconscious, and Miriam—"

Alan hesitated.

"Alan, no!"

"She's alive, Dorothy. Only just. Injuries to the head, the spinal cord, multiple internal injuries. They can't even assess all the damage until she's stabilized. If she survives, she may be brain damaged, or paralyzed. Sit down, love. Here."

He handed me a cup of tea. "I don't want it."

"Drink it."

I took an unwilling sip. It was very strong and very sweet and laced with brandy or whiskey or something. "But how did it happen? And where were they?"

"Brentford, near Kew. Drink your tea."

"So they'd gone to stay with Gillian after all."

"Perhaps. More likely with a friend who could be counted on not to talk. Derek will ask Gillian, of course, as soon as the doctors will let her be talked to. As to what happened—" Alan held up both hands. "Anybody's guess. Gillian lost control of the car, somehow, on a busy double roundabout at the edge of Brentford. It happened just an hour or so ago, so the traffic was heavy. By some miracle no one else was hurt. She ran the car, at high speed, into the wall of an abandoned brewery by the side of the road. Accident, suicide attempt—"

"No. Not suicide. She isn't the type, and anyway, she'd never, never endanger Amanda and Miriam."

"I meant," he said gently, "suicide on Amanda's part. It's easy for a passenger to snatch a steering wheel, and at the speed Gillian drives . . ."

I shook my head. "Not with Miriam in the car."

"What sort of life do you think Miriam would have with her mother in prison for murdering her father? And don't you suppose Amanda might have thought of that?"

I put down the tea. "She didn't do it, Alan. She didn't murder John, and she didn't cause this accident. It was probably just that, an accident. Weren't there witnesses?"

"Well . . . there were lots of other people there, but you know what roundabouts are, especially at rush hour. No one's paying attention to anything but getting through the thing as fast as possible. Once they heard the crash, it was too late to see what caused it. And face it, Dorothy. Human nature being what it is, most of them would simply drive on anyway."

"Except," I said, feeling ill, "for the ones who would stop and stare at the carnage."

"As you say." He sighed heavily. "Derek's people are busy interviewing the drivers who did stop, and a few passers-by.

They'll get about as much out of it as they usually do. A mass of vague, contradictory reports that will have to be sifted through as carefully as though every one of them contained nuggets of gold. And at the end of the day, who knows? Maybe something, maybe nothing at all."

"But Gillian isn't badly hurt. She'll be able to say what happened."

"You know better than that, Dorothy. She may remember a bit, but even then, her evidence isn't to be relied upon. Were you ever involved in an accident?"

"Once, when I was very young, twenty-one or so. It was a one-car accident, like this one, only fortunately not serious. I was visiting my California sister and lost control of the car on a freeway."

"Did you remember afterward exactly what had happened?"

"Not very clearly," I admitted. "I remember thinking someone was going to sideswipe me, and the next thing I knew I was stopped up against the median railing, headed in the wrong direction."

"So you see."

We were silent for a moment; then I began to cry. "Alan, she has to be all right. She has to be!"

He didn't ask who I meant. He just stood next to my chair and held my hand.

29

WE waited all that evening for word. We watched the news on television, both early and late. The reports gave fewer details than we already knew, along with pictures we turned away from as soon as they appeared on the screen.

On both broadcasts, the accident gave way to yet another sound bite by Anthony Blake against the familiar Big Ben background. I lost my temper.

"Alan, how *can* he! Here are both his daughters in the hospital, and his only grandchild fighting for her life, and he stands there and makes an inane political speech! He's the most egotistical, cold-hearted, self-righteous . . ." I ran out of adjectives.

"Bloody bastard," Alan finished for me. Neither of us uses that kind of language much. It seemed appropriate to me.

We stayed up late, both hoping and fearing that the phone would ring. When it did, around midnight, Derek could report only negatives. No useful information from Gillian, no change in the condition of Amanda or Miriam. "That's good news in a way," he said. He sounded exhausted. "The doctors half expected a rapid deterioration, especially in the case of the little girl. The fact that she's holding her own raises some hope."

But not much. He didn't say it, but it was there in his voice. We thanked him and dragged ourselves up to bed.

"Alan, I've got to go see them," I said, sitting on the bed and kicking off my shoes.

"First thing in the morning, I'll find out which hospital. I'll go with you; you won't want to face it alone. You do realize they probably won't let you actually see anyone but Gillian, not unless the other two are greatly improved."

"I know." Neither of us felt like speculating on the possibility of that near miracle.

I fell asleep, finally, curled up close to Alan's warm bulk. It wasn't quite as comforting as usual, but it helped.

I would gladly have caught the first train in the morning, but there was no sense in it. Visiting hours in English hospitals are, as a rule, strictly limited, and what would we do, hanging around London, waiting to be allowed in? So we slept, albeit fitfully, as long as we could, and then took our time over a breakfast neither of us felt much like eating.

"Derek will call if there's any change?" I asked.

"He promised he would."

But there was no change by the time we had to leave for the station.

The train was late, of course, but no later than we had come to expect. "I wish I'd thought to stop by Amanda's house and pick up one of Miriam's toys," I said when we were finally under way. I always think of these things when it's too late.

"My dear, you wouldn't have been able to get in. And I was rather under the impression that toys were frowned upon in that household. In any case, Miriam . . ."

He trailed off. There seemed to be a lot we didn't especially want to say. Why, I wondered bitterly, did we feel that not talking about Miriam's condition would make it any better?

We took a taxi to the hospital. It was a long ride from central London, nearly to Kew Gardens. I had expected a dark, dreary Victorian edifice, but the hospital was relatively modern. Sixties vintage concrete, now looking streaked and dirty and infinitely depressing, especially on a gray December day.

At least it was brighter inside than out. We sought a source of information. When we found it, what we learned wasn't good. No one's condition had changed materially. We would not be allowed to visit either Amanda or Miriam. "But how is she? Miriam? That poor little girl. Can't we even *see* her, if we promise not to talk or anything?"

But my passionate pleading had no effect on the adamant heart of the nursing sister. "Family only, I'm afraid, and that only for a few minutes. Of course we allowed her grandfather in this morning."

"Her grandfather?" My mind wasn't working very well.

"Yes, he's Anthony Blake, you know. Ever such a nice man, for all he's so important. Not a bit condescending."

"Anthony Blake came to visit Miriam?" I still couldn't twist my brain around the fact.

"And his daughters, of course. He was in a state, poor man, all of them being so badly hurt that way."

"But I thought he was in Edinburgh, and going on to America after that."

"Well, he'd come back when his family was so badly hurt, wouldn't he? Do you know, I never knew he had a family before this happened."

"But—"

Alan took my hand and pressed it firmly. "We may see Gillian for a moment, though?"

"Oh, yes, Ms. Blake is doing quite well, really. In a good deal of pain, of course, so she may be a bit muzzy from the medication."

We were shown to her bedside, in a six-bed bay. The feeling was far more institutional than an American hospital, and more crowded, but the staff seemed both competent and sympathetic.

Gillian in a hospital gown and several casts, bereft of makeup and her usual dramatic clothing, her hair lying limp, looked utterly unlike herself, but quite a lot like Amanda. She had also shed most of her abrasiveness, though that might have been the pain pills.

Her eyes were closed, but they opened when I sat down in the hard white chair. "Hello," she said without interest.

"Hello, Gillian. I'm so sorry about all this."

She moved her head restlessly. "How are Miriam and Amanda? Nobody will tell me anything."

"They're still unconscious, so it's hard to tell. They're getting excellent care." I had no idea whether they were or not, but the hospital had a good reputation, and Gillian didn't need to worry about them right now.

"I wish to God I knew what happened, but all I know is what they've told me. There was an accident, I ran into a wall. I can't remember anything. Was it my fault?"

"I'm sure it wasn't, Gillian. Accidents happen. Don't worry about it."

"Right," she said, and for a moment there was a trace of bitter sarcasm. Well, she was justified. It had been a stupid thing to say.

"How are you feeling?"

This time she just looked at me. Okay, another dumb question. I began to wonder what I was doing there.

"They won't let us stay very long, but is there anything we can do for you? Anything you want?"

"How bad is my car?" She addressed Alan. Well, Derek might have told him. I assumed it was totaled.

Alan shook his head. "I have no details, but not good, I'm afraid. They towed the wreckage away, of course."

"Can you find it, and see if any of our things are still in it?

We were going to stay with some friends of mine, and all our bags were in the boot. I'd stopped at my flat to pack. Most of the clothes I own are in that car, and I can't afford to replace them, especially now I can't work for a while."

She sounded angry and depressed and near the end of her rope. Well, that wasn't good for her. I looked appealingly at Alan.

"Of course I can do that," he said in that calm, reassuring voice that I so love. "What shall we do with any luggage we find?"

"Keep it, I suppose, until we get out of here. Or, you might bring my toothbrush and bathrobe, if you can find them. They've threatened to have me up and walking soon, and I don't fancy giving the whole ward a view of my backside."

"We'll bring all of them," I told her. "I'm sure Amanda and Miriam will need theirs soon, too."

And may that lie turn to the truth, I prayed fervently.

We checked again on Amanda and Miriam before we left. There was no news.

"Are you really going to be able to find Gillian's car?" I asked as we left the building.

"Given the high profile of this whole matter, it won't have been taken to a junkyard. The police will still have it so they can check for tampering. I'll find out where from Derek, and we'll go and have a look. I'll have to throw my weight about to get them to release the luggage, but I still have some influence."

"It would all be easier if we had a car."

"Not really. Taxis are the only answer in London."

"And the Underground. I love the Underground."

"Except at rush hour."

Alan called Derek on the cell phone and learned where the car was. "Can you give them a ring, old boy, and tell them I'll be coming 'round to fetch some necessities from the bags in the boot? If they're intact, that is?"

"A bit scratched and so on, but essentially intact. It was the front and the passenger side of the car that took the worst of it. I'll tell them to expect you."

We had to go all the way to Balham, beyond Wimbledon. I pulled out my pocket guide to the tube and discovered that Wimbledon was on the District line, the same as Kew, but Alan nixed the idea. "Look, darling. We'd have to go all the way in to Earl's Court and get another train. Wimbledon's on a different branch. It would take forever, and there'd still be a very long walk. And Balham itself is on an entirely different line, with complicated changes. We'll have to take a cab, but if you want to play tourist, I'll ask the driver to take us across Richmond Park. It's rather pretty in summer, though there won't be much to see this time of year, I'm afraid."

"No, it's all right. It's the rush and bustle of the tube that appeals to me. It takes my mind off . . ."

He gave me a quick hug and stepped into the road to hail a taxi.

30

Some London suburbs are quite attractive. The place where the car was being held was not in one of those. Or perhaps it was only my mood that made the surroundings seem sterile and chilling. I knew for certain, though, that Prince Charles would be appalled by the modern architecture that was everywhere. Both houses and commercial buildings were square, skimpy, and utterly un-English, at least to my eyes.

Looking at the buildings, however, was preferable to looking at the mass of crushed metal that had once been Gillian's car. It didn't seem possible that any human could have survived the forces that could do that to steel. I glanced at it once and then concentrated very hard on hating the bank across the street, while Alan dealt with the bags.

"You know," he said when we were back in a taxi, the bags piled around us, "we'll either have to find a hotel, or take this lot home and come back. We can't roam about London with this sort of luggage."

"You're right. Or, no, there's another alternative. I could

210 + ♦ JEANNE M. DAMS

find what we want right now, and then we could go to Victoria and put the bags in Left Luggage."

"If it's open. If there hasn't been some security alert that has them nervy if one drops a handkerchief." He sounded grumpy, and I knew he had been as deeply upset as I by the wreckage.

However, he redirected the driver to Victoria Station, and I opened each bag in turn and rummaged.

Miriam's was the hardest. Those few little skirts and blouses, the worn sweaters, the prim, plain underwear, all were so pathetic I nearly lost my composure. Her bathrobe was like the rest, plain and well-worn. It was also a size or two too small. Bought big, I guessed, so she'd grow into it. She'd done that and more. I promised myself I'd buy her a new one, a pretty one with flowers on it, just as soon as I could get to a store.

And if she never needs it?

Angrily, I pushed the thought away and concentrated on the other two cases. It was perfectly easy, of course, to tell which was which. Gillian hadn't taken the time to pack carefully. Everything was tossed in at random, black miniskirts gathering wrinkles next to wads of panty hose and extra-brief briefs. Almost everything was black, with an occasional splash of bright poppy red. The bathrobe was red and skimpy and slinky. I pulled it out, wrapped it up with a toothbrush, comb, and washcloth. I didn't know if English hospitals, unlike their hotels, provided face cloths, but there it was if Gillian needed it.

Now Amanda. Her bag was neat, her clothing as drab as Miriam's. She would probably hate the idea of someone going through her things, though they were certainly respectable enough, depressingly so.

I wondered, not for the first time, what John Doyle had done with all the money in the household. He had a job, Amanda had a job, they had only one child and lived in an inexpensive house. Why did he allow his wife and child to live in such grinding poverty?

The chapel, I supposed. He must have given it all away to those appalling Rookwoods, who had apparently done something nefarious with it. I wondered if there was any chance of retrieving any of it for Amanda and Miriam. Probably not, though.

They certainly needed money. I studied Amanda's bathrobe. It might have had some color at one time, but it had been washed so often it was now an indeterminate greige sort of color, and nearly threadbare. I found the toothbrush, comb, and washcloth, and rolled them up into the same kind of bundle I'd made of Gillian's and Miriam's things.

This one crackled, though. I unrolled it again and poked. There was something in a pocket of the bathrobe. I pulled it out.

It was a small piece of paper with a fold in the center. In black ink and dashing, pretentious handwriting, it read: "Not tonight. Lydia's home."

"What on earth?" I murmured to myself.

"Hmm?" said Alan.

"I found a note in Amanda's pocket. I have no idea what it means, and I suppose it's none of my business. I'll keep it and give it back to her later. I don't imagine it's important, but there's no telling what the hospital would do with it."

"Odd place to put a note," he commented. "Unless she's the sort of woman who goes about the house in a robe all day."

"I wouldn't think so. She works very hard. And her husband had all sorts of rules; I don't think he would have approved of anything that smacked of laziness."

"Ah, well. If she's conscious you can ask her what to do with it."

We said no more about the note as we went about the tedious business of leaving the luggage at Victoria and then sped back to the hospital, but it was the first thing on my mind when we checked on Amanda.

She was not conscious, however, or not completely. She had opened her eyes, the nurse said, and was talking a little, but not yet making any sense. "She's coming along very well, though. She'll be fully awake by tonight, I expect."

"May we see her?"

She considered. "It might do her some good to see a friend. Might bring her a little closer to the surface. Only for a moment, though."

Alan went with me, staying in the background. I laid her belongings on the bedside table and put a hand on one of hers. They were lying neatly folded on her stomach, rising and falling ever so slightly with each breath.

"Amanda," I said softly.

Her eyes opened. They looked at me without apparent interest.

"Amanda, it's Dorothy Martin. I've brought you your robe and a toothbrush."

She moistened her lips.

A plastic cup of cracked ice sat nearby. I remembered that semiconscious patients could not be given water, for fear of choking, but could be fed small chunks of ice. "May I give her some?" I asked the nurse, who nodded.

So I spooned a piece or two into her mouth. She seemed grateful, but turned her head away when I offered more.

I tried once more for a response. "Amanda, do you know someone named Lydia?"

"Of course." Her voice was hoarse and very quiet, but perfectly clear, even sharp.

I think I jumped. "Who is she?"

This time Amanda just looked at me, her eyes dull. Then she closed them and curled into her pillow.

I gave up and left her bedside.

"That's the clearest she's been," said the nurse approvingly. "For just that moment, she was quite all there. Well done."

It didn't seem to me that I had done well at all, but if the nurse was pleased, I supposed I could accept that.

We went next to the pediatrics ward, where I left Miriam's things and talked to the nurse in charge.

"You mustn't worry too much," she said. "She's shown no signs of consciousness yet, but her vital signs are steady. There's no internal bleeding, and you must remember that as long as she's unconscious, she's in no pain. It's the body's own anesthesia, in a way. There's every hope that she'll come out of it soon."

"And her brain?"

"Well, as to that, of course we won't know until we can check her ability to communicate. We think she has sensation in her limbs, at least, and that's good news."

"It's amazing," I said to Alan in an undertone, "what passes for good news in a hospital."

I got no response. His attention was elsewhere. He gestured with his head and I followed his glance.

"He marches forth, a long Processional of one." Somebody said that once in a poem. It perfectly described the arrival of Anthony Blake in the pediatrics ward. Carrying a large Paddington Bear, he made an entrance, as if for an adoring audience, a crowd of reporters, a studio full of television cameras.

The nurses responded accordingly, almost curtsying. "Oh, Mr. Blake," said the one who had been talking to me, "this kind woman—I'm sorry, I don't know your name—brought Miriam's things to her."

The processional turned my way and favored me with a five-hundred-watt smile. "Are you a friend of my poor Amanda, then?" he asked in a voice that would have graced any Rolls-Royce commercial.

Alan, who can be very smooth himself when he wants to be, smiled gently and said, "My wife knows your daughter, yes. We live in Sherebury. My name is Alan Nesbitt, sir, and of course I know yours." He held out his hand.

Blake shook it gravely, and then raised his eyebrows. "Nesbitt, Nesbitt. Surely I know you?"

"I don't believe we've met, but I was commandant at Bramshill, briefly, a couple of years ago. You might have heard the name then."

"Yes, of course. And do I remember that your lovely wife is American?"

I smiled stiffly. "American born, yes. I've lived in England for some time, now."

"And have you had the opportunity to visit a debate in the House of Commons?"

"I'm afraid not. I've tried once or twice, but the line—"

"Ah, we can't have that." He thrust the teddy bear into the hands of the nurse and reached into his pocket for a small notebook and a fountain pen. "Here you are." He scribbled something on a leaf of the notebook, tore it out with a flourish, folded it, and handed it to me. "This will admit you any time you like, without having to stand in the queue. And thank you for your kindness to my granddaughter." He smiled graciously. I almost expected a regal wave as he turned to retrieve his bear.

"That bear is ridiculous," I said to Alan as we walked away. "Much too big, and Miriam's too old for such a present anyway. And why is he paying such attention to his family now, after ignoring them for so long?"

Alan shrugged. "Political expediency. He can no longer ignore them, now that his connection to them is known. Especially not when they're in hospital. So he makes the most of the opportunity. I'm surprised he didn't bring along a cameraman."

"Pompous phony!" I started to unfold the note he had handed me. "Handing out passes to Parliament as if they were—" I stopped, moved into a better light, and studied the note carefully.

"What?"

I pulled him along the corridor and around a corner. "Look at this."

He took it, looked at it and then at me.

"Well?" I demanded.

"I'm not a handwriting expert, Dorothy. But yes, it looks the same to me."

"Then would you please tell me why Amanda, who claims not to have seen her father for years, would have a note he wrote in the pocket of her bathrobe?"

31

FRANKLY, I haven't the slightest idea. Shall we ask Gillian?"

"I admit I'm pining to know, but it depends on how she's feeling."

Gillian was feeling terrible. As a consequence she was also in a fractious mood. The pain medication they had given her when they first set her bones had worn off, and she hadn't taken any more.

"When I can't bear it," she said fiercely. "Not before. I know too many people who got started on drugs that way. Not little Gillian. I have my vices, but that's not one of them, and it's not going to be."

"You know, they do say that today's pain pills very seldom cause addiction in cases when they're really needed."

She just glared at me.

I sighed. "Well, if you won't, you won't. I brought your things. What shall I do with them?"

"I don't care. Give them to the nurse." She closed her eyes.

"Gillian, do you know someone named Lydia?"

Her eyes opened. "Why?"

I improvised. I didn't want to tell Gillian about the note, not just yet. "Because Amanda's conscious, sort of, and she's been rambling a bit about Lydia, whoever she is. Lydia, the tattooed lady, for all I know."

"The only Lydia I know is our mother. Though why Mandy would be talking about her, I don't know."

"She probably won't either, when she wakes up. People say all sorts of strange things, don't they? I do hope you'll take some of the pain pills soon, Gillian. You need some rest."

"I could get more rest if people didn't keep coming in and asking pointless questions."

"I'm going, I'm going." Gillian was wrong about the question being pointless, but she was right about the annoyance factor.

Alan and I walked out of the hospital without speaking. We were thinking too hard. He hailed a taxi and said, "Home?"

"Lunch first. I'm starving, and it must surely be lunchtime by now."

"Well past, in fact. Most of the restaurants we like will have stopped serving, but there's always Victoria Station."

So we went to Victoria, collected the bags we had stowed earlier, bought a couple of not-too-bad sandwiches on pretty good French bread, and ate them standing up while we waited for our train. It wasn't a restful meal, but it stayed the hunger pangs.

Our train was late leaving the station, of course. In fact, we had to get out of one and take another, "owing," said the raucous PA system, "to the nonarrival of the driver."

"That's my favorite one yet," I said to Alan as we trudged to another platform, luggage in hand. I collect excuses for the poor service of the railways. "Except maybe for the time in America when they asked for volunteers to get off a small airplane because it was overweight and had to rid itself of nine passengers."

We finally got under way, in a carriage that was deserted except for a young couple who were, almost literally, wrapped up in each other. We sat well away from them and turned our attention to what had been occupying our minds for the last hour.

"The note," Alan said. "Or notes. You have both of them?"

I fished them out of my purse. Side by side, they left no doubt that they had been written by the same person, probably with the same pen.

"Well," he said.

"Indeed." I put away the pass, with a mental note never to use it, and concentrated on the cryptic note.

"'Not tonight. Lydia's home.' Now what does that mean? Plainly he's telling Amanda not to do something, probably meet him, because her mother's at home. Or was she planning to visit her mother somewhere, and this was to say she—the mother—wasn't going to be there. But in that case, wouldn't it say 'Not at' wherever they were going to meet, instead of 'not tonight'? And why would Amanda's father, whom she hates, be making arrangements anyway? Why not just talk directly to her mother?"

Alan thought about it and looked at the note again. "It isn't signed. Now, to a policeman, that's significant. It means that the person who wrote it was well-known to the person who received it."

"I sign notes I leave for you, phone messages and that sort of thing. Just with a D., but I sign them."

"Yes, and that's the second thing this note tells me. The writer wanted to make sure no one else would know who wrote it."

"Hmm. Pretty stupid, really, when he has such a distinctive handwriting."

"No one ever said Anthony Blake was clever about anything except politics."

"True. But I still can't make any sense of this. Amanda's always told us she hasn't seen her father in years. I don't remember if she said, actually, or just implied that she'd had no contact at all. Wait, though. *John* might have seen Blake that day in London, when he went in to see Vanessa. Maybe Blake gave the note to John. Only why would he? And why be so convoluted about it, when all Blake had to do was pick up the phone and call Amanda?"

"You know," Alan said thoughtfully, "you might be going at this from the wrong angle altogether. If I bring into play my long experience of dealing with some rather sordid situations, I get a different idea. Suppose you look at this note and make one minor change. A translation, if you will. Lydia is Anthony Blake's wife. So suppose we make the note read, 'Not tonight. My wife's home.' What does that sound like to you?"

"Good grief! Of course, why didn't I see it? It's the cancellation of some clandestine meeting—rendezvous—assignation—whatever you want to call it. Obvious, once you look at it in the right way."

"Thank you, Watson," said Alan dryly.

"Now, dear. I didn't mean you weren't brilliant. You get full honors for that. However, the question remains: How did Amanda get hold of this? I absolutely refuse to believe that she was involved in something illicit with her own father, and I refuse to allow you to suppose it, either. I don't care how sordid your past is."

"It wouldn't have to be that sort of relationship, you know. It could be political, or even a spot of blackmail. But I agree it's unlikely, given what we know of both parties."

"All right, then, let's think about what we do know of all the relationships involved. *Know*, not surmise. I think it's fair to say we know, from more than one source, that Amanda hated her father. Still does, probably."

"Right."

"We know that John was on somewhat more cordial terms with his father-in-law. Cordial enough that he was going to try to see him that day in London."

"Right."

"So suppose he did see him. Suppose Blake gave him the note—for some reason—"

"No, let's wait a bit for suppositions and go straight on with what we know. We know that John did see Vanessa Thompson, who is a confidential aide to the Honorable Mr. Blake."

"You use the term ceremonially, I take it. I wonder what the lovely Vanessa makes of him? I wonder—wait a minute." I held up my hand, thinking furiously, and Alan obediently waited.

"Vanessa is the most beautiful woman I have ever seen," I went on slowly. "Counting movie stars and Princess Diana and Nefertiti—any competition you can imagine. She is, as you say, a close associate of Mr. Blake."

"Are you suggesting—?"

"You know perfectly well what I'm suggesting. And let me tell you something you don't know. It didn't seem important at the time I noticed it, but Vanessa carries a very beautiful, very expensive handbag. She keeps her appointment book, and other scraps of paper, in a side pocket of the bag. It's a tight fit, and the day I saw her—heavens, was it only yesterday?—she pulled out the appointment book and some other papers fell out and scattered all over the floor. I helped her pick them up.

"Now. I'm back to the realm of supposition here, but see if it makes sense. Suppose Blake, who we agreed is not wildly intelligent, wrote that note to Vanessa. Vanessa *is* intelligent, and would have destroyed it the moment she received it, if she could. But suppose Blake slipped it to her in some place where she could not dispose of it immediately? She would have put it in her purse. And if there had been no time, before she met John, to deal with it, or if for some reason she had forgotten, it could easily still have been in her purse. Suppose she did just what she did with me, pulled out her date book and some other papers with it. John would have helped her pick them up, as I did. Suppose he saw that one and read it?"

"You're doing an awful lot of supposing. But go on."

"We both know what John would do with information like that, don't we? He would immediately see what it was about. Unlike us, he would recognize the handwriting, he would know who Lydia was, he would know who the note was written to. He could put the pieces together. And he would rejoice that he had uncovered a sinner almost in the act of sinning, and, incidentally, that he had an even tighter hold on Blake than before."

32

Alan considered this, and finally nodded. "It's all very iffy, but it's plausible. Do you have an explanation for how the note ended up in Amanda's possession?"

"We can ask her when she's more herself, but I suspect it was in John's pocket the night he was killed, and she found it that morning when she cleaned him up so tidily. And put it away in her pocket and forgot about it. The police might well not have thought to search the pocket of her bathrobe."

Alan groaned. "I wonder if she will ever be able to grasp the difficulties she created by that act of housewifely imbecility. But if you're saying Doyle was killed by Blake, surely he would have looked for the note."

"Perhaps he couldn't. Perhaps something woke Miriam, and he heard her stir upstairs. I think he would have been afraid to look further, would have left in a hurry. After all, with John dead and unable to talk about the circumstances in which he found the note, it wasn't nearly as damning. We can find out if Miriam woke that night at all, if she—when she feels better."

"Yes. Meanwhile, the whole thing is terribly nebulous, and both Blake and Vanessa Thompson will deny that any such thing ever happened, that they are any more than colleagues, that she ever dropped a note. How, by the way, do you imagine—and I use the word advisedly—that Blake found out Doyle had the note? Assuming that any of this scenario is based on reality."

"All right, I admit I'm making an awful lot of bricks with very little straw, but all we have to go on at this point is snippets. The police do that, too, and don't try to tell me they don't. They build up a hypothesis and then go about finding the proof."

"If you say so. So how did Blake find out? Did our righteous friend Doyle try a spot of blackmail?"

"Not of the usual sort, I think. He was a vicious man, but not a thief. He enjoyed pulling wings off flies, always with the excuse that the fly had sinned and was in need of correction, and of course rendered unable to sin anymore. The metaphor's getting out of hand, they always do, but goodness, Blake is such a large, gaudy fly! I can imagine Doyle's delight at the thought of dewinging him. I think he would have waited a day or two to think things over, and then would have called Blake and told him about the note, delivering a long sermon while he was at it."

"And you speculate that Blake, unwilling to allow anyone to jeopardize his career with such dangerous information, would have told Doyle he was quite mistaken and that he, Blake, would come to Sherebury and explain. Is that the denouement of your hypothesis?"

"Of course. He would have come, met Doyle somewhere, and given him a large dose of Lanoxin in beer or coffee or whatever Doyle would drink. I think I remember reading in some book somewhere that it has almost no taste, even in a heavy concentration. Then he would have taken him home when he began to feel ill. Taken him home and watched him die, and then stabbed him to make it look, dear heaven, as if Amanda—Blake's daughter Amanda—was the killer."

"How would Blake have known about the Lanoxin?"

"Oh. I don't know. Wait, yes, I do. Suppose Doyle carried the tablets with him, and Vanessa had seen him take one?"

"Thin, but I'll allow it for now. However, and I hate to do this, my dear, but there is one unanswerable flaw in your reasoning."

"There is not! A hole here and there, maybe, but logically—"

"You have forgotten that Blake has, most unfortunately, the perfect alibi."

I just stared at him.

"On the evening that you suppose Blake was meeting with Doyle, feeding him Lanoxin, waiting for him to become ill, and all the rest of it, he was in fact sitting in Parliament and giving a little speech outside, watched by television cameras, Big Ben, and dear only knows how many viewers across the country, including, I'll remind you, me."

I sat back, defeated. It had all hung together so well. All I'd needed, I'd thought, was to check a few details with Amanda, maybe tomorrow if she was fully conscious by then, and then we could go to Derek with the whole story and he could set the machinery in motion, talk to people, gather evidence, build a case.

But I'd forgotten the alibi. The one small detail that knocked the whole theory into a cocked hat.

"I *wanted* it to be him," I said, half to myself.

"I don't care much for the gentleman myself, but we can't always convict people we dislike. And there's one other objection, too, now that I think of it. Your theory offers no explanation for Gillian's accident."

"It could have been an accident," I muttered, not believing it. We sat in dispirited silence for the few minutes that remained before the train reached Sherebury.

It had been a long and wearying day. I put the three suitcases in the spare bedroom to await the time when their owners would need them, and then put my feet up until hunger drove me to the kitchen. Scrambled eggs made a good enough supper. "It isn't the end of the world, you know, Dorothy," said Alan as he helped me with the dishes. "These things happen. We just have to start over."

"Not tonight, we don't. My imagination, or deductive facility, or whatever you want to call it, has shut down for the day."

We watched the late news. Anthony Blake, thank heaven, wasn't featured, or I think I would have thrown something through the screen. I yawned through it all but came awake for the weather, if only because someone was asleep at the switch and was still showing the map of Scotland in the background while the announcer was talking about the Channel Islands. Then Alan and I went up to bed, and I fell asleep as if I'd been hit over the head. Emotional exhaustion will do that to me.

I woke up about four, though, with a confused dream still racing through my head. It was something about islands in Scotland, and the Scottish Parliament, and Abou Ben Adhem ("May his tribe increase"). There was a sense of urgency about it, somehow, though my fuddled night mind couldn't untangle the images. But it took me a long time to get back to sleep, and then my dreams were the frustration ones, trying to run with heavy legs, trying to find my way out of an endless maze, thinking I had at last found the door only to find it the door to yet another room, yet another corridor.

It wasn't until morning, as I was sipping my third cup of coffee, that my mind suddenly focused. "Alan!" I said sharply, interrupting him as he was reading me an item about Prince Charles.

"Mmm?"

"Alan, when they do the weather, you know those maps? With the little clouds and sun and thunderbolts and all that?"

"On television, you mean?"

"Yes, of course." I was three pages ahead of him and irrationally impatient for him to catch up. "Now the weatherman isn't really standing in front of those maps, is he? Like last night, when they had the wrong one behind him for a while?"

"No, as I understand it he's in front of a blank blue wall, and something called chroma key can combine his image with an image of the map. It's all done electronically. He can point to the right places on the wall because he's looking at a monitor that's out of camera range."

"Right. Now, back home, they used to show reporters standing in front of the White House when they were reporting on a story about the president. Only everyone knew that they probably weren't really in front of the White House. It was done the same way, two images combined electronically. Sometimes they'd get the point of view a little bit wrong, too, so it looked like the reporter was standing too high, or too low, or just somehow not quite right."

"Yes," he said patiently.

"So how do we know, when Anthony Blake was shown on TV standing in front of the clock tower, that he was really in front of the clock tower? Couldn't he have been someplace else entirely?"

"I suppose so, but I remember that the time on the clock was about right. And if he was making a speech *anywhere* at that time, a little after eleven, he wasn't in Sherebury killing John Doyle."

"He could have been if the speech was on tape."

"How would that work?"

"Frankly, I haven't the slightest idea, but I know someone who might."

"Gillian?"

"Gillian. And wait a minute! We know something is odd

about one of those broadcasts, because we saw Blake on TV Tuesday night, apparently in London, when Vanessa said he was in Edinburgh. Now how do you explain that?"

"To tell the truth, I can't. But why wouldn't the TV chaps be there when Blake was making a speech? They'd know, surely, wouldn't they?"

I sighed and looked out the window. The weather had deteriorated even further. It was one of those days when the forecast might include everything: rain, sleet, freezing rain, snow, wind . . . every sort of nastiness that winter can dole out. A trip back to London was the last thing I wanted, but I had to talk to Gillian. I was quite sure she would provide the answers we needed.

Alan wasn't enthusiastic. "Dorothy, my love, this is all the purest speculation. You have no proof—"

"And I never will have, will I, until I can work out a way it could have been done. Anyway, it isn't entirely speculation. There's the note. It's real enough, and it has to be explained somehow."

"There must be a dozen ways to explain that note."

"Give me one, just one that hangs together as well as mine."

"I haven't thought it out thoroughly, but the simplest explanation is often the best. Amanda had that note. Very well, the person who wrote it sent it to her."

"Right. If you can make that idea square with the handwriting on that note, and its content, and Amanda's relationship with her family, I'll buy it. Meanwhile, I'm going to London to talk to Gillian."

Alan grinned and threw up his hands. "There's no arguing with a stubborn woman. Go with my blessing. If you don't mind, I intend to sit at home in front of a nice warm computer. Just try not to get into trouble."

"*Moi?*" I said, tossing an imaginary mane of golden curls to one side.

I wasn't in such a bright and breezy mood when I got to

the hospital. I had been struck by a fit of economy and had taken the Underground most of the way, hoping to catch a taxi for the short ride from the station to the hospital.

The only trouble was, there weren't any taxis. I have been told that, the minute it starts to rain in New York, all the cabs disappear, as if the pavement has swallowed them up. Now if that happened in London, given the English climate, the cab companies would go out of business. But either that particular neighborhood was just short of taxis that day, or the drivers decided that freezing rain was just too much, or *something*, because there wasn't a taxi in sight and I had to walk. I had thought it a short distance. Not on foot, it wasn't.

I reached the hospital wet and cold. The wind had blown me along for the last block or two, and my umbrella, which had been almost useless anyway, had finally blown inside out. My shoes squished. The first thing I did was to find a ladies' room and try to dry myself off. I think I got more shreds of paper towel on me than water off, but my feet and shoes benefited a little. I didn't squish quite so badly as I marched down a corridor to Gillian's ward.

Then I thanked my lucky stars for that wind that had blown me along, for Gillian was in a wheelchair, getting ready to leave. Another minute or two and I might have been too late.

"You must be feeling better," was my greeting. "I can't believe they're letting you go home so soon."

"The damage has worked out to an arm broken in two places, a broken ankle, and assorted cuts and bruises. I feel bloody awful, but I'm well enough to get out of this place," she said sourly.

"How are Amanda and Miriam?"

"Mandy's conscious and making sense most of the time. I saw her this morning. God, I felt guilty! She looks like hell and it's my fault, it must be my fault, I drive like a bat out of hell . . . anyway. No point in rehashing all that. Miriam's beginning to open her eyes and babble a bit. Not what you could call conscious, but they think perhaps she's going to be all right, given time."

I let out my breath, just realizing I'd been holding it. "That's a mercy."

"I suppose. That poor kid . . ."

"Gillian, I don't think any of this is your fault, so stop beating yourself. Now, are you going to be able to manage? You're going home, I presume?"

"Not much point in going anywhere else now the whole world knows where I am, is there? I'll be okay. My flat's only up one flight, and the visiting nurse will come for a while. I can walk on crutches; they're only taking me down in the chair because of hospital rules."

"You're going home with friends?"

"Taxi. I had to prove to these cretins that I could get home under my own steam, or they wouldn't let me leave."

"Then let me go with you. I want to talk to you anyway, and the cab's on me. I just hope they've sent for a radio-dispatched one. There aren't any out on the streets, believe me."

She looked at me, drenched and disheveled, and said, "I believe you."

"Right. Then I'll meet you at the front door in five minutes. I want to say hello to Amanda."

Amanda was awake and looking, as Gillian had said, pretty terrible. She was obviously in a good deal of pain, but seemed reasonably alert. I hated to have to question her, but there were answers I needed.

"Hi, Amanda, nice to see you looking better."

"You were here before?"

"A couple of times, but you were pretty well out of it. I just wanted to let you know you have a bathrobe here when you're able to get out of bed and want it. Gillian had me retrieve it from your luggage—and I have the rest of that at home, so it's yours any time. There was a note in the pocket of the robe, and I didn't know if it was important, so I saved it."

I pulled it out of my purse and handed it to her.

"Oh, that. Yes, that was in John's pocket when I—found him. I don't know what it is. I suppose I should have given it to the police, but I forgot."

Good Lord deliver us, as the Litany says. The woman's naivete was amazing, but bless her, she'd confirmed one part of my theory.

"Shall I do that for you, then?" I asked.

"Oh, yes, please." She plucked at her bedclothes for a moment. "Did you know Miriam's doing better? They won't let me see her, though. Have you seen her? How is she? I wish they'd let me see her."

"No, I haven't seen her, but Gillian says they think she's going to be all right. Gillian's going home, did you know?"

"She told me this morning. She told me everything. I can't believe I don't remember anything about it."

"Probably just as well. Look, you're getting tired and I'm seeing Gillian home, but I'll be back later. Get some rest, and try not to worry about Miriam."

Her face, before she turned away and closed her eyes, clutched at my heart.

33

'D had some time, on the train, to think about how I was going to approach Gillian. She didn't like me very much, and
I wouldn't have called her my favorite person, either, but we
had, I thought, established a certain level of wary mutual respect. So the truth was probably best.

The truth, up to a point.

"Gillian, are you feeling well enough to answer some
questions?" I asked when she was installed in the taxi as com-
fortably as her injuries would allow.

"I feel like hell, but my head is on straight, if that's what
you mean. No thanks to types like you who tried to push pain
pills. Why should I answer any of your questions? Why don't
you just ask your police friends?"

"They didn't ask the same questions I'm going to. And I
can't think of a single reason why you should answer me, unless you're interested in finding out who killed your brother-
in-law and tried to kill you."

She glared at me, then winced as the taxi went over a
rough patch of road. "Oh, get it over with." She sighed and

waved her hand in a gesture of resignation. "I suppose you want to know where I was taking Mandy and Miriam, and why."

"Well, actually—"

"It's rather funny, in a way, really. Dear Papa phoned me at the flat, when we were all there for a few minutes getting some things together. I hear nothing from him for years, and then suddenly, when I have no time, when I'm only interested in getting Mandy and Miriam away, he rings up. I didn't tell him much, only that I was taking them for a rest, and he actually volunteered a place he owns, a cottage in Hampshire. It's usually rented out, but he said it was vacant at the moment, and we could use it, that no one would disturb us there. He gets philanthropic, and look what happens!"

"I see. I had wondered where you'd go, but I wanted to ask you something quite different. I need answers to some technical questions about television production. I know you're a writer, but you do know something about the technical end?"

"I'd have to, wouldn't I? But why—"

"I'm not even sure why, myself, but what I want to know is this: Suppose someone shot a videotape and sent it to a television station. If the tape was shot against a blank background, a white wall or something like that, could the station chroma-key in a different background?"

"You do live in the dark ages, don't you? You can do anything with electronics these days. You can put the prime minister in a cage with monkeys at the zoo if you want to. It doesn't matter what the original background was. They just zap it out and put in anything they want to, and there are lots of techniques for doing it. Chroma key is pretty much used only for live studio production, the weather, that sort of thing."

"I see," I said with satisfaction.

"But if you're saying you want to make some sweet little tape of your grandchildren and get a station to mix it in to a royal garden-party scene, forget it. There are production companies that do that sort of thing, but no TV station would bother with it. They're not interested in amateur stuff."

"I was thinking of something a little different. Suppose someone videotaped something newsworthy. A plane crash, say. They might have scenes that the station would want, mightn't they?"

"Oh, well, yes, that is a different matter. A disaster, where the first person on the scene shot some distinctive footage—right, the stations would be fighting over that."

"And if the background was bad in some scenes? Out of focus, or simply too gory for public viewing—"

"There is very little that is considered too gory for public viewing these days."

"Well, you know what I mean. If part of a scene was good, and part not so good, would they clean it up electronically?"

"That depends. Sometimes the amateurishness gives a quality of spontaneity to that sort of footage. Then, too, there's the question of truthfulness. The BBC won't edit news film except for length, because of ethical issues. Some of the other stations aren't quite so particular, but they all try to be careful not to show something that never, in fact, happened. If they don't care about fooling the public, they certainly do care about lawsuits, and the legal departments won't let them mess about very much."

She waited. I remained silent.

"Well? Are you going to tell me why you've taken such a sudden interest in television production?"

"I can't, Gillian. Not quite yet. I haven't quite worked out what it all might mean."

It was fortunate that we arrived at her flat just then, and she had to occupy herself with the exhausting business of getting out of the taxi and up a flight of stairs. I helped her as much as I could, but we were both out of breath by the time I got her settled in an armchair, with her crutches and the telephone within easy reach.

"Would you like some tea, or something stronger?"

"What I want is a great deal of whiskey, but they say I can't have it. Do you know how to make coffee that's drinkable?"

"I do. How strong do you like it?"

She had apparently lost interest in my questions, which was fine with me. When I left her, coffee in hand, she looked as if she might doze off before she had a chance to finish it.

I was, despite the previous restless night, very wide awake on the train home. My still-damp clothes and shoes weren't conducive to a nap, but worry was really what kept me awake. I had all the pieces now. I was convinced of it. The problem was what to do with them.

Anthony Blake was looking more and more like England's next prime minister. It was going to take some very delicate maneuvering to accuse him of murder.

When I looked at my problem from that point of view, it almost took my breath away. It was one of the most important men in the country I was dealing with, here. Not quite the Prince of Wales, but an heir apparent, all the same. And my only proof, the only foundation for my shaky structure of if-and-maybe, was an extremely ambiguous note.

I went over it all again in my mind. Doyle goes to London. He finds a note. He mulls it over and then gets in touch with Blake. How? Telephone, probably. He could have broken through the protective wall of secretaries simply by saying he was Blake's son-in-law.

It didn't matter how. He had talked to Blake, probably on Tuesday, or maybe early Wednesday. Blake had soothed him, said he had put the wrong interpretation on the whole thing. Had said he couldn't explain it over the phone.

Why not? Well, the simplest lie, the lie I would have come up with, was that the note had to do with a delicate political situation. Then Blake could go on to say that he would be happy to meet Doyle somewhere and explain in detail.

Okay. So Blake and Vanessa between them make plans. I

was willing to bet that Vanessa made most of them. They arrange a lovely alibi. He makes a few comments, on video-tape, about some genuinely important issue. Then how do they get it to the TV stations?

Well, I could see Vanessa phoning the stations, in a huff because they hadn't shown up for an arranged taping session. With her efficiency, she could quite easily convince the television people that it was someone on their staff who had messed up. That would put them on the defensive. They would then be delighted to accept the tape Vanessa had made, and air it as she asked, with the clock tower as background.

Or maybe she just phoned and said some important personages, unnamed, had dropped into Blake's office, and he had made these comments to them. No, she was not at liberty to say who the other people were, and they were not seen on the tape, but they were very highly placed.

She'd managed it somehow, leaving Blake free to be discreetly somewhere else. Maybe in London, more likely closer to Sherebury. The number of small, discreet pubs in southern England is amazing, and it would take the police a long, long time to find the place, unless they got very lucky.

So. Blake and Doyle meet. Blake (undoubtedly briefed by Vanessa) manages to get hold of Doyle's heart pills. They're probably in a coat pocket, and he must have found a way, knocked the coat to the floor or something. Then he doctors the coffee or whatever. Doyle begins to feel ill, his heart begins to beat erratically. Blake manages to get him home, waits for him to die, and then stabs him.

Why stab him? So Amanda will be blamed, of course. Why after he's dead? Because Blake doesn't want to get blood all over himself.

Why doesn't he take the note? That damning note, right there in Doyle's pocket for the police to find. They didn't, of course, but Blake couldn't have anticipated Amanda's actions.

Oh. He had asked Doyle for the note earlier, but Doyle had said he had destroyed it. Blake might not have believed him, might have looked, but something changed his mind. A noise from upstairs, from outside? I'd probably never know, but almost anything might have spooked him. At least, it would for me, if I had just committed murder. I would want to get out of there as fast as humanly possible.

And then—and then what? Then Blake, or more probably the invaluable Vanessa, watches developments. Amanda is arrested; very good. She is released; not so good, but not terrible. The police take no further obvious steps. No one approaches Blake. He appears to have escaped notice.

But then this nosy American woman appears from out of nowhere. She wants to know what Doyle did in London. She says she doesn't think Amanda did it. Maybe worst of all, she sees Vanessa drop things out of her purse.

I thought back to that brief meeting. Vanessa had been cool, capable, very much in control. She hadn't reacted in any unusual way to anything I'd said. What, in fact, *had* I said?

I couldn't remember saying anything that was at all incriminating. I'd certainly said nothing to suggest that I thought Blake might be up to something, because I'd had no such idea, then. My suspicions had all been of the chapel people, those thoroughly unpleasant Rookwoods.

I'd rather lost sight of them, hadn't I? Was it possible, still, that they were responsible for Doyle's death? If they really were raking a lot of cash off the top of the chapel's operation, they had an excellent motive. For one delightful moment I pictured them at one of those Wednesday night prayer meetings, with Doyle standing up to denounce them in front of the whole congregation.

In a way it was almost a pity it had never happened. If anyone ever deserved that kind of pillorying, it was the Rookwoods. I would have liked to be there.

Which was an unworthy thought and one that put me in the same basket as them, glorying in someone else's downfall.

Shame on me. All the same, if they had known such a thing was a possibility, they would have done a lot to prevent it.

Of course, the police knew that as well as I did. They were certainly looking very closely into the movements of that pair on the night in question.

What the police didn't know about was a note found in John Doyle's pocket. A note in Anthony Blake's distinctive handwriting.

I wrenched my thoughts away from the Rookwoods and back to my scenario. After Vanessa and I meet, she tells Blake that I'm asking awkward questions. She doesn't think I know anything, but I have to be silenced.

I shivered. Why was I still alive? Perhaps only because I had a noted policeman for a husband. Or perhaps it hadn't been easy to follow my movements. But Blake could easily find his daughters and his granddaughter, because he had told them to go to his cottage in Hampshire. And they might hold important knowledge, important keys that could lock him out of the future he wanted. Gillian with her knowledge of television, Amanda with whatever John might have told her, Miriam with her memory of whatever she might have seen or heard that night . . .

I'd tried not to think about that part. I didn't want to believe that anyone could be callous enough, cold enough, to kill his family out of political ambition. But as I sat there nearing home, I knew as surely as I knew the train route that Anthony Blake had not been in Edinburgh when Gillian's car was wrecked. I was willing to bet money that he had been in a car on that roundabout, or perhaps that Vanessa had been there, making sure in the fast, heavy traffic that Gillian's car was crowded off the road and into a nice brick wall.

34

I WAS, I realized as the train pulled into Sherebury station, right back where I'd started. How could I prove any of this?

Oh, there was undoubtedly evidence out there. Some phone calls to the right people at the right TV stations might elicit the information that those Blake tapes had been supplied by Blake, not the station cameramen. Very sophisticated analysis of fibers and so on collected at the murder scene might match up with clothing, or hair, or whatever. There was always DNA, too. Blake would not, of course, have left any fingerprints. Unlike his repressed daughter, he lived in the real world and understood about forensics. He would have worn gloves. On a late November night, it was a normal thing to do.

He would have left something behind, and taken something away with him. That's the first rule of forensics, that a person cannot go to a place without leaving something—a hair, say, or a few flakes of dead skin, or a trace of shoe polish—and removing something, perhaps carpet fibers or a little dirt from a muddy patch on a path.

The evidence could be obtained, all right, but first the police had to look for it, and match it up. And there was the problem.

English police are, I believe, as incorruptible as any in the world. But that doesn't mean that they are not influenced by politics. Of course they are. When the government pays your wages and sets all the rules by which you operate, of course you're careful not to upset whoever represents "the government" in your particular bailiwick.

Anthony Blake was, of course, not the MP for Sherebury. But he was a powerful man, the leading Tory in Parliament.

How many policemen were willing to stick their necks out far enough to offend Anthony Blake? Oh, if they were certain he was guilty, most of them. I'd give them that. They wouldn't shield the guilty, not even if the guilty was a Royal. But launch an investigation on the strength of some unsupported allegations by an elderly American woman?

I didn't think so.

I took a taxi home, still pondering.

Alan greeted me with a kiss and made me a sandwich when I said I'd missed lunch again. After I'd changed into dry clothes, I settled down at the kitchen table to eat, while Alan had some coffee to keep me company.

"Was it worth it?" he asked.

"Well, I learned some things." I detailed Gillian's information. "Oh, by the way, I was able to talk to Amanda for a few minutes, and I was right about the note. Amanda's part in it, I mean. You should have heard her tone of voice when she said she supposed she should have given it to the police."

Alan groaned.

"Miriam's still not quite conscious, but she's getting there. According to Gillian, the doctors are pretty optimistic now."

Alan made suitable noises.

I nibbled at my sandwich and then put it down, suddenly no longer hungry. "Alan, what am I going to do?"

He might have said, "About what?" He might have said, "Why do you have to do anything? Leave it to the police."

Bless his heart, he simply shook his head.

"What's happening with the Rookwoods?" I asked after a while. "Has Derek told you anything?" I was hoping that, perhaps, after all . . .

He shook his head again and waved a dismissive hand. "They're in a good deal of trouble, of course. They kept two sets of books for the chapel, and one shows quite clearly how much money they'd been stealing over the years. They'll be charged with various kinds of fraud and so on, but not murder. They both have alibis for that Wednesday night. And before you start your speech about alibis being suspect, let me say that these are vouched for by their congregation for the early part of the evening, and later on by the staff of that dreary mission down by the river. It seems the Rookwoods went there directly after the prayer meeting and stayed until well after midnight, supposedly to minister to the homeless but really, the director says, to harangue them about their evil ways. They were most unpopular, and quite irrefutably there.

"They didn't do it, Dorothy. Much as I'd like to see them behind bars, they didn't commit murder, at least not the murder of John Doyle."

"No." I had already been sure, but it was so much the easier, less painful solution, and hope is not easily defeated.

"He mustn't get away with it, Alan!" I burst out after another moody silence. "A man like that in high office—the damage he could do—"

"Yes. Something must be done."

His tone jolted me out of my frustration. I stared at him.

"You won't like it," he went on.

"Try me. I'll do anything."

"It doesn't involve you. That's one reason that you won't like it."

"For heaven's sake, Alan!"

"Very well. It's the old trick. I ring him up, tell him I know what he did, imply blackmail, arrange a meeting. I carry a microphone or a tape recorder. When he has incriminated himself, the police close in."

Alan was right. I didn't like it, not one bit. Blake was a dangerous man, and I didn't want Alan in danger. If it was the only way, I argued, I wanted to be in on it. I wanted to be there to make sure Alan would be all right. "Besides, I want to see that smarmy smile wiped off his face. I admit it."

"Dorothy," said Alan wearily, "if the positions were reversed, what would you say? How much do you like it when I try to keep you from walking into danger?"

"Oh."

There were a lot of angry answers to that: But this is completely different, I've never put myself in real danger, that isn't the only reason I want to be there. Et cetera.

There was only one honest answer. "I don't like it at all. And it's been a long time since you've done that, even though I know you've wanted to. So I won't try to stop you, and I won't pretend I'd be of any use in protecting you. Who am I kidding? At my age, in my sort of shape, with arthritis and too much weight—no, I couldn't exactly be Superwoman to the rescue."

He smiled and took my hand.

"But."

He stopped smiling.

"I still want to be there, for another reason. I think I should be the one to make the phone call, and therefore I should be the one he sees first when he comes to wherever we meet. He knows me, Alan, and he knows I've been poking around in this. I'm the logical one to have found out something. He doesn't know you, except as my husband. Let me make the call. Then you can come with me, and I can say you insisted. I'll fade into the woodwork whenever you say the word, but I should be there."

We argued about it, of course. I had to admit that I had ulterior motives as well. I'd been in on this from the beginning; I wanted to see it through. I also had the nasty longing to see Blake toppled from his pedestal. I even admitted my worry about Alan and my desire to be wherever he might possibly get into trouble.

He conceded, finally. "*If* Derek agrees, Dorothy. *And* the chief. This is a highly irregular procedure we're proposing, and it has to have everyone's approval from the top down, or we may find ourselves without a case to take to court. And you must do exactly as you're told when the time comes. You have to remember that we are trained to meet dangerous situations and you are not."

I promised. I would have promised to stand on my head if he'd asked, now that I had won my point.

Alan began the process with a long phone call to Derek, to which I was not privy. I imagined them exchanging male commiseration about stubborn women. I didn't care what they said, as long as Derek agreed in the end.

He did, of course. Alan had been his boss for a long time. Derek also, somehow, managed to gain the approval of his bosses all the way up to the chief constable.

It all took time. It would have taken more time but for Alan's quiet insistence on all possible speed. Both of us seemed infected by a curious notion that events were moving fast, that delay could be disastrous. "He's killed once and tried to kill again," I kept thinking, and often saying out loud. I didn't know what was coming next, only that it had to be averted.

It was evening, and we had eaten a sketchy supper, when the call finally came. I beat Alan to the phone, but turned on the speaker so Alan could hear, too.

"Derek here, Dorothy. It's been arranged. I had rather a tough time with the chief, but seeing as it's you and Alan, he finally agreed. To tell the truth, he doesn't believe a word of the accusation, but he's authorized the use of the microphone, and allowed me one man."

"One man! But—"

"Besides me, that is. I'm on my own time, and a few other officers who know enough about you to believe in your story are willing to join me. Don't worry about that part of it. There will be enough of us. All concerned made one point, however, and it's this. When you ring the bloke to arrange the meeting, make it as soon as possible. We want to give him very little time to make any little arrangements of his own."

"Yes, I can see that. Alan and I have been talking about where to meet. Do you have any ideas about that?"

"Yes. You want a place that seems private but actually affords hiding places for our men. The Cathedral Close comes to mind. Spacious, open, but surrounded by buildings. After dark it has all the privacy anyone could want, but we'll be watching from the shops, and houses, and of course the Cathedral itself, and remember that we'll hear every word you say, just as long as you stay inside the Close. The equipment has the range for that, but not a lot more."

"What if he wants to meet some other place?"

"You'll insist, and you'll have the upper hand. He'll think you're trying to blackmail him, remember. He'll know you can always simply not show up if it doesn't suit you. He'll try to negotiate, of course, but stand your ground."

"I can do that. Tomorrow, then?"

"Yes, call him in late afternoon, as late as you think you can still reach him, and make it for, say, seven o'clock. It'll be good and dark by then, and there won't be many people about. And let us know as soon as you're set."

With a distinctly fluttery feeling somewhere inside, I agreed and hung up.

35

I was very nervous as I walked out of my door and through the gate into the Close at seven o'clock the next evening. The Cathedral clock was chiming the hour in reassuring fashion, and Alan was only a step or two behind me, but still I was nervous.

No. I was scared.

The phone call to Blake, that afternoon, had been simpler than I'd feared it would be. English MPs are more accessible than their American Congressional counterparts. They don't have a huge staff, and they have a tradition of responsibility to their constituency.

I'd felt wildly melodramatic speaking my piece, once I'd reached him. I tried not to let my voice shake as I said, "I know what you did, and I'll tell the police unless you make it worth my while."

There was a pause. Then, "I haven't the slightest idea what you're talking about, but perhaps we'd best sort it out. What do you want?"

"Oh, no. Not on the phone. Meet me tonight."

We'd set the time and place. He'd protested, as expected, but I played tough and he finally agreed. Derek had already been to the house to wire me for sound.

"Are you sure this thing is working?" I asked Alan now in an anxious undertone.

"Thoroughly checked out this afternoon," he murmured. "Fresh batteries and all. But if you want to be absolutely certain, just ask Derek to step outside for a moment. He's in the Rose and Crown."

"Derek," I whispered, "could you come out? There's no problem, I'm just—uh—testing the equipment."

On the opposite side of the Close, the door of the pub opened, spilling light out onto the cobblestoned pathway. A man stepped out, looked at his watch, looked to left and right, made an annoyed little gesture and stepped back in again.

"Picture of a man who's been stood up," said Alan next to my ear. "Derek has always been good at amateur theatricals."

"Very reassuring," I whispered back, and then we were too near our meeting place to talk anymore.

I had chosen a stone bench very near the center of the Close. It was right out in the open, with no shrubbery or trees or buildings anywhere near. I would ordinarily not have chosen to spend any time in such a spot on a damp, chilly December evening, but it had all the privacy Anthony Blake's heart could desire. He wasn't there yet, however, so Alan and I sat down to wait.

The stone was very cold. I could feel the cold seeping right through my coat and my slacks, into my flesh, to my very bones. It met the cold fear that lay deep inside me. Maybe I would freeze there into an ice statue and never move again. I would become a monument, a statue of a martyr, and they would put up a bronze plaque, and after a year no one would remember who I was or what I'd done . . .

"He's late," said Alan, quietly cross.

I returned to the world of the living; the ice inside receded a little, though outside the air grew even colder. "Or else he's not coming. Maybe I was wrong after all. What time is it?"

"Twenty past."

We returned to our silent waiting. The dampness coalesced into a fine mist, and from that into a drizzle.

It probably wasn't five minutes later that a car drove slowly along the one public roadway in the Close. The Rose and Crown is an inn—a hotel as well as a pub—and guests have to be able to get there with their luggage, so the public is allowed access along one narrow street. There's no parking except for inn guests, so I assumed that was where this car was headed.

But it stopped, just opposite where we sat, and a woman got out.

There is always some light in the Close, from streetlights and the spotlights that illuminate the Cathedral at night. The light along the roadway was dim, but where it was possible to see at all, no one could have mistaken the form and face of Vanessa Thompson.

My husband let out a low—a very low—whistle.

"Yes, isn't she? I told you. But where's Blake?"

I couldn't tell if there was anyone else in the car. From this distance it looked like one of those murderously expensive models that often have tinted windows.

We stood and waited, uncertain. Vanessa had stopped directly under one of the no-parking signs. She pointed at it, raised her arms in a shrug, and beckoned to us.

"No car," said Alan. "Shake your head, and tell Derek what's happening. The Rose and Crown's right down at the bottom of the street, and that blasted rain's turning to fog. He probably can't see."

I complied. Vanessa gestured some more, finally gave up, and with one more anxious glance at the sign, stepped over the low white chain barrier and walked over to us.

"Mrs. Martin, Mr. Blake has a frightful cold and is wait-

ing in the Rose and Crown. He said to say he's sorry to inconvenience you, but you can choose your spot in the pub."

She sounded as if she hadn't the slightest idea what it was
all about. Or as if that was what she wanted us to think. I
couldn't decide which.

I looked at Alan. He nodded. "Very well," I said, and
started across the grass toward the pub.

"Why don't I drive you?" said Vanessa.

At that Alan quite firmly shook his head, and I was about
to do the same when the wind rose and the rain changed to a
hard, stinging sleet.

The last time that happened to me, I was walking alone
on a narrow road at the top of a rise on Dartmoor, with no
house anywhere in sight. I thought I was surely going to die,
and I might have, in fact, if I hadn't blundered against the
side of a sort of shed, a low, flimsy building that kept the
worst of the wind away until the sleet changed back to rain.

One never knew how long this sort of weather would last,
a minute or an hour, but we certainly couldn't stay outside in
it, even for the few hundred yards between us and the Rose
and Crown. We followed Vanessa to the car, heads down,
huddled inside our coats, trying in vain to keep dry. When we
reached the edge of the grass, I tripped over the chain and
nearly fell. I grabbed Alan's arm.

That was unfortunate. Alan slipped on the grass, slippery
with rain and ice, and sprawled awkwardly, falling with an ex-
clamation of pain.

"Are you all right?"

"Twisted my ankle," he muttered. "Just as well we're not
walking. It's not serious, but it hurts like the devil."

We managed to get into the car, which was warm and lux-
urious inside, and collapsed gratefully onto the soft leather
seats in back. "We're getting your car all wet, I'm afraid."

"Oh, this is Mr. Blake's car, not mine, the official one, you
know. Don't worry about the water. It doesn't matter, and it's

only for a moment." Her voice sounded hollow, and I saw that it issued from a speaker. There was a glass partition between the front and back seats.

She put the car in gear and drove slowly down the street, windshield wipers beating away the sleet. Their noise was the only sound one could hear. A very expensive car, indeed.

We approached the pub. We reached the front door. We drove past. I objected. "Um—if you wouldn't mind letting us out at the door, instead of going with you to the car park? It's behind the inn, anyway, not on down—Ms. Thompson, where are you going?"

"Oh, I'm sorry if I misled you, but Mr. Blake isn't at *this* Rose and Crown. Very common name for a pub, that, isn't it?" She steered the car smoothly around the curve of the street, which was only a loop issuing from and returning to the main gate to the Close.

We were still moving very slowly. Alan gave me a look that said "get ready," and lunged for the handle of the door.

It was locked.

"Childproof locks," said Vanessa in her musical voice. "Such a sensible invention. The door can be opened only from the outside, and before you try it, Mr. Nesbitt, the windows won't roll down either."

Mr. Nesbitt. Not Mr. Martin, as she would naturally have assumed. She'd done some checking.

"Ms. Thompson," said Alan, "exactly where are you taking us?"

"I believe the phrase your wife would recognize is 'for a ride.'"

The inside of the car was suddenly colder than the stone bench.

"Where is Mr. Blake, then?" said Alan coolly, and a little more loudly than necessary.

I remembered the microphone I was wearing, the mike that would be useless outside the Close. "Yes," I chimed in, "where is he? Our business is with him."

She laughed gently. "So far as I know, he's sitting at home working on a speech."

"At home? In Hampshire? You're taking us all the way to Hampshire?"

As the car passed smoothly through the open gate and out of range of the listening equipment, she laughed again. "No, he's not in Hampshire. Our London flat. To which I am indeed going later this evening. You, on the other hand, are going to quite a different destination."

She stopped at the traffic light, signaled, and made a left turn onto the High Street. Her driving was impeccable. "Now, let's see," she said conversationally. "This does become the Brighton Road, doesn't it? I understand there are enthusiasts in America who fancy a dip in the sea at this time of year. I've never thought it my cup of tea, but I daresay you two will enjoy it. At least for a brief time."

The cold settled in. I could think of nothing to say, nothing to do. But I must, or soon Alan and I would be past thinking at all.

Alan nudged my foot with his. He looked at me intently, trying hard to communicate something, but I couldn't read his face. "What?" I said, and my impatience edged a little of the cold away. Surely it didn't matter what he said to me now, what she overheard, when shortly . . . I wouldn't think about that.

Alan said nothing, and I looked at him even harder. He was breathing fast. And surely with an irregular tempo? That, now—that was a gasp. "Alan? Alan, what?" I had whispered, but I raised my voice. "Alan, what's the matter?"

His right hand came up to clutch his left arm, above the elbow. "I can't—I think I'm—"

He fell heavily against me, his breath coming in short gasps, his face an alarming purple.

"Vanessa! Vanessa, stop the car! I think Alan's having a heart attack!"

The words that came to those lovely lips were short,

Anglo-Saxon, and ugly. She doesn't care, I thought in despair, she doesn't care at all, she's going to kill us anyway, she'll be delighted if Alan saves her the trouble—and then the car was slowing and stopping and she was getting out, just before we reached the lights of the railway station parking lot.

The door on Alan's side opened. Before I could react she had seized his ankles and was dragging him out of the car. She was going to get help after all! Eagerly I lifted his shoulders and pushed as she pulled. It isn't easy to move a large, completely inert man, but the slippery leather upholstery helped.

And then he was lying on the ground and I was leaning over him anxiously, trying to get past him and out of the car. Vanessa stepped close to me. "Oh, thanks, give me a hand, will you?"

She lashed out and caught me on the temple with—surely that was a gun!—and that was the last I knew for some time.

When I opened my eyes, we were rolling smoothly, quietly, along a dark, winding road. My head ached violently. Alan was nowhere to be seen.

I pounded on the window separating me from her. "Why? WHY?" I screamed.

She was in control of herself again. "There's no need to shout, you know. I can hear you perfectly well. And surely you don't really think I wanted him to die in my car," she said in a reasonable tone of voice.

"But you were going to kill him anyway, so why did you have to—"

"This is not a good road, and I must concentrate. Be quiet."

I sat back and tried to marshal my forces. What could I do?

Nothing. My husband was dying, dying of a heart attack and exposure, and I couldn't lift a finger to help him.

Frank, my dear Frank, husband of forty years, had died of a heart attack, neatly, tidily, in a nice, clean, warm hospital, and nobody had been able to help him.

Now I was going to die, somehow. She'd said something about Brighton and the sea. I was going to be forced into the sea, forced at gunpoint to walk out into the choppy, freezing English Channel until the chill paralyzed me and the waves took me, and I might never be found.

Oh. That was why she hadn't wanted Alan to die in the car. A body is hard to dispose of. She couldn't have carried Alan to the sea. Much better to let him die of natural causes, and by a station, too, where some reasonable explanation could be invented. And Vanessa was inventive.

Now, when it was far too late, I saw the truth. "You killed him, didn't you? And tried to kill the others. I was all wrong about faking the speeches and all that."

"Of course. I don't know what you mean about speeches, but dear Anthony has neither the brains nor the guts to commit a successful crime. He did drive the car at that roundabout; that's why the job was botched. The ideas have always been mine. Really, you know, there is no Anthony Blake, in any practical sense. I do it all, the speeches, the ideas. One day I'll expose the puppet and then I'll have the glory as well as the power. For now he's useful, though his stupidity causes trouble from time to time. Now do shut up, dear Mrs. Martin, and let me drive. It's not far, now, and I don't want to miss the turn in this filthy weather."

It was even less far than she had supposed. I began to realize that the roaring in my head was not simply the pounding of my terrified heart. There was a car close behind us, a car traveling without lights, until suddenly the lights were on, all the lights, including a blue light on top, and the car shot past us, and a voice from a loudspeaker commanded Vanessa to pull over, and there were more police cars, they were everywhere, and in one of them was—surely not Alan?—and I slumped down in my seat and had to be helped out of the car and into his arms.

36

IT was the next day before we sorted it all out. Alan knew most of my story, but I needed to hear his, once I'd had a very good night's sleep.

"I had to get out of the car, and it was the only way," he explained. "I couldn't attack Vanessa with that blasted glass panel in the way. I couldn't kick out the car window, not with that stupid ankle swelling by the minute. So I had to use my wits. I'm sorry I frightened you so badly."

"It was only—Frank looked just like that, you see, when he—Alan, you were *purple*—" I picked up my coffee cup and then put it down again. My hands were shaking and I needed another pain pill.

"I was purple from all that gasping, and then holding my breath. I did try to tip you the wink, literally, but I suppose you were too upset to notice." He sneezed.

"Upset! I was frantic! But what did you do, once you were out of the car?"

"Lay where I was, getting extremely cold and wet, until you were out of sight. Then I limped to the station and commandeered their telephone. Derek, fortunately, had stayed where he was rather than try to follow us blindly. I simply told him where Vanessa was taking you, and he was after you at once. I followed in a later car. Derek brought the receiving equipment along in the car, by the way, so we have a lovely tape of everything Vanessa said. It's unfortunate that you never mentioned names of the victims. Her lawyers will make a meal of that, but the fact that she left me, as she thought, to die, will work against her. I think we have a case." He sneezed again, and coughed.

"You're going to get pneumonia if you're not careful."

"I have every intention of being careful."

"And what about Blake?"

"Blake, of course, claims to know nothing whatever about any of this. Yes, he did get a crank phone call, but he paid no attention. People in his position are subject to that sort of annoyance. And so on."

"He'll get away with it, won't he?"

"In a sense. There'll be very little, if anything, that he can be prosecuted for. But his career is finished, of course. The publicity will put an end to any chance of his getting elected to anything, ever again."

"And I expect his marriage is over, too."

"You're probably right. Mrs. Blake may not be terribly keen on having her husband's adultery splashed all over every front page in the country. I wouldn't be surprised to see her setting up housekeeping with Amanda and Miriam."

"Oh! How's Miriam? Have you heard anything?"

"Amanda rang up, actually, while you were still asleep this morning. She—Amanda—is being discharged today, but she'll go to Gillian's flat for the time being, so as to be close to the hospital. Miriam's conscious and there's no apparent brain damage, though she'll need a good deal of physiotherapy if she's to regain full use of her limbs. It'll be a rough road ahead, but that child knows how to deal with adversity.

And with a supportive family as a nice change, I think she'll do well. I think they both will."

The phone rang. I was closest.

"Dorothy, good! Catherine Woodley here. I wondered—of course Amanda Doyle will be convalescent for a good while yet, and our list of supply teachers is so short—do you think you might be willing to bone up a bit and take the qualifying exams? We'd love to be able to call on you regularly, and the children adored you that one day, and—"

"No, Catherine," I said quite firmly. "I'm flattered to be asked, but no."

"But—"

"No. The last time got me involved in a situation that very nearly killed me. Have you read your morning paper?"

"No."

"Read it. Good-bye, Catherine." I hung up the phone. "There. Aren't you proud of me?"

He kissed me and sneezed. "You'll find another way to get into trouble, but I took you for better, for worse. The difficulty is that I can't always tell which is which. Hand me a tissue, will you?"